Critical praise for

FLEUR DE LEIGH'S LIFE OF CRIME

"It's a rare voice that succeeds in bringing to life the bitter comedy of childhood under siege from unreliable adults—and succeeds without the victim's whine. In Fleur de Leigh, Diane Leslie has created that voice: wry, ironic, still trusting, still touchingly tolerant. It's an even rarer voice that can bring to life a period as dated and overdone as Hollywood in the '50s. This, too, the author pulls off. . . . It's all there, bright and crisp, like a lovingly restored cut from a grainy old classic."

—Wendy Law-Yone, *The Washington Post*

"Anyone who has ever been a child has something to complain about; celebrity is no criterion. But Leslie's sprightly prose precludes dwelling on her heroine's dissatisfaction. Rather, by summoning the same resourcefulness she attributes to Fleur, Leslie prescribes an age-old remedy: Have a laugh and move on."

—Sunil Iyengar, *San Francisco Chronicle*

"If you've ever dreamed of living a Hollywood life, you won't anymore after reading this breezy first novel."

—*The Wall Street Journal*

"Witty, sweet, curiously moving . . . rare, lovely, and slightly outrageous."

—Mark Johnson, *San Jose Mercury News*

"An enchanting, believable, and wickedly funny tale. . . . The tales are related with such sparkling writing and told with such verve that it is impossible not to enjoy them."

—Robin Vidimos, *Denver Post*

"Leslie's breezy tone turns what could have been a bitter, morose tell-all into a wickedly funny, readable kiss-and-tell."

—Brenda Gunter, *Houston Chronicle*

"Crisp, clear prose . . . she mingles wry comedy and genuine pathos. . . . With an appealingly wide-eyed, tongue-in-cheek innocence, Fleur relates her surprising adventures."

—Merle Rubin, *The Christian Science Monitor*

"[A] wonderfully droll and cynical picture of Tinseltown . . . unlike most movies today, Leslie manages to craft a cohesive Hollywood story that makes us laugh and reflect while she entertains us."

—Sue Pierman, *Milwaukee Journal Sentinal*

"This novel is truthful, funny, poignant. Fleur navigates the odd terrain, gains strength, retains humanity. Go, Fleur."

—Sarah Sarai, *The Seattle Times*

"Leslie brings Fleur to very believable life."

—Mandy Davis, *St. Louis Post-Dispatch*

"An often hilarious, semi-autobiographical tale of a young girl coming-of-age in the glittery environs of Beverly Hills and Hollywood."

—Paula Friedman, *Chicago Tribune*

"[Leslie's] sly wit and offhand candor unite to create a charming and memorable protagonist. . . . The questing, curious, ever-growing character of Fleur is a delightful creation—a fictional character well worth meeting and remembering."

—Diann Blakely, *Nashville Scene*

FLEUR DE LEIGH'S LIFE OF CRIME

A NOVEL

Diane Leslie

SIMON & SCHUSTER PAPERBACKS
New York London Toronto Sydney

SIMON & SCHUSTER PAPERBACKS
Rockefeller Center
1230 Avenue of the Americas
New York, NY 10020

For information about special discounts for bulk purchases,
please contact Simon & Schuster Special Sales at
1-800-456-6798 or business@simonandschuster.com.

Designed by Ruth Lee

Manufactured in the United States of America

3 5 7 9 10 8 6 4

The Library of Congress has cataloged the hardcover edition as follows:
Leslie, Diane.
Fleur de Leigh's life of crime / Diane Leslie.
p. cm.
I. Title.
PS3562.E8173F58 1999
813'54—dc21 98-53353

ISBN 978-0-684-86741-0

The first chapter of this novel originally appeared in *Nimrod*.

ACKNOWLEDGMENTS

In recent years I've had the good fortune to link up with many remarkable people who eased my way as a writer.

I am deeply grateful to Joan Friedman, who is a wonder of compassion, insight, wisdom, memory, good humor, patience, and persistence; Doug Dutton, whose goodness, knowledge, love of books, and friendship perpetually inspire me; Jonathan Kirsch, who has been unflaggingly generous with his time, advice, praise, and practical help; Jim Krusoe, whose benevolent criticism saved me years of floundering. Within his workshop Lynn McKelvey, Liza Taylor, Peter Elbling, Nancy Krusoe, Charles Eastman, and Susan Morgan were especially helpful.

I also wish to thank Jill and John Walsh, who transformed the city of Los Angeles and my life as well; Fran Ringold of *Nimrod International Journal,* along with Timothy Findley; Katherine Minton, Isaiah Sheffer, and Sarah Montague of Selected Shorts at Symphony Space and the Getty Museum; and Sarah Spitz at KCRW.

My appreciation goes to Elizabeth (in memoriam) and Alan Mandell for providing friendship, honesty, and, for many years, a setting akin to Yaddo; all my fellow booksellers at Dutton's Brentwood Books—Lise Friedman, Ed Conklin, and Eileen Lynch are only three of the many—whose friendship and passion for reading have heartened me; Tim Farrington, Larry Leamer, Nancy Hardin, Gaye Richards, Susan Chehak, Tony Velie, Ron Hansen, and Linda Ashour, who so kindly read various chapters and made invaluable comments.

Thanking my agent, Laurie Fox, a splendid novelist herself, is hardly sufficient. She has been my literary nanny, tutor, and fairy godmother. She has unselfishly given of her knowledge, writer's acumen, empathy, and time. I'm also grateful for Linda Chester's astute guiding hand. And then, what luck, to connect with the energetic and sagacious Laurie Chittenden, who has made the experience of being edited both edifying and fun. Denise Roy inspirited me with her goodness, optimism, and decisiveness, as has the delightful Marah Stets. Jackie Green has also been a godsend.

However, the man who actually lived with me while I wrote deserves my deepest gratitude. A more magnanimous, humane, adaptable, attractive, funnier man I haven't met. My sons, Brendan and Dana Alan Huffman, have bolstered me as well.

Enfin, I thank my mother, Aleen, who has an amazing capacity to laugh at herself and has taught me the value of humor to get through the tight squeezes of life.

for

Fred Byron Huffman, the find of a lifetime,

and

Roy London and Daisy Belin, who remain alive
in frequent thoughts and dreams and,
I hope, on the pages of this book.

Beverly Hills School Days

School days, school days
dear old swimming pool days
The chauffeur will drive us to school and
back
Each girl and boy has a Cadillac
Everyone gets an A or B
We pay our teachers well you see
Though our parents are famous and
lousy with dough
we still love you dear El Rodeo.

Hazel Shermet Rhine

CONTENTS

I

Glendora

3/17/57–6/12/57

We'd been studying Bedouins in my fifth-grade class, how they carried only what they needed or loved on the backs of ornery camels, and how other, territorial groups kept them hopping. In my experience nannies were far more nomadic. They had time at our house to knit just one argyle sock, complete just one jigsaw puzzle, or paint (by numbers) just one seascape before my mother made them repack their belongings and move on.

I therefore paid little attention when prospective nannies came for interviews, but I can still remember my mother's words after her first encounter with Glendora. "She could play the wisecracking assembly-line worker who never gets the guy," Charmian said. "Because she's too fat to be anything but a supporting character."

"A nanny *is* a supporting character," I recall my father, Maurice, pointing out. He was between pictures and temporarily finding domestic matters a kick. "But we aren't casting a picture," he reminded her.

"C'est vrai," Charmian agreed, using the death-defying remains of French she'd learned when she'd played, as she put it, second banana in *Ivan the Marriageable.* "I won't hold the woman's girth against her."

Charmian herself was exquisitely petite. She described herself to casting directors as the cute-as-a-button type. "It's best for actors to be small," she had explained to me, "so they fit gracefully into the frame."

Charmian's *fame,* however, had been acquired on the radio, and it had left her discontented. "What's the good of having the perfect turned-up nose or saucer eyes or hair the color of sunshine? Who's to know?"

"But everyone knows *of* you," I tried to console her with a statement I believed to be true.

"And I'm sick of driving an Oldsmobile just because that's who sponsors my show," she complained. "Imagine how *jolie* I'd look on that little screen behind the wheel of a Cadillac or, better, a Rolls."

My mother had created *The Charmian Leigh Radio Mystery Half-Hour,* and her audience soon numbered in the tens of millions, she said. Charmian played an actress who, after appearing in dozens of detective movies, had taken up private investigation as a hobby. "I simply play myself," she liked to say in interviews, "except for the IQ. Our writers—the dimwits—gave me a one hundred sixty-five IQ when actually mine is one eighty. Like Einstein. I had lunch, you know, with Einstein before he died. He said he wished he had my beauty."

Once Glendora assumed her duties as nanny, Charmian spelled out more instructions. "You'll make the beds, clean the bathrooms, dust and straighten up daily. At least twice a week you should vacuum the entire second floor."

"So, really, I'm the upstairs maid," Glendora noted.

"Not at all. It's just something to do while Fleur is at school. You'll be chauffeuring her to and fro. But before she steps out of this house, you have to make sure she's bathed, her clothes are ironed, and her hair is clean and combed. If you curl her hair and dab on some rouge, you can get her looking like Shirley Temple."

I had to laugh. I saw myself as a skinny ten-year-old with chlorine-tinted hair and eyes slightly inflamed from the swimming pools I frequented. And with a vast, gray grillwork of braces and rubber bands bridling my mouth, no amount of primping was going to make me into Charmian's china doll.

"Please don't depend on Fleur to accomplish such tasks for herself. She is maddeningly . . . delinquent," Charmian persisted.

Glendora's left eyebrow journeyed halfway up her forehead; I couldn't be sure if it signaled dismay or disapproval.

"Let's see. . . . Oh yes. Always remember, we treat Fleur as an adult. She may be ten years old, but we don't coddle her. No baby talk. No dolls or childish games. Is that understood?"

"If you don't mind, Mrs. Leigh," Glendora said flatly, "I fly by the seat of my pants."

It was a shame she couldn't actually fly, because wherever Glendora strolled, her footsteps broadcast vibrations across the hardwood floors, through the tiles of our Spanish colonial domicile, and up the faux adobe walls, making the chandeliers jingle. When she reached full stride, the objets d'art and the antique furniture artfully arranged throughout the interior rattled or wavered. This caused Charmian to fret over a particular sixteenth-century statuette.

The Sleekèd Boy, as we called him, had been chiseled out of Italian marble. Almost a foot tall, he stood with knees pressed together and hands on hips. His head was cocked provocatively, as though he knew something no one else could fathom. The Sleekèd Boy was vigorous, stalwart, proud, and, except for a rounded helmet he wore à la Donatello's *David,* he didn't have a stitch on. This was the only one of Charmian's treasures I wasn't allowed to touch—*"trop cher,"* she said. Nevertheless, I'd kissed this naked man and rubbed his smooth and compact backside, as well as fingered his creases, crevices, curves, crannies, cracks, and protrusions numerous times.

His genitals astounded me, and I speculated untiringly about how they worked.

"Glendora's clumping about is bound to topple my little man. I'll have to set him out of harm's way. *Quel dommage,*" Charmian tsked as she pushed him against the back of the shelf and stuck him down with museum gum.

When Glendora was on the move, her spidery, hennaed hair wriggled around her face. She had a face that wasn't stingy with its features. *You want eyes, a nose, lips, you want full cheeks, then look at me,* it seemed to say. Her wide lips twisted into a different shape with almost every word she spoke, as though she found her own thoughts droll. I listened attentively to her speech, enriched by a midwestern twang, as it boldly rang out and echoed through our cathedral-like living room.

Though she had an extravagant bosom, there was nothing maternal about Glendora, and the white heavy-duty bra, as glimpsed through her nylon uniform, insisted, *Don't touch.*

My mother found it astonishing and seemed annoyed when a tall, handsome-in-his-uniform Beverly Hills cop fell for my nanny.

"There's no accounting for taste," Glendora explained his attraction to her.

Jeff parked his gleaming black and white motorcycle in our driveway and hung his helmet from the handgrip. His radio turned up loud, he strode to our front door. From my upstairs bedroom window I spied on Jeff and Glendora as they laughed under the portico at the side of our house. I could have watched for hours though all I could really discern was the patch of skin, like an orange slice, glistening though Jeff's dark, curly hair and Glendora's sturdy fingers that squeezed Jeff's neck when he kissed her.

Sometimes our gardener, Constantine, had no choice but to pass the lovers when he carted weeds and debris down from our hillside. He whistled, warbled, and chirped like a loquacious parakeet to alert them of his approach. And from my vantage point I observed Glendora, her face reddened, nod amiably to Constantine. I assumed that all our help held our gardener in as high esteem as I did. "He tickles my funny bone," Glendora had said of Constantine, though Jeff, conversely, ignored him.

"Why do you make birdcalls the minute you see Glendora and Jeff?" I asked Constantine.

"Is bad thing embarrassing police," he explained.

"But why don't you just cough or clear your throat?"

"Because lovers making world go 'round," he said with a wink.

Whenever *I* passed their way, I came down with a case of the giggles.

"There are only a handful of men in *tout le monde* who are actually attracted to women . . . of tonnage," Charmian commented pointedly. "They're neurotic as hell, of course, fixated in infancy or something. But imagine the odds of Glendora finding one of them, here in Beverly Hills. A million to one, *oui*?"

It occurred to me that this was precisely why previous nannies had always chosen to meet their dates away from our house—they were dodging Charmian's judgment. "Jeff's very nice to me," I tried to defend him. "Why shouldn't he like Glendora? *I* like her a whole bunch."

"He's the strong, silent type" and "Still waters run deep" is how Glendora characterized Jeff; it was true he never said much. But several times, at an hour when other children were in bed, Jeff took me gallivanting on his motorcycle. We roamed the fire roads up beyond the old Chaplin estate. Pickfair with its endless, high, white walls hovered over us like a medieval castle, and the Barrymore villa by moonlight could have been designed by Gaudí. These mansions were all but deserted now—or served no other purpose than to shelter dipsomaniacs, my mother claimed. If she was right—if they *were* cobwebbed and dingy—I found them that much more intriguing.

Then too the desert-scented air shooting through my hair, the throbbing of the motor, the sweep of landscape in my peripheral vision, the smell of Jeff's jacket thrilled me just slightly less than having my arms around Jeff's leather-clad waist and my head against his broad back.

"God is Jeff's copilot," Glendora said reverently.

When Glendora had time, late afternoons before dinner or after dinner when my parents were out, we climbed into the broad-beamed Buick my father provided for the help and declared ourselves "on the prowl." Glendora knew the Beverly Hills police routes as well as anyone on the force, and we followed them as faithfully as pilgrims. We drove with the windows rolled down and the radio turned up. We pretended we were spies, hired guns, or detectives. I treasured those outings because, for their duration, I could pretend I was beautiful and smart; I could pretend I was an actress, a writer, and a private investigator all in one; I could pretend I was Charmian Leigh.

Jeff worked north of Wilshire Boulevard, but we never knew if he would be patrolling the flats or tacking his bike in and out of the irregular canyons. Jeff might be hiding behind a clump of ivy on Pamela Drive, where Pamela and James Mason lived, or wedging his bike between the stucco wall and the garbage cans at Lucille Ball's. Once, we found his motorcycle leaning against an ivy-covered wall on Summit Drive. It took an extended search to discover him crouching in the shadow of a pillar that held up Fred Astaire's house. Another time Jeff concealed himself, bike and all, behind Danny Kaye's eugenia hedge, and on another occasion he parked between the white-streaked, spiny plumes of Jerry Lewis's dinosaur cactus. Each time we ferreted him out, Jeff would ask, "How do you two do it?"

"Your guess is as good as mine," Glendora invariably responded. Then they would throw their arms around each other and have a good laugh.

I never knew if Jeff was playing a game or if all the Beverly Hills motorcycle police purposely stationed themselves in celebrity hideouts, but I knew my job was to cajole Jeff into escorting us to Dolores's, a local drive-in that stayed open late, at the end of his shift. If I succeeded, Glendora rewarded me with a hamburger, a cheese-smothered slice of apple pie, and a chocolate shake.

One afternoon Charmian chided Glendora, saying, "You ought to watch your weight." (This embarrassed me terribly. I had been taught by previous nannies never to mention anyone's physical disadvantages.)

"Why should I? I've caught my man," Glendora retorted, gaily waggling her thick finger so that the jot of diamond on her engagement ring caught the light. She was letting Charmian know she wasn't shaken by her remark.

"But will he stay on your line, *chérie*?" Charmian needled her.

"That's for me to know and you to find out" was Glendora's tactical rejoinder.

"Peut-être," my mother said, placing an emphasis on the *pooh* sound of it.

"What do you want me to do? Stand on my head and spit nickels?" Glendora joshed. Yet she must have taken Charmian's jeering to heart, because she stopped eating starches and commenced an exercise regime. Every morning, wearing nothing but her sensible white underwear, Glendora positioned herself, feet apart on the speckled linoleum, in the middle of the cubicle that was the nanny's room. She breathed noisily for several minutes. Only after she'd "oxygenated herself" did she begin the difficult task of reducing. This entailed her spreading her arms as wide as they'd go and making torpid little circles. She reminded me of a rooster attempting flight, though *her* wattles hung down from her arms, and I knew that the feeble motions she made would never get her airborne. Still, with a grimace she persevered; maybe, given a little time, she would have achieved real muscle tone.

One Monday evening, when Charmian felt exceptionally relaxed because it was the day after her weekly broadcast, she magnanimously offered Glendora and our cook her Academy card. "I'm giving you the evening off so you can attend a showing of *The Three Faces of Eve,*" she told them. "I already saw it at the producer's house, and since Mr. Leigh is out of town, I think I'll just relax tonight. *Je suis très fatiguée,*" she yawned.

"It doesn't sound like my kind of picture," Glendora said. "Geraldine Page gives me the willies."

"Then you're in luck. Joanne Woodward is the star of this particular vehicle," Charmian proclaimed.

"Oh, well, maybe Jeff would like to go with us."

"Only two can get in on my card," Charmian said.

"Well then, what about Fleur?" Glendora asked.

For just an instant my mother wore a look that seemed to say, *Who's that?* It was a look I'd seen before and one I found unsettling.

"As I said," Charmian announced, "only two can go in on my card. Besides, Fleur wouldn't comprehend a story of this nature. It's a cerebral drama, loaded with psychological snafus. What does Fleur know of ids and libidos?"

"What do *I*?" Glendora asked. "But what I mean is, who'll keep an eye on Fleur?"

"Is it as hard as that?" Charmian inquired.

It wasn't hard at all. Although I did have a habit of dogging my mother's footsteps when she was at home, I'd spent so much time alone, I was used to amusing myself. That night, however, my mother cheerfully suggested we indulge in a few rounds of gin. (Charmian adored games.) "And you can make some cocoa too," she proposed. (Charmian also adored sweets.) "Put it on a tray and we'll drink it upstairs while we play."

Generally speaking, the kitchen was off-limits to me (my parents thought it degrading for girls to learn to cook) unless there was something my mother particularly desired. Naturally, I found the kitchen irresistible. Once there, I followed the directions on the Hershey's cocoa tin, carefully stirring salt, sugar, and cocoa into four tablespoons of water. Then I heated the mixture in a pot and slowly added milk. I took pride in the fact that I could do something Charmian considered worthwhile. Because I was rushing to carry the tray upstairs before skin formed atop the chocolate, I didn't bother to soak or wash the pan or wipe up the trail of cocoa I'd left between the cupboard and the stove. No matter—no one expected me to clean up after myself.

The silver tray I'd prepared with the porcelain chocolate pot, Haviland cups, dainty teaspoons, and lace-edged napkins bedecked with a single scarlet rose looked as nice as the trays any of our cooks arranged, and I considered it praise from heaven when my mother classified the cocoa "divine."

"Do you really like it?" I asked, trying to snare a second compliment.

"It's the best I ever had," Charmian said with unusual largesse.

My mother played cards intently, and I found her face more interesting than the game. Her eyelids fluttered and her lips hugged a cigarette as she rapidly dealt the cards. Charmian wore this same alert expression when she was studying a script or writing one. Since I personally didn't possess much power of concentration, I admired my mother's single-mindedness even though it meant that for her I'd ceased to exist.

And inasmuch as I was grateful to spend time in my mother's presence, I really didn't care that she won every round. (Years before, Charmian had explained, "The parents who *let* their offspring win games give them nothing but delusions of grandeur.") Eventually, cold chocolate sludge covered the bottoms of our cups, and the game seemed to hold no more surprises for Charmian. She gathered up the cards and said, "All right, that's enough. I'd forgotten how dull gin can be when no money is involved. Anyway, the cocoa should have made you sleepy, so you better get to bed."

This meant my mother had grown tired of me. I didn't remind her I had no set bedtime, because since February fifth I'd made it a habit not to complain. On that fateful day my best friend Daisy had been whisked off to a boarding school against her vehement protests. The threat of meeting a similar doom had commandeered my every thought for the last four months.

Daisy Belmont was two whole years older than I, but since she was also the daughter of movie people, the two of us had been what Charmian called *confidantes.* We were flowers growing in the same field, Daisy said. I admired her for being self-assured and taking her celebrity parents in stride. "In a few more years we'll be driving. My parents will give me something stylish, no doubt—to suit their *own* images of course. Probably a Karmann Ghia or an MG. A car will spell our freedom from all this hypocrisy. We'll drive up to San Francisco and marry poets as soon as possible," Daisy promised. "Poets don't give a fig about appearances. They only care about heart."

I'd received only one letter from Daisy since she'd been banished from Beverly Hills. She'd said the girls at her Swiss boarding school were as icy and dull as the country itself. She'd said she was hellishly homesick for California, where there was sun, and saw no reason to go on living without it. I'd called Daisy's parents many times since reading her letter, but the caretaker said the Belmonts were out of the country and the house was closed. "Could you just tell me if their daughter is alive?" I asked. She'd been hired by an agency, the woman said, and knew nothing of the property owners.

No, it was essential that Charmian remember our evening together in the best possible light, so I retired graciously. Soon, I was in bed pretending sleep had overtaken me, but actually I'd lodged a flashlight between my chin and shoulder and tucked the bedcovers over my head. I had no reason to hide—no one was going to discover me reading *True Confessions* magazine; no one but Charmian was home. And if she found me reading what she called "prurient literature," she would hardly care. I hid under the blankets only because I liked pretending I was a normal American child.

A story about a young, raven-haired ballerina who had "proved her love" to a teacher of flamenco dance captured my attention. Like all the females in *True Confessions,* this one keenly regretted her "error of the flesh." Why should this magazine be considered trash, I wondered, when each tale of passion ended with a dire consequence? Sex was definitely something *I* planned to put off until old age.

The ringing of our doorbell was a happy distraction. I slid from the bed, crawled across the floor, and peeked out between the bottom row of slats in the shutters.

Constellations of moths formed and re-formed around the porch light. Jeff stood back from them in the shadows. Charmian had evidently changed her clothes—I heard her feathered mules clack down the stairs, and when the door finally opened, she was framed in a golden light. She had on a low-cut, gold tulle negligee, and her yellow hair was pushed back behind her ears so that I could see the sly smile she bestowed on my uniformed friend.

I couldn't hear what she said to Jeff, but after several

minutes he nodded, turned, and walked away. I knew he would return, however, because Charmian remained poised in the doorway.

I found it odd that my mother cared to spend time with a cop. "Having written about *gendarmes* for years, I can tell you their conversational skills are, at best, scant," she'd told me. Maybe Charmian planned to ask Jeff about his intentions toward Glendora. Maybe she wanted to know if he'd resigned himself to setting a wedding date.

Like Charmian Leigh on a surveillance case, I lay down flat against the tapestry runner on the creaky balcony that crossed our two-story living room so that when Charmian and Jeff came inside, the architecture of our house rendered me invisible.

"A drink?" my mother suggested.

"Is a beer okay?" Jeff asked, sounding as though he was seeking my mother's approval rather than saying what he wanted. "I just finished work, so it's not as if—"

"What kind?" Charmian interrupted.

"Oh, anything." He busied himself by pretending to look at the dark oil paintings that lined the walls of our living room. He stopped in front of the étagère.

Charmian set her martini and Jeff's beer on ivorine coasters so as not to mar the Italianate table in front of the couch.

"This little statue is real pretty," Jeff called to my mother from across the room. "Why do you hide it way to the back?"

"C'est un bijou précieux," Charmian said, sitting down.

"You have good taste, anyone ever tell you? Although I've never met anyone who didn't like that statuette." The long blue sofa ran perpendicular to the balcony, and Charmian happened to sit where I could easily see her. She smiled at Jeff, cocked her head, and patted the cushion next to her.

Jeff sat on it.

My mother took a cigarette out of the creamy white Meissen basket she kept on the coffee table. She picked up the silver Ronson lighter and snapped it; a celestial glow momentarily lit her face.

Jeff, looking stiff, took a nervous gulp of beer. "Nice beer," he said as though he were talking to a pet.

Silence on the radio is called dead air, and Charmian couldn't abide it even outside the studio; she didn't wait long for Jeff to attempt conversation.

"Do you ever listen to my show?" she asked, sucking the heat from her cigarette and letting it go. "*The Charmian Leigh Radio Mystery Half-Hour*? I like to know what my average listener thinks. Do *you* enjoy it, *chéri?* You can be honest."

Jeff shrugged; from my vantage point I thought he looked tense. "I'm no critic," he said hesitantly as he wiped away a mustache of foam. "Guess the boob tube's got me hooked."

"But you *have* heard my show?"

"Once or twice. Glendora thinks it's swell."

"I am its star," my mother said in a morose tone indicating the burden she bore. I watched in fascination as she shifted her eyes back and forth in their sockets as though Jeff's thoughts were printed out and she was reading them. This was a technique actors often used in two-shots when they wanted to upstage the actor who had the lines. "The audience always looks toward the action," Charmian had explained to me. She'd become such a practitioner of this ploy that she even used it off-camera.

"You *look* like a starlet," Jeff said bashfully.

Charmian cheered up. "But did you know I created the entire *concept* of the show?" She tilted her head just so and opened her eyes wide like Debbie Reynolds.

"Well . . ." I thought Jeff was going to say "shucks" like a movie cowboy, but he held back. "I think Glen maybe mentioned it."

"From now on, Jeff, I want you to tune in every week," my mother said, twirling the bowl of her martini glass so that the olive oscillated, "because you've already given me quite a few ideas."

"Me?"

"*Mais oui.* You see, *The Charmian Leigh Mystery Half-Hour* is soon to be on television, so I've begun to think in visual terms. Guess what kind of character I'm going to add to the cast?"

"Dunno," he said.

"He'll have a stunning uniform with a stripe down the leg. He'll have tall black boots, a gun, and a very powerful machine between his legs," Charmian said and then winked.

Jeff made a sound I couldn't interpret and raised his eyebrows.

"In order to write this character—this good-looking, robust motorcycle cop—I'm going right to the source. And what would you think of my asking the very man my new character is patterned after to play him?"

"You don't mean me?" Jeff asked, sincerely surprised.

"*Absolument*—will you accept?"

"Well, um, yeah, I suppose." Even the circle of skin on top of his head blushed, and I wished he hadn't removed his helmet.

This was the first I'd heard of a TV show in the works; in my amazement I inadvertently shifted my weight and caused the balcony to creak. But as deafening as it sounded to me, it didn't break Charmian's momentum. "I think I can talk the network into it," she said. "Especially if I convince them I know you . . . inside and out. I'd like to be able to say that I've had access to your entire . . . mind and heart." She gave him her very practiced Jennifer Jones stare. "You would, wouldn't you? Give me access?"

"Um, eh, I think so."

"Let's see."

"How do you mean?"

"Come here," she said in the lowest tone in her register as she crooked her pointer finger back and forth and grinned.

Jeff glanced around as though he thought she was speaking to someone else. It was awhile before he moved closer.

Charmian placed her cigarette in the ashtray, her drink on the coaster, and her arms lightly around Jeff's neck. Then she kissed him, or he kissed her; it appeared to be by mutual consent. Within moments she had disarmed my policeman friend completely.

My lips formed words: *Wait a minute. What's going on?* I wished to scold them, but the image of Daisy pining away in a boarding school dorm hovered over me like a cartoon bubble. If I wanted to remain at home, I would have to champion my mother's activities, no matter how outlandish they were. Besides, a fascinating exhibition had begun to take place: Charmian and Jeff seemed to be in a contest. I thought of those played in Roxbury Park at Fourth of July picnics, but this competition entailed undressing each other while keeping their lips in constant contact. It required much more skill than a two-man gunny sack race, or putting on layers of funny clothes before crawling through barrels. Charmian struggled with Jeff's belt, a button, and a zipper, while Jeff got his fingers caught in my mother's tulle negligee. He pulled his lips away from her long enough to say, "Oh damn."

It wasn't easy but they worked as a team: Charmian managed to slide Jeff's pants down his legs, while he got hold of her lacy French undies and didn't let go. Finally, they were both disrobed from the waist down; they sank onto the sofa and melded into one another. The tableau they created would have elicited a symphony of birdcalls from our gardener, Constantine.

I'd often overheard Charmian on the phone whispering sugary sentences to would-be wooers. And returning home from parties, she frequently awakened me to describe in sensational detail each of the men who'd made passes at her that night. Charmian *was* one of the most sought-after women in Hollywood; I knew because her publicity said so. But I'd assumed that what she called her *affaires des coeurs* were realized in words, not action.

As seen from my position high above them, Jeff and Charmian seemed to metamorphose into a beautiful though dangerous insect. It had a blue-black thorax outlined in gold. Neither my mother nor Jeff had pincers, but their "antennae" fluttered and their legs flailed. If only Jeff had left his helmet on, it would have been perfect.

Even the noises they made didn't sound human. I heard growls, gurgles, mewls, snorts, crackles, and yips. They were so busy, so absorbed, I had the leisure to fully observe them. I saw that Jeff's backside was as nicely shaped as our statuette but that his legs were dark, hairy, and a little too thick. By Sleekèd Boy standards they were a disappointment, so I was relieved when he and my mother changed places. Then Charmian's pretty, heart-shaped backside appeared to be waving at me, or just waving indiscriminately, with glee.

As the realization of what was really occurring, the downright ickiness of the act, penetrated my consciousness, I felt disgusted. Naturally, I had seen Charmian commit far more heinous acts on-screen. As a small child, I'd watched her in a circus thriller called *Bigger Than Life* as she stabbed an aerial acrobat in midair. That same year, in *A Note for the Teller,* Charmian eased the feet of a policeman into cement shoes before she and her bank-robbing boyfriend tossed him into a lake. (My mother's part was abbreviated since she'd spent the rest of the picture in jail.) On-screen, Charmian had kissed numerous men. If not, she made it clear that kissing them was her utmost desire.

"It's just a movie. It's not real. Your mother is *acting,*" I had been told by nannies when I voiced anger or disgust. And that's what I told myself now. My mother was *acting.* She did a lot of acting, even in everyday life.

If only I could have shut off my thoughts at the spigot. But the word *why* flooded into my brain. Why would Charmian bother to pretend she loved Jeff when she said that only men like my father, men like David O. Selznick or Bill Paley, men who could advance her career, truly interested her. Of one thing I was certain: unlike the girls in *True Confessions,* Charmian would not regret her act.

Finally, I had to admit that the specter of my mother's coupling with a man other than her husband—my father—frightened me terribly. Did this mean she was leaving Maurice? And if so, what would happen to me? I would receive a life sentence in a boarding school, wouldn't I? Like Daisy, I'd be looking for a fast way out.

My fear made me squirm and I unwittingly attracted Jeff's attention. In the stupefying moment in which we gawked at each other, I realized I was guilty of a crime. Early in the game I could have pretended I'd heard a burglar and shouted "Help, police!" I could have cried "Fire!" or set one. I could have simply coughed and it would have stopped them. But I was so immersed in the spectacle of Jeff and my mother on parade, I had forgotten all about Glendora.

For the next few days Jeff didn't come around. Glendora and I couldn't find him no matter how many hours we spent circling his routes. "What's the story, morning glory?" Glendora kept asking the air. As she drove, I tried to formulate words that wouldn't hurt. I didn't dare ask if we could drive by Daisy's house, as we did sometimes, just to see if there were any signs of life. No matter, there never were. On the fourth night I was paying no attention to our itinerary until I heard the squeak of the emergency break. "End of the line," Glendora said, rolling her top lip toward her nose. I looked up to see that we were parked behind the Beverly Hills City Hall, where the police and fire departments were housed.

Like many children in the fifties, I had been taught to consider the police as friends. The idea was reinforced when my class paid a visit to headquarters, where kindly officers served milk and Oreos. Before we left, a sergeant had locked us in individual cells. For a few minutes he let us experience the just deserts of criminals. Some girls shrieked, some cried, but I calmly tested the cot in my cell, paced the cubicle, and scrutinized the lidless toilet. The bars of the cell seemed familiar, and I found them oddly comforting. If the officer had said I would have to remain inside them forever, I might not have minded.

Everyone seemed to know Glendora at headquarters, and we walked right through to the garage. Motorcycles roared past, the squeals of their tires echoing. Pungent gasoline fumes befouled the air. Whether they were whizzing in or revving up, all the policemen looked alike in the polluted atmosphere. How Glendora spotted Jeff I had no idea, but she made a beeline toward one of the dark figures who was putting his bike away. Jeff flinched when he saw us. "So where've you been? You hibernating or something?" Glendora assailed him. She had to yell to be heard above the din.

Jeff hung his head low and shouted back, "I didn't suppose you'd want to see me."

"You didn't, huh? Why not?" Glendora asked, looking perplexed.

"You haven't heard?" he shouted, eyeing me with suspicion.

"You thought a little birdie would tell me why you haven't shown your face?"

"Well, yeah, I guess I did. I thought Fleur would have . . ."

"What's Fleur got to do with the price of eggs?" Glendora drowned out the rest of his sentence as well as the ruckus around us. She was clenching and unclenching her fists. "You better be your own birdie," Glendora told him.

"Yeah, okay, I just thought you knew all about . . . everything."

"Hell's bells," Glendora said angrily, "I know zilch."

"Oh gee, oh damn, okay, I guess I owe you an explanation." He looked around furtively as though someone else could hear him through the roar. "We can't talk here. Let me go change my clothes."

"While I stand here with egg on my face," Glendora said, but I knew she was suffering from more than embarrassment. "He thought you would have told me . . . what?" Glendora confronted me as we watched Jeff walk slowly toward the locker room.

I racked my brain but couldn't think of a single appropriate word. Finally, I shrugged.

A few minutes later a very ordinary man emerged from the locker room, and I wondered, Where's Jeff? Only when the man said "Let's go" did I realize he *was* Jeff.

Without his uniform, Jeff lacked what my mother called "élan." His polo shirt was crumpled and slightly bleach-stained, and his arms weren't quite as muscular as I had expected. He seemed shorter, less ruddy, less manly.

Without his uniform, Jeff was a big disappointment. Could such a plain sort of person know how to soothe the woman he'd spurned?

The three of us walked so silently to the street that our footsteps sounded like drumbeats. When we got to the Buick, Jeff asked gruffly, "Mind if I drive?"

* * *

We could see the glow from Dolores's Drive-In a block away. Three tiers of cars encircled the diner, so we had to take a spot in the back, away from the activity on Wilshire Boulevard. Jeff parked behind a gray-green Studebaker, my favorite make of car. None of us said a word until a pretty waitress in a very short, yellow uniform stuck our menus through the window. The name embroidered on her pocket was "Bunny."

"I think we know what we want," Jeff told Bunny.

"I'll have a cheeseburger—hold the tomato—and fries and a strawberry shake and a slice of apple pie," Glendora commanded, thus terminating her diet, such as it was.

From the back seat I ordered much the same, but Jeff said, "Just coffee for me." Then he turned on the radio. We sat quietly for minutes seriously pondering the words of "Who Wrote the Book of Love?"

"So, what gives?" Glendora confronted Jeff when the record ended.

Jeff postponed the inevitable. "Let's eat first."

Bunny arrived with our food, but she'd obviously forgotten who ordered what or didn't see me because she put my milkshake, hamburger, and pie on Jeff's tray. This caused much passing of plates and cutlery back and forth; without a tray, I could only hold one dish at a time. Glendora ate very quickly, Jeff becoming increasingly nervous with every one of her bites. Finally, he blurted out, "Look, Glen, gee, I don't know how to say this. The long and the short of it is, I've fallen for somebody else." He turned and looked at me quizzically, to see if I approved.

I tried to turn myself into a statue so they'd forget I was in the car, but I saw Glendora's face redden as though Jeff had slapped her hard on the cheek. I thought she might be choking on her pie; in fact, she set her plate back on the little outside tray and handed her untouched milkshake to Jeff. She had a fork in her hand and it looked like a weapon; but, amazingly, when she spoke, her voice retained its usual vigor. "Who's the lucky lady?" she asked.

Jeff looked very uncomfortable and seemed to be stifling a belch. "You shouldn't take it personally."

"What's that supposed to mean?"

"To be honest," he gulped down some coffee, "it's just plain old ambition that's raised its ugly head."

"Do you mind speaking plain old American?" Glendora said huffily.

"The thing is, I've met someone who likes me. She likes me enough to want to put me on TV."

"TV?" Glendora sounded as though she'd never seen one.

"You can't live here, in Hollywood I mean, well, anyway *I* can't, and not have a bee buzzing in your bonnet that says: Wouldn't it be great if someone spotted you and liked your looks and wanted to put you in pictures?" This was the most I'd ever heard Jeff say.

"It's *girls* who think stuff like that," Glendora chastised him. "Not men."

"Some men do," he said defensively.

"Who's leading you down this primrose path?" Glendora asked contemptuously.

Jeff set his coffee cup back on the tray, perhaps anticipating that Glendora was going to hit him. "Well . . . I guess you're going to find out sooner or later. It happens to be . . . Mrs. Leigh."

"Fleur's mother?" Glendora asked, aghast.

"Charmian," he said buoyantly as though he found it a pleasant sensation to have my mother's name on his tongue.

"Yeah, okay, I got the picture." Glendora's eyebrow, the one I could see, lifted away from her eye into an arch of skepticism. I'd always admired her ability to express it visually. "All right, that's it," she said under her breath, "I've had it." Then she tugged the engagement ring off her fleshy finger and handed it back to Jeff. "There's no use fighting City Hall," she told him.

"I'll get the check," he said.

"Don't bother," Glendora warned him.

"Bunny, Bunny," Jeff summoned as though he were calling for help. He tapped the horn and flashed the headlights several times.

"I think you better just scram," Glendora snapped.

It took Jeff some time before he understood that Glendora meant he should get out of the car.

"I said, scram!" Glendora shouted at him.

Jeff reacted by giving the door a push, but before he could actually extricate himself from behind the wheel, there was a terrible clatter—he'd knocked all my dishes and his coffee cup off the tray. They smashed noisily on the pavement. People in the cars around us stared at him and then hooted and honked their horns. I had to fight the giggles. Jeff's face turned no-parking red; he was so discombobulated he forgot to close the door. Glendora watched impassively as Jeff retreated through the messy glob of milkshake and pie, over the shards of dishes and glass.

The next morning I awoke to discover Glendora's battered suitcase sitting on top of her bed. Its lid was angled upward. No matter how Glendora leaned on it and redistributed her weight, the latch teeth would not bite. And no wonder—a mélange of my mother's finery prevented their union. I could see the sleeves of a silver fox coat, the ivory satin hem of a negligee, a collar of mauve silk, and a strand of sapphires curling through the perfumed tangle.

"Those clothes will look funny on you," I told Glendora, hoping she would put them back. I didn't want her to get into trouble with Charmian or the law. She'd suffered enough as it was.

"Climb up and sit on my suitcase so I can snap it shut," she ordered.

I did as I was told.

Glendora threw her entire torso across one side of the suitcase lid. "Bounce a little," she commanded me through gritted teeth as though she were instructing the suitcase how it should act. Counting three, we pounced on her suitcase together. There was a satisfying click.

"Are you leaving?" I asked.

Glendora rolled her eyes at my stupidity.

"What about your uniforms and your day-off clothes? They're still hanging in the closet." I pressed her on this because I still hoped she wanted to stay.

"They're up for grabs," Glendora said, raising an eyebrow and thrusting her lips.

"Please don't go," I begged. Unbidden tears surfaced and I became the whiny, clinging, loathsome child my mother sometimes said I was.

"I have no choice," Glendora said indifferently. Then she yanked her uniforms from their hangers and tossed them into an immense leather satchel.

Glendora had also forgotten an elaborate, manila accordion file, tied with a pink satin ribbon. This was something I coveted because inside it, folded and refolded like road maps from a long trip, were mementos of her life before us. I still remember her flower garden, photographed in black and white, with an empty swing dangling above it. Wicker rockers in a breeze had made blurs on the porch. Glendora also kept a daisy pressed in a gold-edged Bible that was bound in white leather. Her file contained paper doll cutouts from a niece, and a brown blob that was their mutt Moe as drawn by her young brother. A recipe for Scotch butter biscuits, written in her mother's thick, fountain-penned strokes and barely contained between the lines on the card, was stapled to a letter promising to make them as soon as Glendora came home.

I was ten years old and had already noted that all nannies carried an envelope or a shoe box or a cloth pouch akin to Glendora's file. Those envelopes were the hope chests of domestics, and now Glendora had no hope. I was going to miss touching these letters and pictures as much as I would miss Glendora. Despite my longing, I reminded her, "Don't forget your accordion file."

She moaned as she yanked out a dresser drawer, grabbed her file, held it briefly against her chest, and then placed it lovingly inside the satchel. Then she regarded me with large round eyes. "You're a thoughtful child. You can rest assured, you don't take after your mother."

The shutters on the tall, narrow, arched windows had been closed against the morning sun so that horizontal slats of light whittled and reshaped Glendora's ample figure with every step she took. I watched from the balcony as she lugged her suitcase, her satchel, and a large purse down the stairs.

On the landing Glendora set everything down but her satchel. Then she tiptoed across the room. She stopped at this end table or that vitrine and inspected the objets d'art. She hefted and turned over in her hands all the decorative items on the coffee table. I thought this was Glendora's way of saying farewell, but she pulled some uniforms out of her satchel and proceeded to wrap them around a small bronze bust of a milkmaid, a porcelain hunting hound, an enameled Fabergé egg, the Meissen cigarette basket, and the silver Ronson lighter, as though they were kidnapped children and she was stifling their cries.

My audible gasp startled her, and she looked up at me.

"Glendora, that's stealing," I whispered.

"An eye for an eye," Glendora said. "Now, don't be a busybody," she warned as she wrapped and packed several more of Mother's bibelots. She scanned the room with her big eyes and, with a furtive smile, snapped the satchel shut.

I waited until she left the room before I went downstairs. Then I checked to be sure: yes, the Sleekèd Boy still smiled in darkness at the rear of the étagère.

When I entered the kitchen, I found Glendora carefully rolling Charmian's best silver into tea towels. "I don't think you should do that," I warned, picturing Glendora squeezed into one of the Beverly Hills jail cells.

"A tooth for a tooth," she said. Then she gave me a wry smile and hinted, "Right now, I'd walk a mile for a Camel."

Smoking in the kitchen was a no-no, but this was the cook's day off so I brought her a pack from the butler's pantry. "Where are you going to live?" I asked.

Glendora blew an oval of smoke that looked like a visual sigh. "Be it ever so humble . . ." she gave me a clue.

"I think your home must be very nice," I told her, trying to make going home seem like a prize instead of a retreat. "Your mother will make you Scotch butter biscuits."

Charmian rang for Glendora from the bedroom. "That's my cue," Glendora said. Galvanized, she stubbed out her cigarette in the sink, switched on the percolator, and picked up the phone. "Have a cab here in exactly twenty-five minutes," she instructed Celebrity Taxi Service. "As for you, stick around and watch the chips fly," she advised me.

My mother's good china looked diminutive in Glendora's hands. I trailed behind her listening to the rhythmic tapping of porcelain cup against saucer as she strode through the butler's pantry, the dining room, and the living room. I listened for the last time to the furniture rattle. Again, Glendora didn't glance at the dark, lonely spot where the Sleekèd Boy hid. She went on upstairs, kicking the tiles with her heavy feet, and crossed the balcony noisily to Charmian's room. Once there, she knocked on the door and, without waiting for an answer, let herself in.

My mother had to get up early on Mondays for her standing appointment with her analyst. It wasn't so much that she needed the analysis as that David O. Selznick had the appointment before hers. He was an important connection and this was Charmian's way to connect.

I lingered near the door as Glendora handed my mother a glass of orange juice and a red amphetamine pill. Charmian, angled on one elbow, neck straining to hold up her head, stared at us with soupy eyes and silently swallowed. Any other time of day my mother was beautiful.

Glendora took the empty glass back from Mother and then plumped some pillows behind her. Leaning against them, Mother received her ritual cup of hot coffee and a cigarette lit for her by Glendora. Just because my mother was awake didn't mean she was ready to talk.

While Glendora returned to the kitchen for tray number

two, I ventured closer to Charmian's side of the bed, lured there by the remnants of last night's box of chocolates. My mother must have nibbled quite a few before her "sleep" pill had taken effect. Fishing though the candy wrappers, I found several savaged confections. They lay like wounded children with their hearts of cherry syrup and raspberry cream oozing onto their rumpled, brown, crinolated wrappers. Wishing to put them out of their misery, I devoured them.

"Mommy," I said, knowing she didn't like me to call her that, "something's wrong."

My mother's eyes looked at me scornfully for, as they said in radio, a beat. Then they closed.

Glendora appeared with a second, more substantial tray. On it was half a grapefruit with a silver serrated spoon by its side, a four-minute egg upended and indented in an egg cup, a crustless piece of toast already buttered, and another, fresher cup of black coffee. Glendora stood by while her cooking was silently consumed. "Mrs. Leigh," she said softly as my mother dawdled over her egg, "I don't want to rush you, but . . ."

Although I hated to miss Glendora's explanation, I slipped away from the room and tiptoed downstairs. Those two women had stolen from each other, but I felt I'd suffered a bigger loss. I was losing Jeff *and* Glendora. Why couldn't *I* have one little thing I wanted?

I found Glendora's luggage where she had placed it outside the breakfast room door on the flagstone steps. Her bags had heated up in the sun, and I patted her leather satchel affectionately as though it were a dog. Then I unsnapped its leather flap and pulled it open.

Deep down under the shrouded artworks and silver, I found Glendora's manila accordion file. The pink satin ribbon had come untied and it looked slightly crumpled. I extricated the file from out of Glendora's loot, knowing full well that mine was a crime too petty to ever be dramatized on Charmian's show.

With the accordion file tucked under my arm, I hurried to find a place to stash it. On *The Charmian Leigh Radio Mystery Half-Hour* my mother was constantly unearthing well-concealed objects—my hiding place would have to be exceptional. And then I remembered the dog we'd once had. He'd been a purebred Saint Bernard named Cocteau, and although my mother got rid of him because he shed, no one had ever thrown away his enormous sack of Dr. Ross dog food. It still stood on end in the service porch closet. I pulled at the string that held its sides closed and plowed my fingers through the hard, dry pellets of feed until I'd made a deep depression. I squirreled Glendora's accordion file down into the hole, and covered its shape with kibbles. Then I neatly closed the sack. Only when I'd concluded this criminal activity did I feel guilty.

Good riddance to bad rubbish (or its equivalent in French), Charmian would say when she learned of Glendora's departure. It would make no difference to my mother that she had been the cause. I knew it meant risking being sent to boarding school, but I wanted to compensate Glendora for all that she'd lost and, while I was at it—as Charmian often said of the criminals on her show—teach my mother a lesson.

The house had already grown larger now that Glendora was leaving. I walked back through the kitchen, through the butler's pantry, and into the dining room, which was two steps higher than the living room. Despite the recent plunder of decorative objects, the living room did not look bare. From where I stood, I could see the Sleekèd Boy beaming his smile from out of his dark corner. I remembered my mother saying he was a priceless chef d'oeuvre, a gift she'd given herself. For quite awhile I admired the Sleekèd Boy's exemplary silhouette. Then I slowly crossed the living room and lifted him off the shelf. I pressed his cool marble skin against my lips.

I retraced my steps, caressing the Sleekèd Boy once again, wanting always to remember his firmness, his density, and the smile that seemed to pervade his entire body. I held him so tight his marble flesh warmed in my hand. When I opened the French doors that led outside, the sun shone down on him and I saw for the first time fine, glistening streaks of gold that ran through his marble flesh.

Rummaging in Glendora's satchel again, I found an extra uniform, which I wrapped slowly and meticulously around the statuette. Then I braced his swathed body between some of the other artifacts and closed Glendora's satchel once and for all.

Just as I entered the kitchen, Glendora did too. She banged down Charmian's tray. "My swan song," she said, then added, "If you weren't jailbait, I'd take you along."

I followed behind Glendora when she carried her baggage out to the cab. She hardly looked at me as she climbed into the back seat, but her big, bent body spoke of dejection. Just before the taxi reached the first curve in the canyon, the window next to Glendora rolled down a crack. Her thick, ringless fingers reached over the edge and wriggled a listless good-bye.

11

Glo

9/12/57–9/13/57

The expression on my father's face worried me. It said we had a disagreeable task to perform, something akin to discarding dead animals, something best left for a maid. In fact, his secretary had been assigned to this chore, but at the last minute she'd demurred—it was a Sunday night. Then, as he was leaving the house, Maurice decided to take me along. "You could use an airing," he said. I linked this phrase with the old frocks and outmoded furs Charmian sent to a charity shop. For the deduction, she routinely explained.

Maurice and I watched as the airplane rolled to a stop. Before the propellers stopped spinning, a hatch opened and passengers emerged carrying babies, books, toys, a cat in a cage, and baggage of countless shapes and shades. When two uniformed men disembarked, I asked my father, "Is there a war?"

"They're the pilots," he explained wearily. He had no patience with ignorance.

Stepping into the atmosphere of Los Angeles, the passengers rubbed their eyes, contorted their bodies in uneasy stretches, blinked, and quickly lit cigarettes. They looked as stunned and amazed as house pets set free in the wilderness.

I scrutinized every female who left the plane, but when the last passenger had disembarked, not one of them had hailed us with a hello.

"A fine how-do-you-do," Maurice snarled.

A cleaning crew mounted the stairs to the plane. I heard their buckets and carpet sweepers thud against the metal railings. On reaching the top, they began to back down: a large woman had commandeered the hatchway. Her torso, I noticed, was covered by a scarf fashioned of fur-bearing animals. Little sets of toenails curled at the ends of dangling feet, barbed teeth gnawed idly on tails, and mean pairs of eyes glowered out of narrow heads that leaned slyly on her bosom. These were muskrats, I surmised, skins my mother never deigned to wear.

At the end of the fifties, when traveling by air, people still dressed as though they were attending a theatrical event. This particular woman wore cotton gloves and a hat shaped like a biscuit with a prune-colored veil that drooped over her eyes. It didn't entirely hide the bluing in her gray hair, which hunkered around a big, demanding face. She wore a dark old lady's dress with no particular style or shape, and her legs reminded me of upholstery.

My father groaned and bent the jacket collar of his suit upward as if trying to hide his face.

The woman was flanked by stewardesses, so smart in their orange uniforms with gold piping and matching caps that I wished I could join their ranks. The stewardesses were toting a selection of crumpled grocery sacks and threadbare carpet- or knitting bags—obviously *hers* since the woman had similar ones hooked over each arm. The whole business took a long time, and when she and the stewardesses reached the ground, the old woman looked around and quickly set her sights on my father. The baggage she carried prevented her from holding out her arms, but I saw her use them to make a sort of flap. "Morrie," she cried out.

Maurice put his finger to his lips by which he meant, "Pipe down." He didn't move, so she came up close to him. For a minute I thought she was going to lick him with her tongue. Maurice must have thought so too because he took a step backward.

"Morrie," she admonished.

"I'm Maurice now. Out here, I'm known as Maurice," he said sternly. Then he made a show of taking charge of her bags—his way, it seemed to me, of keeping his distance.

I saw her shrug before she looked at me. "So, this is the little one?" she asked.

"This is Fleur de Leigh," Maurice announced as though she might never have heard of me.

"That's supposed to be a name?" she frowned.

I agreed with her. I said, "Pleased to meet you," and curtsied, just slightly, as I had been taught.

"He told you I'm your Grandma Glo?" she introduced herself. When I giggled, she frowned. Then she bent toward me, leveling her eyes with mine. "So, how much do you love me?"

My fifth-grade teacher had told the class that all questions deserve an answer, and since my own questions so rarely were answered, responding to inquiries had become my credo. I looked into my grandmother's eyes, avoiding those of the beasts on her chest, and tried to determine if she was thinking in terms of a seamstress's tape or in ounces, the way our cook measured flour. Since I wasn't sure how to answer, and the word *love* embarrassed me—I'd only heard it in movies—I turned to my father for guidance.

His lips were pressed together. He wasn't going to be much help.

"I . . . love . . . you . . . as much as I . . . love . . . God . . . and my country," I murmured, borrowing a portion of the Girl Scout pledge which I had committed to memory. I hoped it was an answer that would satisfy both the mother and the son.

Maurice's face relaxed; I thought I saw a glint of approval. He was an atheist, so for him God counted for nothing, and as for "the country," he must have known I had no clear conception of it, rarely having crossed beyond the borders of Beverly Hills. In fact, each Monday at Girl Scout meetings, I squirmed with guilt as I vowed to love these two mysterious entities.

My grandmother was pleased. She lowered her body disjointedly as though it were attached to a crane. Then, as one of her paper sacks thumped to the ground, she swaddled me in a hug. Her moist warmth and her pleasantly pithy scent surprised me. But it didn't make me forget that my parents believed physical contact of any kind was undignified, and because we were in a public place I felt extremely ill at ease. Then, as my grandmother's purchase on me tightened, I felt the prick of sharp teeth at my shoulders and chest, and stifled a cry. Not wanting to embarrass her, I whispered, "Your muskrat bites."

Once I'd wriggled away, I saw that one of her carpetbags had flapped open and in it were dozens of tiny, potted cacti. Even in their mishmashed condition, I could see they were shaped like ears, noses, and thumbs. Though stunted, each was fitted with a noteworthy set of spines. She *collected* cacti; she was a kindred soul. However, as much as I cared for the many inanimate objects *I* collected, I'd never considered taking them on a trip.

Though I didn't collect *live* vegetation, cacti weren't entirely out of my frame of reference—next to our house there was an immense cactus garden. Facing the street, where the sun spent its longest hours in our canyon, a wall of cactus at least ten feet thick delineated the entire length of the neighboring estate. It had been a monastery, I'd been told, erected even before Pickfair or the Chaplin estate. Our gardener, Constantine, said that a wise old monk must have collected and established the prickly plants as a kind of decorative Maginot Line to segregate the forces of good from those of evil.

I hadn't known the meaning of Maginot, and he'd explained, "Is wall being impregnable." Until I looked it up, I thought he meant a wall that couldn't get pregnant.

My parents considered cacti so ugly that they were an affront to Beverly Hills. My nannies said cacti were too dangerous to touch. To Constantine, however, cacti were precious and full of mystery. The most exquisite of their blossoms opened only under the cover of night, he said, and he had promised to take me sometime soon to see the rarest cactus flower of all. He said cacti were practical too, and once, in daylight, before my awestruck eyes, he slashed a cactus in half to reveal the storage tank of juices hidden beneath its spikes. Desert nomads knew this secret and, now, so did I.

But when my father beheld Grandma Glo's succulent booty, he sneered. "Are you crazy, lugging that junk around the country?"

Don't talk to your mother that way. You could get sent away to boarding school, I wanted to warn Maurice.

Grandma Glo took the time to crank herself into an upright position. "You don't like I got a hobby?" she asked. Her voice was loud and raspy.

"Let's get out of here," he decreed.

He had parked his car at the curb right in front of the terminal, and already a ticket flapped on the windshield. Maurice didn't *pay* tickets, he had them *fixed,* but just the same he reached across the windshield and angrily tore it away from the wiper. Then he yanked open the passenger door, demanding that his mother "Get in."

Grandma Glo tentatively stuck one rag-doll leg out into space. It hesitated as though deciding whether to step down into the street from the curb or to try to bridge the ample gap between the sidewalk and car.

"If you'd put down those damn weeds, you could use your hands for leverage," Maurice told her impatiently. "Here, give them to me." But she wouldn't. "They'll scratch the upholstery," he warned, his voice climbing the same scale of intensity as it did when she called him on the telephone. When I was small, I'd thought he had to yell at her in order to be *heard* long distance.

As he pushed me into the back seat, Maurice asked his mother sarcastically, "Can you keep yourself out of trouble for two minutes?" Then he went back into the terminal for the suitcases.

My grandmother spread her carpetbags on the wide front seat. She opened their maws and set each of the little pots straight. Their contents looked like tiny, plucked birds waiting for a beak. But instead of dangling a worm over their heads, she spoke to them. "He wants I should leave you behind, but don't fret," she said. At least that's what I thought she said. She had an accent I couldn't fully interpret, an accent I'd only heard when my parents told jokes.

"They lead a terrible hard life, my cactuses," Grandma Glo sighed, "with maybe an eyedropper of water a month, and under a cruel sun."

I understood her to say "cruel *son.*" "Grandma Glo," I told her, "I'm sure my father won't hurt them."

My grandmother's suitcases were as bulky and misshapen as her body. Maurice deposited them in the trunk. Then he climbed into the car, and we sped away from the curb.

"Where'd you get such a smart little girl?" his mother inquired, and then I knew she liked me.

There was a pause. "How do you like my car?" Maurice asked. "It's a Cadillac. I'm a producer now. I can buy anything I want."

"You think I never seen a Cadillac? Your sisters married doctors. *They* have Cadillacs." It amazed me to hear someone talking back to Maurice.

Maurice drove silently in a direction away from our house. As usual, I was experiencing what Charmian called *mal de mer,* but I knew better than to say anything. Fortunately, we soon stopped at a cheerful duplex apartment on Olympic Boulevard. Set back behind a pretty lawn and a camellia bed, it had tall, graceful windows, some of them set into fanciful turrets as if to remind passersby that every man's home is his castle. From the outside I could see into the lighted apartments. They had high ceilings and spacious rooms, but most appealing were the sidewalks with people walking on them, evidence to me of a bona fide neighborhood.

It seemed as though Maurice had to tug and yank to extricate his mother from the car. We ambled in fits and starts toward the building, stopping several times to wait for her legs to work and to pick up the tiny pots of cacti that kept dropping to the ground. She was purposely slowing the action so that my father would have to give her a hand, and I couldn't help smiling a little.

"*This* is where you live?" she asked, sounding disappointed.

"This is where *you* are going to live," Maurice said, making a grimace that was his stand-in for a smile, as he led her up the step. Then he threw open the front door and turned on the lights. The apartment was nicely furnished; even my mother would have approved. We walked, or rather my grandmother bobbed and hobbled through the commodious rooms, as my father pointed out the comfortable couch, the easy chair that rocked, the modern kitchen, and two TVs.

"See, the refrigerator is groaning with food. The larder is stocked," Maurice bragged as he opened the various cupboard doors to demonstrate. "You've got all the staples, toothpaste, toilet paper, Calso water, Epsom salts, whathave-yous to last a month." He really had gone to quite a bit of trouble.

His mother didn't put down her cacti and she didn't sit in a chair. "When Poppa died, I lived five years with Zipporah and five with Muriel," she said. "How can I be a Democrat if I don't live with you?"

"Not a chance," he said firmly.

"Your little girl can't use a baby-sitter?" she answered back.

"She has a *nanny*," he told her.

This wasn't strictly true. So far, no replacement had been found for Glendora, but I didn't care to brave Maurice's wrath by revealing this information.

"So I can cook."

"We have a professional taking care of that."

"She makes borscht good as me?"

"We don't eat borscht," he responded sourly.

"Grandma Glo, it's nice you like to cook," I broke in. "Maurice cooks too. He must have gotten it from you. He doesn't make meals or anything you'd eat everyday, but sometimes, if he sees I'm sad, he makes super-duper milkshakes. He puts everything in them I'm not supposed to eat: chocolate ice cream, strands of coconut, poppy seeds, little pieces of graham crackers or Toll House cookies, or maybe Grape-Nuts—you never know what—so that drinking his shakes is like being on a treasure hunt."

"So you learned a new trick, Morrie?" Grandma Glo exclaimed. "The way to the girl's heart . . . ?"

"Ma," Maurice began with forced calm, "I picked this neighborhood because you can walk to a market, a bridge club, a department store, and this area is crawling with temples. You'll meet people you have something in common with. On the street where we live, you won't see a soul."

"You think I'm here for making friends? I come to be with you." She wasn't sassing my father now. There was a plaintive sincerity to her voice.

It made Maurice cringe. "There'd be absolutely nothing for you to do. We live way up a canyon, and you don't drive. Or *walk*," he said, attempting to terminate the subject.

"You think I *mind* being waited on hand and foot?"

"The fact is we have no room," Maurice responded, sounding quite glad.

"In your big Beverly Hills mansion? This I gotta see." She began walking briskly—her hobble miraculously cured—toward the front door.

As I've said, my parents didn't indulge in physical contact, not publicly at any rate. Oh, Maurice smacked my mother on the backside sometimes when she was dressing, as a joke, he said, but that was the extent of it. They weren't demonstrative in love *or* in anger; in fact, they seemed to have neither sentiment in common, so it jolted me when Maurice lunged toward his mother. His face glared with a bestial threat as he grabbed her arm and spun her around, but he'd forgotten the sharp-toothed mammals covering her chest and the spikes that lurked in her bags. Within seconds Maurice jumped away and took a moment to rub his skin. Then he wheeled around her and grabbed her shoulders from behind. "I paid good goddamn money for this apartment, it's a helluva lot of rent, and you're damn well going to stay here," he shouted as he pulled her over to a couch and bent her into it.

I was shocked: I couldn't believe Maurice would manhandle his own mother in that way, but before I could decide how to defend Grandma Glo, Maurice yelled at me: "I'm getting the luggage out of the car, so you're in charge. Don't let her out of your sight. Don't let her budge."

"Orders from headquarters?" my grandmother asked as she let her body slump further into the couch. "You get old, you lose your vim," she said with a shrug as though her only regret was that she hadn't been able to physically hold her own.

A new sensation overtook me: Where were my loyalties supposed to lie? If Grandma Glo was Maurice's adversary, was she mine too? Was I supposed to take my father's side or just pretend nothing was wrong? I recalled a motto set forth by Miss Nora, the first and longest-lived of my nannies: "When in doubt, apologize." So I said, "I'm sorry Grandma Glo. I don't know why my father is acting up. I guess he's just in a very bad mood."

"So when isn't he? You shoulda seen the way he bullied his big sisters. And their friends. He bullies you too?"

"Maurice is really busy. He runs out of time. He gets bothered by how little I know."

Then, as if to make up for all the injustices he'd heaped on me, Grandma Glo pulled me onto her lap with strong, friendly hands. I regret to say I stiffened; I wasn't used to being touched.

But my grandmother had made an undeniably amicable gesture and I believed she deserved a response. "It's nice in this neighborhood, Grandma Glo, with lots of people around. My nanny could bring me over to visit. Every day if you wanted. I'd be happy to spend the night. At *our* house you'd get lonely."

"Do *you*?" Grandma Glo asked.

This was a question I'd never been asked, and one I refused to pose to myself. Indeed, the very *word* brought tears to my eyes. "Well, my parents are away a lot. My mother works," I explained.

"You think I don't know? Haven't I heard her on the radio? Haven't I seen her pictures?" she scoffed. "Outsiders raising you while *she* diddles in B pictures?"

"Charmian's career is very important; it's why she has to be away from me."

"Ha-ha-ha, that's rich."

"She has a true artist's soul." I quoted my mother's own words.

"Soul. Mole. Down a hole."

It seemed like a good idea to change the subject, so I asked, "Were you and my father born in the same country?"

"No, no, he had it *easy*," she piped up. "*His* country never went after his hide."

And then Maurice was in the room, having carried the last of her suitcases in. I no sooner scrambled off my grandmother's lap than my father began pulling me toward the door. "Everything you need is here. Just look for it," he told his mother, "and tomorrow my secretary will take you wherever you want to go."

With amazing spryness she raised herself from the couch and started after us. "You think I'm an invalid? You think I can't catch a bus? Maybe I'll get to your house before you," she taunted him.

Maurice steered me over the threshold. "Let's get out of here," he said with an urgency that made it appear that he was afraid. Then he tugged the door tightly closed behind us.

It took Maurice several aggravated minutes to brush the sand off his leather upholstery. He was as fussy about his car as he was about his apparel. Then, just as he started his engine, the fluttering movement of a dark figure caught my eye. It was traveling toward us from the lawn of Grandma Glo's new apartment. My father saw it too and shook his head as if to clear his eyes of sand.

Grandma Glo was scrambling toward the front of Maurice's car. All of a sudden I saw her eyes—or were they those of her muskrat?—gleaming spitefully in the beam of the headlights. She was standing directly in front of us wriggling her shoulders and hips and shuffling her feet as though burrowing herself into the ground, her very stance daring Maurice to run her down.

I expected him to curse and snarl, but instead he pushed the heel of his hand, ever so casually, against the horn. He must have meant to scare her off, to say *Go home,* but the blare had the opposite effect. Maurice should have known. She dodged away from the sound, momentarily blocking the headlight on the driver's side of the car, but in a second she was back. I watched her slap both her hands down hard on the enamel paint and was amazed by her pluck. Then I felt the Cadillac sway; she must have placed one foot on the bumper and stepped up to meet our stare. She grabbed hold of the Cadillac ornament and rested her torso on the hood. I could see the teeth and claws of her muskrat scrape against the paint.

"The old bat thinks she can stop me," Maurice growled.

"My teacher says the force of a mother's love has been known to actually *lift* a car if her child is pinned under it," I offered to explain the phenomenon.

"Your teacher should shut up." Maurice was declaring war. I could tell.

Even so, I assumed we would be getting out of the car to reason with Grandma Glo. But as I felt for my door handle I noticed a sudden smirk warp Maurice's lips. He lifted his foot from the brakes and began to move it as slowly and deliberately as a record player arm ferrying a needle to a precise groove. I observed how lightly he settled the toe of his shoe on the gas pedal.

"Please don't hurt her," I whimpered, but he didn't seem to hear.

Maurice inched his Cadillac along Olympic Boulevard, then executed a painfully slow turn. I doubt we traveled as far as three blocks, but in my ten-year-old mind it seemed we were driving for miles with Grandma Glo's backside facing the oncoming traffic. My mother would laugh if I described the incident, but I wasn't going to say anything.

"Please stop, Maurice. Please let her down. She could get hurt."

"What do you care? What's she ever done for you?" he seethed. "It's exactly what she deserves. She's a . . . shrew. A shrike. Goddamn it, she's destroyed just about everyone she's come in contact with."

Just then I noticed my grandmother's hand slipping away from the hood ornament—she was sliding off the fender. "You've got to stop. You have to let her down. Right now. Please, Maurice, please," I begged my father.

When Maurice finally coasted the Cadillac to a standstill, I looked around the solitary side street where we'd landed. Now that the engine was off, we could hear Grandma Glo's cries. So could the people in the adjacent apartments: within seconds porch lights snapped on and people were stepping onto their balconies and their stoops. Someone must have called the police because a siren tuned up in the distance. Soon dogs were mimicking its whine.

My father slowly removed himself from the car, too livid to hurry even though the apartment-dwellers were moving out onto their lawns. They walked gingerly as though we might be escapees from the asylum at Camarillo, as though the least deviation in their gait might provoke us to attack. They were too timorous to offer help, so I climbed out of my seat and walked around to meet Maurice by the radiator grille.

"We'll have to lift her down," my father yelled at me. "I'll grab her by the waist. You take hold of whatever you can."

As I have indicated, my grandmother was a large women, but it hadn't crossed my mind she'd be wearing a girdle. I remember the stiff feel of straps and stays overlaying triangular chunks of soft flesh. It was hard to know where to take hold of her and then what to do with the force of her weight.

Grandma Glo's body felt like a leaden Raggedy Ann when Maurice and I shouldered more of her ballast. To my amazement her carpetbags of cacti were still hooked over her arms, and I made sure to dodge the needles poking through the cloth. Once Grandma Glo was standing on her own, she grinned at my father sheepishly.

The stoop of her body or maybe the expression on her face reminded me of the Piltdown Man, whom I'd read about when I'd skipped ahead in our science book at school. I'd treasured the photographs of his mysterious, blackened jawbone and the artist's conception of the whole man. But when we finally arrived at *his* chapter in class, our teacher gave the order to x him out. Our textbooks were old, he'd explained, written and published before the Piltdown Man had been exposed as a hoax.

The siren had closed in on us, shocking me when it stopped in mid-reverberation but emboldening the onlookers to skulk closer. "Was there an accident? Did he try to run you down?" a policeman asked my grandmother, bypassing Maurice and me.

Grandma Glo straightened up. "My son wouldn't give me a ride in his luxury car. So I thought, why not go steerage? Wouldn't be the first time."

Instead of pulling into our driveway, Maurice parked down the hill near our front door because Grandma Glo insisted on entering our house as an honored guest. The entry steps were steep, but I'd learned that my grandmother could walk rather well if she so desired.

I ran around to the breakfast room door, which was never locked, and hurried through the living room to unlatch the front door. "Charmian," I called out excitedly, sure she must have arrived home after the *Mystery Half-Hour* broadcast. "Guess who's here?"

Just as Maurice piloted Grandma Glo through the tiled entry hall into the newly carpeted living room, Charmian was descending the stairs. I couldn't tell if it was the mean little countenances leering out from her bosom or Grandma Glo herself that caused my mother to gasp.

The two women came face-to-face. Charmian was wearing a spotless white tulle negligee. The ends of her gleaming blond hair curled upward like the petals of a hothouse flower. Next to her, my grandmother looked like one of the refugees I'd seen in the pages of *Life* magazine, someone who'd hastily grabbed all her clothes just before a foreign army invaded and was still wearing everything she owned.

With an actress's self-possession, Charmian smiled tolerantly and held out her hand to be shaken or kissed. "*Bon soir, chérie,*" she trilled.

Grandma Glo avoided Charmian's hand and threw down her statement as though it were a glove. "Bet you didn't dream you'd be seeing *me* here tonight."

"*Mais non, vous n'avez pas de raison,*" my mother said. "I'm an actress, *chérie,* a creature plagued by a creative mind. I dream of *everything,*" she sighed with the burden of it all. "Although, I must admit, I had no idea you were in town. Did you mention it, Maurice? I can't recall."

"You dreamed of me staying here with you? I had that dream too," Grandma Glo said with a broad smile which was not returned. "So where do I sleep?"

Charmian looked bewildered and turned to my father for help, but he merely shrugged.

"How about I take a bath while you get to work on it?" Grandma Glo suggested.

Where Grandma Glo procured scented soap I never found out. Its cloying bouquet seeped out of the downstairs powder room where she was bathing (Maurice had refused to maneuver her up our steep staircase) and permeated the air with a saccharine bubble-gum scent. She must have smuggled it into the house under the cacti in her carpetbag, because our house was scrupulously devoid of anything that smelled. My father said that cooking odors, perspiration, perfume, scents of any kind, were an intrusion on his inalienable right to privacy. Over and above that, he was *allergic*. Indeed, while the three of us listened to Grandma Glo splash and warble foreign-sounding songs, Maurice started to sneeze.

"What ever possessed you to let her come to Los Angeles?" my mother asked my father.

"Don't blame me," he said defensively. "My sisters put her on the plane. They only told me they were going to do it a week ago."

"Did you stop sending them money?" Charmian accused him.

"They don't want money. They want out from under . . . you know who."

"Morrie, Morrie, come and get me," my grandmother called. It sounded like a tease. "You have to get me out of the tub."

"You managed to get in it all by yourself," he shouted.

"But now I'm wet," she whined.

"Well, I'm off to bed," my mother said, which didn't surprise me because she didn't like to involve herself in imbroglios. She'd hardly spoken to her own parents since she'd left Pittsburgh for Hollywood; she sent them money instead.

Before she went upstairs, Maurice asked Charmian if our cook had returned from her day off.

"Highly unlikely," my mother said.

"Where the hell does she go on a Sunday night?"

"Church," I told him.

"Jesus," he said, and went to look for himself.

I followed Charmian and waited until she stretched out on her bed. Only then did I ask, "How come Maurice hates Grandma Glo? Why's he so mean to her?"

Charmian looked thoroughly annoyed. "If you must know, the woman is an ogre. All she cares about is herself."

"She likes her cactus and I think she likes me."

"Take my word on her character."

"Tell me what makes her so terrible."

Charmian surveyed the room in a way that was uncharacteristic of her, as though she were afraid of hidden microphones. Then, in a quiet but contemptuous tone, one usually reserved for the lawbreakers on her show, she confided, "Glo was a bootlegger."

"A boot*legger*? What's that? Is it like a boot*licker*?" I asked, already in love with the word.

"If you must know, during Prohibition, Glo and your grandfather got very rich making gin and selling it on the sly. Glo masterminded the entire operation."

"But you always say Prohibition was asinine, that it made law-abiding citizens into criminals."

"Your father and his sisters—they were just little kids—were forced to . . . mull the gin, bottle it, and make deliveries after school."

"Did they cook it in their very own kitchen?" I asked, imagining the five of them, costumed in matching aprons and chef's hats, stirring aromatic liquid in oversized vats. I couldn't help feeling envious of families who did *anything* together. "So *that's* how Maurice learned to cook."

"Oh please."

"Shouldn't Maurice forgive his mother? She's just an old lady now. Lots of children work for their parents after school. I'd be glad to help *you,* for instance."

"Your father could have been shot," Charmian said scornfully, as though I'd proposed shooting him myself.

"By who?"

"By *whom.* That's all I have to say about it," Charmian said, meaning that I was dismissed. "And don't breathe a word to your father. Don't tell a soul."

"Soul. Mole. Down a hole," I said.

The downstairs powder room had no heat; situated on the shady side of our house, it was always colder than the out-of-doors. Just this afternoon I'd played jacks on its cool tile floor to evade the scorching September weather. I assumed that party guests, the only other people who used the room, and always at night, shivered when they peed.

I saw right away that Grandma Glo's teeth were chattering and the large expanse of her exposed skin was covered with goose bumps. She had achieved a squatting position, and her big, blotched breasts, with their wide, seemingly all-seeing nipple-eyes were visible above the water. If this was the tip of the iceberg, I didn't want to think what lay in the soapy depths.

"You ever seen such a big girl?" my grandmother asked when she saw me looking at her.

My father might as well have had his hands clamped over his lids, he was averting his eyes so vigorously. I turned to see what he was looking at and discovered that the only towels in the powder room were small and appliquéd. I raced to the upstairs linen closet to find something more appropriate.

"You want my legs should slip out from under me?" Grandma Glo was toying with Maurice when I returned. "You want I should break a hip?"

My father grabbed one of the bath towels I'd retrieved and threw it around her as though to protect me from the spectacle. I saw the ends slide into the water and hungrily sop it up.

"Give me your hands," he demanded of his mother. Once he had his hands around her red, wet wrists, I saw that his eyes were closed. Too curious not to look, I beheld a life-size rag doll with all the pleats, tucks, and stitches sewn on the outside.

"You hopped onto my car. You walked all the way up our front steps. How can a little old bathtub hold you back?" Maurice griped. Nevertheless, we had to lift one of her legs, bending it at the knee, to raise it over the bathtub wall. Her leg rubbed against the enamel and made the room echo with tuba sounds. When both her feet finally found a safe harbor on the bath mat, Maurice rushed to drape her with more towels.

"Pat me dry, Morrie?" she asked coquettishly.

"Not now," he responded. His eyes shown with disgust and he quickly left the room.

I had to borrow a nightie from the cook's room. Lulu wasn't nearly so big as my grandmother, but she owned a muumuu purchased in the Hawaiian Islands before she came to work for us. And from the upstairs linen closet my father had gathered a pillow and two blankets, which he pitched onto the long, blue couch closest to the staircase. I helped Grandma Glo tuck their satin-lined edges into the couch to simulate a bed.

"Grandma Glo," I asked, seeing her now as a bootlegging mastermind, "why did you make such a fuss?"

"The squeaky oil gets the wheel, at least until they throw the wagon away," she said, or so I thought she said, as she dropped her body onto the couch.

No matter what, I had strict instructions never to knock on my parents' closed door, not even if I smelled smoke in the house or awakened from a nightmare, even if I saw light shining through the crack. "Wake the nanny," they told me. "That's what we're paying her for."

Instead, I would sit on the step in front of their bedroom door. I sat there in the dark and listened, my ears like little antennas pressed against the wood. This was my only means of obtaining information, because my parents told me nothing of importance. Unfortunately, their door was extremely thick, and I rarely heard them speak to each other when they were alone.

Later that night I was at my station when Grandma Glo began to snore. I leaned way out over the circular iron pinwheel shapes of our banister and listened attentively. The sound she made was as steady as a heartbeat. I liked the way it filled up the house, the way it told me someone was there. And it carried with it an unexpected reward—her snoring roused my parents and obliged them to talk.

"I haven't heard *that* sound in years. I'd forgotten she snores," Maurice grumbled.

"Even when she's asleep, she monopolizes the conversation," Charmian complained. "You've got to get her out of here."

"You don't need to rub it in. I'm getting her on a plane in the morning. I'll call my sisters *after* she's safely on her way."

The news of her imminent departure came as a blow. It wasn't that I'd learned to love my grandmother in this short period; I didn't know if I should trust a bootlegger. Nevertheless, I believed Grandma Glo had come to visit us with good intentions, and I wanted to compensate her for a wasted trip.

"What is it, little one?" Grandma Glo asked, surprisingly cheerful when I awakened her in the middle of the night.

"Please whisper," I told her, "so my parents don't hear us. And please get up. There's something I have to show you."

"It can't wait till morning?" she yawned.

"It can't. It only comes out at night." My broken whisper betrayed my urgency. "If we don't see it tonight, in the morning it might be dead."

"What?" she asked.

"You have to see."

"So, where?"

"Outside. Next door. I think I can find it, but I'm not one hundred percent sure. Please come with me."

"How long will it take? Should I wear my corset?" She was going to comply.

I helped her pull her dark dress over her shoulders. I prodded the flesh around her ribs in order to tease her zipper closed. I twisted her shoes on without a horn just as nannies in the past had done for me.

Even though this was a summer night, at the last minute she threw her muskratty fur around her shoulders. I saw its crippled feet beat against her chest as we descended the wide, flagstone entry steps and was relieved she'd left her carpetbags behind. The flashlight I carried lit her toes and previewed the next step in a small but effulgent circle. Grandma Glo loped down the steps like a colt.

Soon we were standing on the dark street with the entire panorama of the neighboring cactus garden before us. Though I stopped to admire the sculptural forms of the cactus every day, by moonlight it seemed that the black, spiny shapes might be a forest of spears, swords, and knives.

My grandmother flinched and looked away, and I considered calling off our expedition. On the other hand, Constantine had told me this was an event that everyone should experience at least once in a lifetime. So, trying to mimic the enthusiasm of our gardener who had told me the names of every living thing, I piped up, "Look, that's an organ pipe, and that one's called a prickly nipple." I traced their outline with the flashlight beam. "And that one is called old man of the Andes. The tallest one over there, it's a saguaro. I wish you could see all their flowers," I exclaimed as I captured brilliant scarlet petals and magenta stamens in a ring of light. I moved the glowing orb so that it illuminated this dewy orange-tinged blossom or that spray of yellow flowerets, blooms that looked like giant asparagus and blooms that looked like plumes, at least in daylight. Hesitantly, I asked my grandmother, "What do you think?"

"To tell you the truth, the only cactuses I like are the ones I can carry with me," she said.

"Well, Grandma Glo," I urged her, "maybe when you see this one really special . . ."

"So point your flashlight, I'll take a gander, and then we'll go back," she interrupted me.

"We have to walk through the cactus wall to get to it."

"You want me walking in a briar patch?"

I wasn't sure I wanted to either. I'd never seen that most special of cacti; I only had our gardener's word that it was there. And I wasn't sure I could trust everything that Constantine had to say. But then, this one rare blossom—if I could find it—was all I had to offer my grandmother. "Each flower blooms for only one night in the year," I said earnestly, "and Constantine says tonight's a good night for them because there's a full moon."

"So this Constantine character, who's he?" she asked.

"Well . . . I guess he's my best friend. My first best friend, Daisy, has gone away for good, I'm afraid."

"Where is she?" Grandma Glo asked.

"That's the trouble. I just don't know."

Because a few tears began to dot my face, my grandmother did me a kindly turn and allowed me to lead her through the thicket of bristles and briars. I guided Grandma Glo carefully, stopping several times to unhook her clothes from a needle or two. Thorns scratched my cheek and pierced my forearm. When a lizard scurried across our feet we screamed. Finally, we penetrated the cactus wall far enough for me to detect the dreamy scent.

Grandma Glo smelled it too. "Is that a dandy smell or what?" she said, deeply inhaling the fragrance.

We had to squeeze our bodies between a devil's claw and a Turk's pincushion. When the flashlight beam fell on our prize, Grandma Glo bent down her head. Her old myopic eyes and my young ones beheld a flower bigger than her hand, comprised of the subtlest pastel shades of lavender and white. Its petals, pistil, and stamen were so fresh and tumescent, yet delicate too, it seemed to be more alive than any animal.

"It's a night-blooming cereus," I whispered its name proudly and said a silent prayer of thanks to Constantine.

Grandma Glo pondered. Then she turned her body toward me as much as she dared with needles everywhere. "I'm thanking you. Such a night I'll never forget. This night-bloomer is a beauty, but no more beautiful than you."

Receiving a compliment of such quality was a new sensation for me, and I longed to preserve it. If only I could have placed it in a satin-lined jewelry box and tucked it into my secret dresser drawer. I wanted to be able to take it out and cherish it whenever I pleased.

The following morning, Maurice inveigled his mother into the car. He didn't say anything about the airport, but I felt certain she knew where he was taking her. She didn't protest this time, I thought, because her son's bad temper had worn her down. Grandma Glo must have realized Maurice would never let her live with us. And maybe it occurred to her that if he did, it certainly wouldn't be fun. I wanted Grandma Glo's remaining time in California to be as happy as possible, so I told Maurice, "I'm going with you."

"Absolutely not," he said. "You can't miss school."

"It won't matter if I miss a morning. School's just started again and we aren't learning anything."

"I won't let you miss school."

Emboldened by my grandmother's presence, I walked around to the front of Maurice's Cadillac and put my foot on the bumper. I was taking a foolish chance, but I felt I owed it to a relative.

"You're not gonna try stopping the little one from going

with me if she wants to?" Grandma Glo yelled at my father loud enough for me to hear. "Not her. The kid's got guts."

Grateful for the encouragement, I gave a little push with my other foot and climbed atop the bumper.

"Get down, get down right now," my father fulminated.

"Only if you let me go with you," I cried victoriously. Then I jumped down and climbed into the car before he had the opportunity to argue further.

At the airport I felt certain Grandma Glo was going to infuriate my father, and, I regret to say, I remained a few steps behind as we walked to her gate. Before I knew it, the propellers were rotating and it was time for her to embark. Grandma Glo bent down and set her rumpled grocery sack and two carpetbags on the pavement. She grabbed hold of my arms and pulled me close. Before she hugged me, she made a show of twisting her muskrat scarf so that the faces and feet hung down her back. "So, how much do you love me?" she asked.

People were pushing past us, hurrying to get on the plane. "It's time to board," my father kept saying. "Let's go."

She was squeezing me so tight it was hard to find the breath to answer, but I did. "I love you as much as I love the most beautiful flower there ever was," I whispered. I didn't care if Maurice heard me or not. And I wanted my grandmother to have something to take home with her, so I stretched my arms as far around her girth as they would go.

Minutes later I watched her climb the metal stairs accompanied by a stewardess. My father was watching her too. He'd fixed his expression into one of scorn, and yet I detected a deeper, more subtle emotion in his eyes, as though a painter, using just the tip of his brush, had dabbed my father's pupils with a few remorseful flecks of gray. I saw Maurice blink as if to wipe them away. Maybe he loved his mother without realizing it. Maybe he wished he could. Maybe, and I hoped this was the case, he loved her but just didn't know how to say so.

When I looked back at the airplane, Grandma Glo was framed in the hatchway. She blew us a kiss and then she was gone.

III

Bettina

9/15/57–10/25/57

All morning, Bettina, Glendora's eventual replacement, had remained in bed, supine under an ice bag. "My head is one big flashbulb," she groaned each time I asked her how she felt. Edgy with pain, she still spoke in a soft, beguiling drawl. She came from that most foreign of regions, the South.

"How do you get a migraine anyway?" I asked each time I replenished the ice bag or provided more aspirin and cold water. I thought it might be a result of the Santa Ana winds that blew their hardest and hottest every October.

"Please," she begged me, "don't ask. Don't ask."

Bettina's welfare was of considerable importance to me.

The nanny job included taking me to swimming practice at the Beverly Hills Hotel. (Ever since Maurice produced a movie about a competitive swimmer called *Steady Stroke,* he'd devoted my life to the sport.) Utilizing every amenity at the hotel's Sand and Pool Club, Bettina and I would eat lunch on the strip of sand by the Olympic-size pool. We liked to order Monte Cristo sandwiches and Cokes—two pleasures my father denied me—and we talked and talked.

On the subject of my mother, Bettina's words were "Grin and bear it, mostly grin," though she expressed no opinion about Maurice. As to Daisy, she was very reassuring: "There's no question the Belmont girl is alive and kicking. If she'd died, especially by her own hand, all the newspapers and fan magazines would have picked it up. Her parents are much too famous to quash a story like that, believe you me," Bettina guaranteed. "You'll probably be hearing from Daisy in a matter of days."

Sometimes, just for a change of pace, Bettina took me to *her* pool club, the even more exclusive Copa Club with its equally imposing pool at the Beverly Wilshire Hotel.

"You're barefoot, so why do you walk on your tippytoes?" I was fond of asking her.

She offered the same explanation each time: "I'm just so used to wearing mile-high heels, my feet refuse to walk flat." And it was true, she was the only nanny I'd ever had who wore heels and stockings on the job.

At home Bettina's duties included mending—"She does a darn good job darning argyle socks," Maurice joshed—light housekeeping, driving, helping the cook, and caring for me. My memories of her, however, are centered in the Beverly Hills and Beverly Wilshire hotels. She had a statuesque figure, and her nut-brown hair stirred and shimmered in a self-made breeze. The wrapper she wore over her bathing suit was woven with twenty-four-carat gold thread and twinkled like an electric sign. She'd bought it to match the flecks of real gold that permeated her custom-made lipstick. "It's my signature," Bettina said. "Every woman should have one."

"Bettina is a triumph of the species," Maurice declared. Certain magazines would have called her a "glamour puss." I remember everyone staring at her as she promenaded toward the Brazilian Room where we sometimes ate lunch.

"How someone of Bettina's station happens to have a membership at the Copa Club, how she can *afford* it, is beyond me," Charmian occasionally harrumphed, but she'd already appropriated the idea of gold-flecked lipstick, using its print as the clue that exposed a home-wrecker on *The Radio Mystery Half-Hour.* "No doubt, Bettina has a sugar daddy," Charmian once speculated with a tone I'd interpreted as admiration.

"What's a sugar daddy?" I'd asked, treasuring the words since they represented two components which were normally missing from my life. I did not receive an answer.

"Bettina is giving *me* a headache," Charmian declared fifteen minutes after she awakened at noon and was informed *she* would have to take me swimming. Not only that, the entire Sand and Pool Club had been closed because Elizabeth Taylor was "entertaining" there.

"I worked with my writers—the dimwits—until three last night so I could have a Saturday *off*," my mother bitterly grumbled to Maurice. "Bettina is stealing my precious time. So Fleur misses a day or two of practice, so what?"

"It's a matter of discipline," my father said, adding snidely, "and besides, she'll get fat."

"In one day, Maurice? Come come," Charmian scoffed, her eyes narrowing with disbelief. On her show, when she exposed a suspect's faulty reasoning, Charmian approached him with a gentleness worthy of Teresa Wright. At home she could be as churlish as Agnes Moorehead.

"Fleur is prone to plumpness, or haven't you noticed?"

"She is?" Charmian sounded dubious.

But Maurice was on what my mother, with a roll of her eyes, called a "perpetual health kick"; he'd invented the No Whites Inside Diet just for me. He also remained adamant that I swim every day. He would gladly take me swimming himself, he said, but he was producing a picture with a budget in the millions. This made his time a wee bit more valuable than Charmian's. As soon as Maurice left, my mother loosened the reins on her crabbiness—she refused to drive longer than five minutes away.

But Charmian couldn't think of an acquaintance in Beverly Hills with a proper pool for actual *swimming*. It took less than four strokes to get across the Adlers' star-shaped pool. Worse, it was cantilevered precariously over a canyon. I wouldn't have known which way to aim in the Martins' pool; built by the previous tenants, it was tiled in pink and was embarrassingly kidney-shaped. The Jaffes, who each year sent Christmas cards of themselves posed in an elaborate Noah's Ark with all their pets, had a nice pool, but it had been usurped by their water snakes. Ever since the last earthquake, the Haphners, who lived at the bottom of the next canyon, had coexisted with a boulder in *their* pool. "Haph has produced three flops in a row," my mother explained. "He doesn't have the money for a crane to pull it out." Mud slides had slid an oak into the Walshes' pool and, since the tree refused to die, they didn't have the heart to remove it. The Cohens had a pondlike pool, more like a puddle, the contents of which spilled down the side of a cliff in an imitation waterfall, while the Starks only had a waterfall, and Edith Head managed with little more than a fountain. Charmian knew that Harold Lloyd had a stunning Olympic-size natatorium only a few blocks away, but she didn't know Harold Lloyd. And maybe he was dead; he hadn't made a picture since only God knew when. The Rosens' pool was also immense, but it mimicked the shape of an oil well. Alas, the pointy end narrowed so sharply, a swimmer could easily get stuck.

"What about the pool at the high school?" Charmian asked in a tone that said, *Ah-ha.*

"It's basketball season, I think. They practice on top of the pool," I explained. At Beverly Hills High School the indoor Olympic-size pool was situated under a basketball court which rolled under the bleachers for swimming events. The gym had been featured in a movie years before, and one rainy afternoon I had seen it run on television. Girls in prom dresses of cotton-candy chiffon with their escorts fitted in jaunty tuxedos had danced to the music of a live band. The dancers were so starry-eyed they didn't notice the floor rolling out from under them until it was too late. A few frames later, they were screaming for help. Their hair had turned into seaweed and their dresses were parachutes as they flailed about in the chlorinated water. Oddly, their dunked boyfriends didn't look so bad.

Given this image, my concentration disintegrated whenever I swam at the high school. I kept waiting for the movable floor to close over me once and for all.

"Don't tell me, *ce n'est pas possible,* that the only conventional swimming pool is in the *Valley*!" Charmian said as though she were referring to the Valley of Death. "*At Suzie Duvic's house?*"

On the winding, carsickening spin through Coldwater Canyon up over Mulholland Drive and down into the Valley, I broached a subject that had become all too familiar to Charmian. "You aren't going to ask me to call Daisy's parents again? They're on a secluded island in the Mediterranean making a picture. I wouldn't presume to bother them at this juncture with trivial questions," she said.

"Then, could you just find out if she's okay. I really miss Daisy terribly. Could you ask them to ask Daisy to write?"

"Not on your life."

Charmian, unless she could use it for material on her show, didn't really have much concern for people who vacated the premises of our lives. She seemed to think that, like nannies, friends were easily replaceable. Charmian reserved her sorrow for the loss of objects. It was conceivable, or so I heard her tell the insurance company, she would never recover from the burglary so craftily committed by Glendora.

To be honest, I had my dalliances with objects too. As I have mentioned, I was a collector of almost anything I could find, scrounge, or beg from Charmian: jokers from card decks, cutouts from cereal boxes, slugs from construction sites, postcards from anywhere, pressed flowers, abandoned birds' nests, eucalyptus pods, stamps, every one of my baby teeth, beads, shells, foreign coins, and buffalo nickels. Astonishingly, I had also amassed five hundred or so buttons of every shape, size, and material.

As a result of Charmian's Edict on Décor, which required me to keep my collections tidy and out of sight, they were housed in raffia baskets we made at school and inside animal cracker, cigar, and match boxes. Only the attractive volumes of the *Wizard of Oz* series I'd been given by a cast member on Charmian's show were displayed on a shelf. In a Whitman's Candy Sampler shell, I had stowed thirty-seven shining silver dollars, souvenirs of Maurice's trips to Las Vegas. I stored minuscule shells, all the nickels, and tiny circles of paper in pastel shades—the effluence of a hole punch I'd found—separately in various coin purses cast off by Charmian. All of these containers were kept in my desk or bureau drawers where they had been perfectly safe for years.

But recently, I'd discovered that many of my possessions were missing. A prized shell from Madagascar, all my birds' nests, and my entire cache of silver dollars had vanished. And oddly, so had several favorite dresses; a beloved, spumoni-colored nightgown; my cherished penny loafers; and the envelope containing all my baby teeth.

Suddenly, I couldn't even count on the *things* which dignified my life. Who would take them, and why? Bereft and enraged, I'd had only one recourse—Charmian Leigh's celebrated investigative method. The very next day I'd set about attaching hairs dipped in glue to my bureau drawer pulls and coating everything with dusting power.

Within hours I espied two hairy, white hands. They belonged to Maurice. But he refused to behave like a crook. Incensed by the stickum on his hands, Maurice confronted *me* before I had the chance to accuse him. "What's the meaning of this goo?" he thundered.

Like a cornered felon on my mother's program, I cowered; seconds later I blurted out the recent history of my losses.

Maurice listened and then quoted an oft-repeated phrase from *The Radio Mystery Half-Hour*: "Sounds like a pip of a case. Why don't you take it to Charmian Leigh?"

Throughout my childhood I was convinced that my parents spoke to me in code. I believed that if I could only learn to interpret their actions and decipher their system of communication, I would earn their love, a love so elegant and refined it defied the English language. As usual, I didn't comprehend the meaning of Maurice's message. But since he'd said it so forthrightly, I gave him the benefit of my doubt.

As our Oldsmobile swooped across Ventura Boulevard, I completed the litany of my losses.

"And here I'd thought you were going to tell me something really pithy. It's probably all there somewhere. You were careless and the maid tidied up," Charmian upbraided me.

I considered arguing this point but changed my mind; it wouldn't have been smart. Instead I said, "It *is* a whodunit, you have to admit. If we could solve it, you'd have material for your show."

"You think a few items missing from a child's room constitutes a mystery plot? Oh please. If only they came so easy. And even if you had a plot, you'd have to come up with a method of relating it. You'd have to decide on a point of view, you . . ." Charmian preceded to wear me out with a familiar lecture on the trials and tribulations of script writing.

Fortunately, we were turning onto Suzie's street. "We're almost here," my mother interrupted herself. "And I must warn you," she added in a hushed voice that commanded attention, "whatever you do, don't pee in Suzie's pool."

"I'm too old to pee in pools," I sassily replied.

"Well, keep in mind, Suzie laces her pool with a dye that turns pee bright pink. *Tu comprends pourquoi?*"

I was supposed to say *non*.

"The dye reveals the perpetrator of the pee," she explained, now using the jargon of *The Radio Mystery Half-Hour.* "Big joke, if it doesn't happen to be you."

Every possible indication that Suzie had thrown a party the night before lay in front of us: Small barges shaped like lily pads clunked against the tiles in each corner of the pool. Remnants of last night's drinks, with stuffed olives and puffy little onions, rocked in smudged glasses affixed to the barges with suction cups. Limp potato chips and soggy crackers caked with a greenish paste were clinging beside them like casualties from a shipwreck. Everything but the bobbing cigarette stubs, their filters now serving as life rings, had a light coating of flies.

Mindful of bits of decaying fruit from a cocktail or the punch, I hopped from one bare foot to the other trying to elude the egg-frying temperature of the deck. I'd grown during that tenth autumn of my life, and my one-piece, no-nonsense, navy blue swimsuit tugged at my crotch. A swim cap girdled my head. I was sweating underneath, but the pool looked no cooler than the air. It was going to be a steam bath, I thought, and seconds later my toes confirmed it. The fiery fingers of the Santa Ana winds left nothing untouched.

"Dive in," Charmian commanded from the side of Suzie's pool. "I don't want to spend any more time with Suzie than is absolutely necessary."

I had thrust one foot into the dubious waters when, from across the acre of crabgrass where Suzie's house roosted in its own nest of dwarf palms, we heard a back door slam. Then a familiar voice shouted, "I meant to clean up before you got here. *Every* party looks like an orgy the morning after, don't you think?"

"That voice," my mother said, and winced.

Suzie Duvic had the loudest, shrillest voice in Hollywood. Unlike Charmian, who could turn softly coquettish when she needed to get her way, Suzie invariably sounded like a naughty child. *That,* and her blowzy, spunky style gave her a quality widely sought after by casting directors.

It had originally attracted Charmian too. Since my mother played a former actress who'd become a formidable detective, who better than Suzie to ham it up on her show as Charmian's wacky, baby-voiced secretary, Miss Golly? Two or three times an episode Suzie answered the telephone: "Charmian Leigh Detective Agency. We're discreet, neat, and elite." And she always got a laugh with that. It was also Suzie's job as Miss Golly to pose pertinent questions so that Charmian could explicate the loose ends of the plot. And my mother's genuine off-the-air attitude toward Suzie, one of exasperated tolerance, sounded funny on radio.

Suzie was not the cute-as-a-bug-in-a-rug type like Charmian; her thin arms and legs stuck out from her thick trunk like the branches of a badly pruned fruit tree, and no cosmetics could compensate for her pumpkin face. I did admire her hair—it looked like a mass of maraschino cherry stems.

Of late, Charmian had been complaining that Suzie's humor was too broad. "She's coarse and *trop vulgaire,* a regular *vrai jambon.* I've warned her that I won't take her along when we move to TV if she refuses to play scenes as written."

In fact, my mother had been furious with Suzie since the death of James Dean. "Not only does Suzie steal stories, but she appropriates dead men too. Really now, what young, virile leading man in this town would take up with an aging, Jewish bit-part actress like Suzie? Certainly not James Dean," Charmian had told various acquaintances within my earshot. "Going to celebrity funerals is her pastime, did you know? Miss Duvic shows up at the mortuary and, suddenly, whoever the famous stiff is—he was her best friend. You should see her. She sobs. She screams. She rends her clothes. She calls so much attention to herself that mourners tend to ignore the grieving widow. And then, forever after, Suzie tells stories accentuating the relationship between the star and herself. If you don't believe me, ask her sometime if she knew FDR."

I watched Suzie trip across the lawn like a comic acrobat. As she approached us, it wouldn't have surprised me if she'd done a cartwheel or touched her heels in the air, anything to amuse an audience. I liked Suzie; I didn't want her to get fired.

Though Suzie was breathless, it didn't stop her from talking. "You know, yesterday when I got home from work, it was so hot I thought I'd been tossed into a pepper stew. If it hadn't been for the pool . . . oh well, I might have keeled over for good. So once I cooled off, I felt it was my duty to invite over everyone I knew in the world who didn't have a pool. Do you mind my asking, why *you* don't have a pool, Charmian? I mean, what with Fleur's swimming and all?"

"You're not *in* yet," my mother scolded me and waited until I had plunked my right foot into the top step brine before she answered Suzie's query. "We're *canyon dwellers, ma chère,*" Charmian grandly explained, as if we were members of a distinguished tribe of Indians. "The way our house is situated, right up against a hill, I had to choose between a pool *or* a garden. And, as you know, aesthetics always wins out with me. Besides, if we had a pool, people would be dropping in all the time the way we've just dropped in on you."

"Well, I *was* sorry you couldn't come last night," Suzie said as she energetically pumped Flit to atomize some flies and therefore missed Charmian's puzzled look. "I guess it was too spur-of-the-moment for you. I'd forgotten you had to rewrite an entire script in one night."

"I worked till three," Charmian sighed theatrically.

"And yet you were generous enough to allow Maurice to come without you."

Charmian and I glanced at each other. This was the first *we'd* heard that Maurice had gone to a party last night.

"You're a lot more broad-minded than I would have been," Suzie laughed knowingly. "But maybe that's why I'm not currently connubially conjoined."

My mother nodded appreciatively at this one of many recognizable lines she'd written for the show. Then, not letting the smile fade from her face, she said, "Maurice and I never caught up with each other yesterday, so I actually didn't know about your little fête. *Mais, vraiment,* Maurice knows I won't go to *pool* parties. He knows I find them . . . *déclassé.*"

"Since when? You always tell me you'll go to any party anytime, anywhere," I pointed out. The only place I dared to contradict my mother was in public where she quickly glossed over my remarks. By the time we got home, she'd usually forgotten them.

"All right, Fleur," Charmian replied, "I'm not going to ask you again, get in the goddamn water, *dépêchez-vous.*"

"You have to understand, I never for an instant imagined you'd be coming over here today," Suzie told Charmian needlessly.

"Neither did I," Charmian muttered, her eyelids dramatically sealing off the bright beauty of her eyes.

I descended cautiously and let my knees absorb the shock, slowly working my way down the steps until my thighs were ringed with the disagreeable liquid. There was a smell to it I didn't like or recognize—at least it wasn't pee—and although I had never in my life washed in someone else's used tub water, the steamy, oleaginous quality of this fluid made me think of it.

"She can't very well swim laps in a pool full of dirty dishes," Suzie's voice rippled toward me.

"Fleur, quickly, go around and clear it out. Just set everything on the deck, and then get your swimming done, *tout de suite,*" Charmian demanded.

Holding the gutter railing with one hand and propelling myself with the other, I paddled around amid slimy slices of vegetables and swollen crumbs of cheese, stopping to lift waterlogged drink barges and someone's lost shoulder strap onto the deck. While I was splashing a sodden bee into the gutter, my shoulder brushed something spongy, wretched, and dead, something as odious as the beige globs suspended in jars of formaldehyde in the science room at school.

I lifted the pulpy mass between thumb and forefinger with as little contact as possible until I saw that the dreaded organism was, in fact, a scummy, foam rubber falsie. Without thinking, I stuffed it under my own undistinguished suit. Had some inebriated lady climbed out of the pool without it? If I swam around some more, would I come across its mate?

I checked to see if Charmian was watching, but she and Suzie had pulled their chaise lounges out of range of the

Flit-resistant flies which were clustered on the spoils around the pool. My mother had placed hers under the umbrella of a sycamore tree. Even so, she'd donned a wide-brimmed hat and had covered her legs with a beach towel. "The sun has no compassion for fair-haired women," she often said, even though, close to the skull, she wasn't all that fair. Suzie, by contrast, lay outside the tree's protective shadow with her neck cocked at an awkward angle so that the sun had access to a broad stretch of flesh.

Now that she was talking, my mother wasn't going to notice whether I swam or not. That was the beauty, and the pain, of going places with her—eventually she forgot me.

As I submerged myself completely, I felt the hot, sticky water wrap around my skin. Trying to ignore it, I set about systematically exploring the shallow end. I'd found five tiny sprays of parsley, a whole slice of cheese, and a celery stalk before something sharp stabbed my heel. "Yeow!" I cried, and looked to see if I'd been heard. My cry went unnoticed, so I reached down quickly and yanked from my skin a small, plastic arrow; its feathery end was still lodged in an olive oozing pimento.

As I looked for a safe place to put the toothpick, an object on the bottom of the pool caught my eye. It was smaller than a slice of peeled cucumber but larger than a carrot circle. I turned myself upside down to investigate.

On the pool floor, my free fingers touched what appeared to be the perfect addition to my button collection. As seen through the blur of chlorine and tidbits of decaying food, it looked very much like the rarest of my buttons, one that, despite my vigilance, I had only missed this morning.

I routinely washed my buttons, played with them, sorted them by color or shape, or into special divisions peculiar to them. And I kept a constant count. I knew how many Bakelites, mother-of-pearls, celluloids, moonglows, aurora borealises, radiants, glass, brass, snakeskin, pewter, and painted buttons I had. It seemed impossible that the rarest one had vanished.

Lifting the object out of the water, I squealed. It was indeed my earthy, brown button, carved from a palm nut which grew in the Amazon. "Vegetable ivory," these buttons were called, and this one, with its primitive-looking carved and dyed face, was rare. My nanny, Miss Nora, on the day of her departure, had given it to me as a fond remembrance. "I wish you button luck and love," she'd said, and then explained it was one-of-a-kind. Here, now, was the same button that only yesterday afternoon had rested on a cotton pallet in its very own matchbox in my middle desk drawer.

Certainly, Charmian would have agreed that its presence in Suzie's pool was a puzzle worthy of *The Radio Mystery Half-Hour.* How I wished I had access to the members of Charmian Leigh's cast: the cool Police Chief and the calculating D.A. and even Miss Golly. I thought of asking Charmian herself, "What the heck is going on?" But something prevented me.

Drifting on my back through the warm, viscid water,

I found myself at one with the imperturbable and insightful character my mother had created for herself. Like Charmian, when confronted with a plot she couldn't tie up, I imagined being a fly (Flit-resistant of course). I buzzed into the matchbox and settled my ugly fly-self next to my button. I didn't wait long before a scenario evolved. Effortlessly, I pictured my father in his room, preparing for Suzie's party, while I ate dinner downstairs. I saw him take a towel from the linen closet and pull his swimsuit out of a low bureau drawer. One look and he was taken aback because his suit was missing its button! Then, recalling my vast collection, he grabbed the first button he found and asked Bettina to sew it on. It was my good fortune that Bettina didn't excel at domestic work. So there it was, as Charmian would have said, a private eye's fly view.

I congratulated myself on my sleuthing and then, not having any pockets, shoved the button under my suit, using my own *belly* button as a kind of niche to keep it in place.

"Excuse me, I need to use the powder room." Keeping my arms folded across my chest, I climbed out of the pool and walked over to where Suzie and Charmian were reclining.

"Just go in the bushes and get on with the swim," Charmian advised me.

"*Charmian, please,*" I sulked to cover my embarrassment. Ever since one of my nannies had branded my young psyche with the rules and regulations of "relieving oneself," I'd been finicky about it.

"You can use the bathroom off the kitchen," Suzie directed me.

"Be quick about it, *vite,* I'm telling you," Charmian ordered.

I opened the back door and stepped out of the Torrid Zone of the Valley into a heat all the hotter for being penned in. I could hear the hiss of flies even before my eyes adjusted to see them, and I recognized the sound of coffee snuffling in the sinuses of a percolator. Judging from the smell, it had been plugged in all night.

There were puddles and ponds of ketchup and mustard on the countertops. Ice cream had melted and flooded over hillocks of hamburger buns, and badly stained plates swelled up out of the sink.

In my mother's repertoire there were five different stories of orgies, but she never mentioned that the houses where they took place got dirty. Our house, even during the throes of a party, never looked soiled. I had never seen our kitchen in disarray because the cook kept cleaning while she prepared meals, and a helper—currently Bettina—kept up with the flow of fouled china.

Then, too, as far as my father was concerned, our house was one big filing cabinet. I was not supposed to know that late at night he spent time in the kitchen organizing the drawers and the shelves. He lined up the breads, the sour dough, white, rye, and pumpernickel in the bread drawer.

He arranged cans alphabetically: pork and beans first for the *B* in beans; fruit cocktail under *C;* corn; peach halves in heavy syrup; tuna; salmon; and then the soup. There were neat rows of Campbell's chicken noodle, chicken with rice, cream of asparagus, cream of chicken, cream of mushroom, vegetable vegetarian (with an alphabet of noodles), then Heinz.

Once, when I'd awakened thirsty and padded into the kitchen late at night, I caught my father in the act. He was embarrassed, I could tell; he didn't realize that I found his zeal for order comforting.

My wet footprints on Suzie's stained linoleum were not going to make a difference. The floor was littered with upended liquor bottles that made me think of spin-the-bottle games, and many of the tipped-over glasses had been embossed with half a lipstick kiss. One of them, I suddenly noticed, shone with flecks of gold. Bettina had been here! She'd left her signature. As Charmian would have said, this plot was moving way too fast. I resolved not to tell anyone about what I'd found, but, under the falsie, my heart began to ache because I sensed Bettina would soon be fired.

There was a small bathroom next to Suzie's washing machine and dryer. I went in so I could look at my button in privacy, but I found the paper hanging off the roll, lying in ribbons on the floor, and excrement in the toilet. I put the seat down quickly and flushed. By chance, I caught a glimpse of my chest in the medicine cabinet mirror, and was distracted from my original purpose.

Standing on tiptoe, I tried on the falsie, first on my left side, then on the right, even in the middle, turning myself for a profile and three-quarter view. I was hoping to conjure up a little of Bettina's allure, or my mother's, but the falsie's hollowness, which was apparent even under the cover of my suit, mocked my desire. The mirror made it clear that a single falsie, or even two, didst not a woman make.

I had just stuck my fingers under my swimsuit to retrieve the button, when I noticed Suzie standing in the doorway. How long had she been watching?

"Hi, Suzie," I said forlornly, but suddenly I was feeling sorry for her. She didn't have anyone around her house to take care of domestic details. "Do you want some help cleaning up in here?"

"Oh, it's nothing," Suzie said. "The girl comes in tomorrow and whisks it into shape. Besides, your mother wants you to finish your laps. She's anxious to go home, and I'm anxious to get her out of here."

"Why?" I asked, surprised. I didn't think people talked that way about my mother.

"You know me and my big mouth. I'm dying to ask how Bettina's doing today, for example. Ohhhhh, I forgot, I *can* ask you now. How is she?"

"Why do you ask?" I used the question Charmian posed when she needed to stall for time.

"Bettina was so sloshed when she left here last night,

I was sure she would be hanging *way over* today. Am I right?"

"She has a headache, if that's what you mean."

"I'm afraid I'll slip and make some crack about your nanny cavorting in my pool last night. So please, finish what you're supposed to do and take your mother home."

If Suzie wanted to spare Charmian's feelings, why tell me? Didn't *my* feelings count? "Suzie, if you want to keep your job," I said slyly, "there's something you should think about. My mother knows you tell her anecdotes. You tell them as though they happened to you."

"Heavens to Betsy, or should I say *Bettina,*" Suzie mugged, displaying very bad acting technique, "I don't know what you're talking about."

For the past year Charmian had been delighting new acquaintances at parties by retelling an incident that took place in a second-story rehearsal hall at CBS. It was the night the studio caught fire. The lights went out, smoke permeated the halls, and the actors who played the ever-unruffled Police Chief, the calculating D.A., the maniacal criminal of the week, the Announcer, and, of course, Miss Golly, fell into a panic. Losing little time, Charmian whipped off her skirt, wet it down with coffee and milk, and then tore it to pieces. Clad only in her blouse, French lace panties, and matching garter belt, my mother handed each member of the cast a swatch of her wet skirt. They obediently covered their noses and mouths while they followed her through the smoke. Coolly, in all that heat,

Charmian led them through the hallways, down the emergency stairs to the air and safety of the parking lot. Even now, I'm very proud of her.

"*Merci, merci, ce n'est rien,*" Charmian liked to say with a modest bow of her head when, at the end of her recitation, listeners remarked on her courage.

One night, while my mother danced at a soirée in Bel Air, she overheard Audrey Meadows narrating the same tale of valor, the only difference being, this time the cast had followed *Suzie Duvic's* lead.

"I beg your pardon, *s'il vous plaît.*" Charmian had had to introduce herself to Miss Meadows, whom she'd never met before. "I really must give you the true provenance of that story. . . ."

As more and more of her yarns rebounded from various directions, Charmian had recently told Maurice in my presence, "I've reached the boiling point. One more falsification and Suzie is fired."

Suzie began to smile broadly. As an actress, she knew how to make her eyes twinkle, and now they did just that on a grand scale. "And how do you know that what your mother calls *her* anecdotes aren't *mine*? How do you know *she's* not stealing stories from *me*?"

"She doesn't steal. She wouldn't. She couldn't," I said in a loud voice. It was the truth so long as I didn't count the thieving of Glendora's boyfriend.

"She gets away with it because I don't happen to care. I'm not a *writer hyphen actress* who has to get credit for whatever I say. I'm just a plain old actress. I give it away for free."

"But . . ."

"Did Charmian ever tell you about how she got her first acting job in Hollywood?"

"Lots of times."

"Was it this?" Suzie asked, and then with a little squirm she assumed a pose. With one hand on her hip and the other poised on her head like a tiny beret, she opened her eyes wide and gave me a pouty smile. "I'd been in Hollywood for twelve long weeks," she said with the same drawn-out tone my mother always used at the start of this story. "My money was running out and I was literally starving"—Suzie grabbed her stomach theatrically as though she was acting in a silent picture—"living on one skimpy meal a day, cinnamon toast mostly, when, by chance, someone I ran into mentioned he knew where Boris Karloff lived. Now, I happen to believe you only get one chance at things—"

"That's exactly what my mother says," I interrupted.

"So I got myself all dolled up, borrowed a really chic cape—wish I still had it—a tight-waisted suit, a cute felt cloche with a feather, and stiletto heels, the whole bit. In those days, if I worked at it, I could be stunning."

Even though Suzie was standing in a bathroom doorway that was painted a rude, powder room pink and she was wearing a shapeless pair of shorts, I could imagine her looking magnificent in her jaunty outfit, even if it was the same one Charmian had described many times. Suzie had grown taller and slimmer before my eyes, and she had, I would have sworn, what the fan magazines called "stars" in her eyes.

"Well, I spent all the money I had left in the world on gas, so you can imagine how nervous I was driving up the craggiest, most tree-tangled canyon in Hollywood—"

"Laurel Canyon."

"—on my way to beg the famous actor for help. I actually found his address, tarnished brass numbers set into a crumbling stone wall, but, for the life of me, I couldn't find an entrance and certainly not any kind of doorbell. After spending some time looking around, I finally spied a twisted tree trunk growing alongside the wall. I decided to climb it. I was doing famously, shimmying between the brick and the bark. *Pas de problème* until, at the very top of the wall, one of my high heels got wedged in the mortar.

"I fell. Tumbled down inside the grounds. Tore my stockings, bumped my head, maybe I passed out, but the worst blow fell when I opened my eyes. A dark, formidable figure was looming over me, blocking out the sun so that I thought there was a total eclipse. Holy moly! It was Boris Karloff himself, scary as ever, even in person. And I was a common trespasser trespassing against *him.* I had to do *something,* so taking a quick breath to gather my wits, I shouted, '*BOO!*' "

"Yes, I know," I said peevishly. "Boris Karloff was charmed and helped get my mother cast in his next movie."

"Is that so? Have you ever seen it?"

"The movie? It's not shown anymore. My mother thinks it was burned up in a studio fire."

"There was no fire," Suzie said in a sarcastic tone. "That picture is my proof. Someday you'll screen it—*then* you'll know whose story this really is."

You're fired; you're off the show, you bit-part actress; I don't have to take your guff, I wanted to tell her. But what was the use? I had no power.

"Charmian has been telling that story since I was a little girl," I defended my mother.

"That's when we met," Suzie insisted with a smile. "But don't judge her too harshly. We all steal from each other. She steals *my* fable; I steal *her* come-hither smirk. As actors and writers, it's our *business* to steal. We steal. We improve the material. Then we play it to the hilt."

In a flash I tore the falsie out of my swimsuit and threw it at Suzie. Then I barreled through the back door and started running across the lawn. I could feel the crabgrass pricking my feet, but if it had been a battlefield, I would have kept running. My mother was standing near the pool. She had her purse strap over her shoulder, ready to go. But when I neared the pool, I leaped into the air, curling myself into a tight cannonball before I slapped down on the water.

My splash covered Charmian, wetting her hair and streaking her dress so that she looked like one of the water-logged prom dancers in the movie at Beverly Hills High. I expected rage. I wanted it. Instead she laughed. "Oh well, it's so hot out here in the Valley," she said.

I would have smacked my fists over and over again into that vile, adulterated water but I remembered the reason I'd originally gone to the powder room. Whether out of spite or of necessity, I let myself go. A streamer of passionate pink followed me as I stroked from the deep to the shallow end. Once I reached the steps, I stood a few moments watching my handiwork fade and dissipate. Then, feeling oddly victorious, I climbed the steps. Bracing myself for her tirade, I informed my mother that I was ready to head for home.

"Well hurry, before Suzie catches you," she said.

Had she been a normal American mother, Charmian would have been furious, but as we dashed across the lawn, she roared with laughter. I felt grateful for her response even if it was at Suzie's expense.

Clouds were leaning against the top of the hills. From Mulholland Drive we could see the Pacific Ocean quilted in gloom. As we snaked down into Coldwater Canyon, where the air cooled, I began to shiver in my wet bathing suit. I was covered with goose bumps, but I couldn't stop looking at the outline of the button over my navel.

At home I found Bettina dressed and upright on bare tiptoes. Her furrowed brow, along with the ice bag pressed against her scalp by a scarf, indicated her head still ached. She moved about as cautiously as a tightrope-walker but she was packing.

"Bettina . . . ."

"Sooner or later your mother is going to figure everything out. She fancies herself a detective, doesn't she? So why should I wait for the inevitable?" Bettina turned her body slowly as if to survey the shabby nanny's room one last time. "I don't need a job like *this*, that's for sure. I like *you*, Fleur, but that's about it."

Bettina stripped her bed, but she didn't bother to make it for the next occupant. "Won't it be fun to watch your mother contend with sheets and pillowcases for once?" Bettina justified, shirking the work.

"My mother knows how to make beds," I countered. "She was poor for a long time, or didn't you know? She worked in department stores on her feet for hours at a time," I quoted an article I'd read about her in a fan magazine, hoping it was truly Charmian's history, not Suzie's or anyone else's. "And she had lots of aches and pains because she couldn't afford good shoes. Then at night—for no pay—she dragged herself to a drafty theater to practice her craft. My mother can do anything she sets her mind to." I lashed out at Bettina, surprising myself with my sudden compulsion to defend Charmian.

After Bettina had vacated the premises and I was certain neither Charmian nor Maurice was in the house, I knelt by my dresser. Deftly, I tugged on the strip that appeared to be its base support though actually camouflaged a hidden drawer. Only my most deserving collector's items had the honor of being deposited in the one place my father had not discovered. The button, lost and retrieved and now restored to its cotton pallet in the matchbox, belonged here along with a new object. Under Bettina's bed, shrouded in a puff of dust, I had found a tube of gold-flecked lipstick.

IV

2/5/58–4/23/58

Early each weekday, before the tourists arrived, an army of Japanese invaded our neighborhood. They wore khaki uniforms with matching rubber boots and drab variations of safari hats. The flora in our canyon was well pruned and trimmed, but the gardeners appeared to be heartbroken. I often saw them bent over their rakes, hoes, and hoses, but they never answered my hellos. Their passion for life had been snuffed out long ago in the internment camps, a nanny had explained.

Charmian didn't want depressives around even if they remained outside, so she'd hired a gardener who personified what she called "Moldavian zest." Considering Constantine's chiseled face, his demeanor, wardrobe, and the sparse words he chose—his vocabulary resembled that of the Lone Ranger's Tonto—I thought the Moldavians were an Indian tribe.

Impervious to the weather, Constantine never wore a shirt—just trousers cinched to his calves by high, tight-laced boots—so that his torso, with its embossed, smooth clusters of muscle, could be readily examined by me. His hairless skin, like that of a statue of Geronimo I'd admired at the Southwest Museum, seemed to be sculpted in red marble. Our gardener was the Sleekèd Boy come alive and fully grown. Yet it was his cap that fascinated me most. It had been fashioned from the thigh end of a lady's nylon stocking.

"Constantine, where do you *get* the stockings?" I asked repeatedly.

"Friends," he said, pronouncing it "friendzzz." Then he winked and adjusted the knot on top of his head.

From the time we moved into Benedict Canyon, whether my mother was off on location or, these days, at the studio working on her radio show, and regardless of the fluctuations in our domestic staff, Constantine's presence in our garden was the one thing I could count on. Three afternoons a week he was the remedy to my loneliness. A hum and a muffled beat caroming through the canyon heralded his arrival in a sun-yellow jalopy, a conveyance that rivaled the chariot of Apollo depicted in my mythology book. In fact, the Greek deity's vehicle lacked the jalopy's deluxe accoutrements: fenders, a rumble seat, and a top that was always down. Whenever I heard Constantine approaching, I dashed to meet him just as he made his turn into our driveway.

"Fleur" or "Fleur Leigh," the great man addressed me, never using the embarrassing play on words my parents had pinned on me. "Fleur Leigh, put bathing suit on. Is going on sprinklers." Then he'd whoop encouragement as we darted together across a field of homemade rainbows.

One afternoon Constantine washed my face with a garden hose and dried it with his handkerchief, which was as large as a tea towel. "Go inside. Get hairbrush," he commanded before he walked me to the leeward side of the big pepper tree and gave my hair a thorough going-over.

While I made a fuss and whimpered, "Ouch, you're hurting me," he made cracks about our chaotic household. He laid odds on how long the new cook and nursemaid would last and voiced contempt for nannies who didn't do their job: "Purpose of nanny is taking care of Fleur."

"I can take care of myself," I said, wishing it were true.

"But hair needing wash. And when was last time of bath?"

"I don't know," I shrugged. "I go to swimming practice every day so the chlorine keeps me clean."

"Swimming pools no good," Constantine strenuously objected. "People born in salt water und need keeping in touch. Constantine swimming in Pacific Ocean every morning. Going in before sun is up."

Charmian didn't find Constantine as bewitching as I, and his refusal to poison the snails exasperated her to the nth degree.

"Plants plenty healthy. Enough flowers for everyone," he routinely explained and, truly, our gardener grew dahlias big as serving platters. He coaxed roses to grow in the shade. He pinched and prodded and forced snapdragons with fat, funny blossoms to grow tall as yardsticks, and I had a feeling they bloomed only for love of him. Constantine mulched and fertilized and aerated so that ferns and ficus, ice plant and lilies-of-the-Nile nestled together in one great green body. Only Constantine, it seemed to me, could combat the rains, the earthquakes, and the constant gravitational force that aimed to pull our hillside into our living room.

"Cooking potash und seaweed und coffee grains into special stew," he proudly described his endeavors. "Then whip into ground."

"Why?"

"Is tired ground." He gestured toward the old Chaplin estate, the Barrymore villa, Pickfair, and a few less notable mansions. "Has sore muscles. Not like when Indians living here. Indians A-Okay. Real cool. Doing what comes naturally," he quoted bywords of the day.

It thrilled me to think of Indians living in Beverly Hills. I'd thought the first humans to reside here had simply moved west from Hollywood. But Indians . . . ! Indians were practically the epitome of nature; they gave historical significance to my hometown. Had they been canyon dwellers too? Soon I was imagining Constantine as the Indians' chief. "Are you sure Indians lived here? Are you positive?" I asked repeatedly.

"Is truth everything I speak," Constantine told me. He told me many things.

Despite his guarantee, I kept my eyes to the ground in search of arrowheads and ollas, tangible proof of the Indians' existence.

One day, in March, a whole year and a month since Daisy had left, when Constantine was pulling out nasturtiums that had "volunteered" to come up where my mother wished they wouldn't, he indicated he found my latest nanny to his taste. "Is stacked Helga. Worth many winks," he said, cutting stalks of pink ladies and bunching them together with a handful of fern fronds. "Here, take to Helga," he said.

Charmian happened to be home that day—on hold with someone at the other end of the telephone line. During the last month she'd spent hours conferring with the insurance company, trying to collect "a sum commensurate with the priceless chef-d'oeuvres" Glendora had filched. Nevertheless, Charmian's eyes were drawn to the pink lady bouquet I was carrying. "Flowers. *C'est jolie,*" she said eagerly, taking them from me. "Now who could my admirer be?"

"They're for Helga," I explained.

Mother looked crestfallen; her eyelids and the sides of her mouth drooped momentarily. Seconds later she peered at the flowers more carefully. "They're from *my* garden, I see."

"Constantine wants to do something nice for Helga."

"Well, it is not his prerogative. Not at my expense."

"What's a prerogative?"

"Look it up," Mother commanded, "and *cherchez* a vase."

"But Constantine will feel terrible if Helga . . ."

"He's just the *gardener,* Fleur."

I approached Constantine full of remorse. I had failed at the task he'd given me.

Constantine shrugged it off. "Other ways to make friend with new nanny," he assured me. Then, inexplicably, he began describing the virtues of yogurt. "Is speeding digestion und elimination," he said. He spoke of yogurt with the reverence I had heard our cook's minister use when speaking of the Holy Ghost.

"Does it taste good?" I asked.

"Is very delicious when I am cook. If Fleur wanting to try, Constantine brings a mother."

"Another what?" I asked.

"*A mother,*" he repeated, emphasizing his rare article with a long vowel. "Calling her *mother* because mother helps child develop into special something." As he said this, I thought he gave me a look of pity.

"Does anyone call it a father?" I asked, thinking of him.

"Is okay," he said.

I could hardly wait to taste his yogurt.

"When Helga in kitchen, Fleur inviting me in," he instructed me. "Constantine explains steps of to cook."

"But Helga isn't the cook," I told Constantine.

"Okay, but is Helga I like," Constantine declared sweetly.

That Helga was gorgeous, young, blond, exquisitely tall—a Scandinavian Amazon, my mother called her—wasn't lost on me. She had arrived at our house, full of life, on the first-year anniversary of Daisy's departure, and I liked thinking she would soon replace Daisy in my heart.

"I guess you want one of her stockings," I teased.

Since Molly the cook was amenable, I invited my guest to lunch. We ate in the kitchen, the coziest place in the house.

Molly, Helga, the great man, and I sat down at the kitchen table where the sun-ripened scent of Constantine's body mingled with the smell of the food. "If we hear your mother come driving up, you run for it," Molly advised me, "and I'll remove your place setting." She, like all the cooks before her, had been warned to keep me out of the kitchen. My parents were taking no chances their child would fritter away her life in domestic pursuits.

It thrilled me to be in such close proximity to Constantine, sharing the same table in an enclosed space where no landscape could distract him.

Constantine picked up a slice of delicious soft, white bread from his bread dish, but he just turned it over and over. He eyed the brightly dyed maraschino cherry which was set, like a gemstone, into the perfect circle of pineapple that crowned his hamburger patty, but he left it untouched. He didn't proselytize about the goodness of vegetables. I liked him for that, and I liked the way he looked at Helga. He let his eyes explore her so we could all see he enjoyed the view. I thought this was very straightforward of him. And amiable.

But Helga was wary.

After lunch Constantine guided her into the garden. I followed. They stood under an arbor that trickled wisteria.

"Constantine making you fine dinner. One night soon? All natural, all California. Also, serving warm, yellow wine from homeland. Very fine wine. Has heart," he said, thumping his own heart with his fist. "You come?"

"I don't know," Helga replied, without any of the smiles and wiggly eyebrows my mother would have used in the same situation. Helga seemed really not to know.

"Showing you very good evening," Constantine urged, looking just a little vulnerable.

"Well . . ." Helga carefully considered her reply. "I will come to your home for dinner . . . on the condition . . . that I can bring Fleur with me. She would enjoy it at least as much as I."

"Fleur is best friend," Constantine said magnanimously, although I thought he'd hesitated for a second or two. "Of course Fleur comes. Saturday night. Saturday night is A-Okay."

Later Helga said to me, "I just don't know if I'm doing the right thing. I never dreamed of keeping company with a *gardener.* Not only that; he's a cuckoo bird, I think." Her lips revealed her pleasure at being so proficient in the American language.

"You like it when he winks at you."

"Winks?" Helga laughed. "I thought he was blinking. I thought he had something wrong with his eyes."

"He's really very nice," I urged her.

"He's awfully old."

"Old?"

"Why the man must be forty-five."

I had never thought of Constantine as old. Old men were never seen without a shirt. Old men didn't saw down trees and chop them up for firewood. They didn't sweep leaves off the roof or pump out the basement when it flooded. They didn't lug two-story-high Christmas trees from the street to our living room. Old men did not drive sporty yellow chariots with the top down even when it was raining.

I couldn't understand Helga's hesitation, and begged her not to change her mind, but I was also very proud that she had confided in me. Furthermore, she didn't ask my mother's permission to take me to Constantine's apartment. "Your mother wouldn't approve of your associating with the baser element," she said. "And, then, I couldn't tell her that you've already associated with him plenty and that, in fact, I'm mostly doing this for you."

It had seemed to me Saturday night would never come, but at last it was time to get ready for our date. Helga dressed in her day-off outfit, an embroidered peasant blouse, a long dark skirt, cinched at the waist, stockings, and low heels. She dabbed on only a bit of lipstick and a fingertip of shadow. Even so, she was as beautiful as Charmian.

"Aren't you going to look at yourself in the mirror? Try out a smile?" I asked, thinking of my mother practicing a few pouts and grins before she left the house.

"I don't find myself all that interesting," Helga said.

She wasn't as witty or flirtatious or successful as Charmian, but I had no doubt Helga liked me. From there my thoughts loped along in a familiar direction: If I loved two people and they loved me, they would have to love each other, wouldn't they? And if they became a couple, they would want to adopt me immediately. Such thinking represented a pattern of mine, a pattern that only worsened now that Daisy had disappeared. On my eleventh birthday this past April first, when I'd blown out the candles on my zucchini cake, I'd fervently wished that Helga would remain in my life happily ever after.

As soon as Helga combed out my tangles, I put on a burgundy polished-cotton dress with puffy sleeves, a birthday dress from Ohrbach's department store—I didn't have much choice. A white organdy pinafore was sewn to it, "just like Alice in Wonderland," Charmian had praised the costume when I'd opened the package. "Well, even if *you* don't like it, *my* friends will. They have good taste."

Helga drove the Buick into Santa Monica. She parked

near the beach, and when we opened the doors, the fishy air, salted with possibility, surrounded us. All these years later I can still hear the rhythm of our soft-shoe routine on the sandy flagstones as we walked through the courtyard of Constantine's apartment building and looked for his door.

Constantine took me by surprise. It hadn't occurred to me that he would be dressed, and I'd never seen him without his stocking cap. He now revealed the object of his conservation: thick, wavy hair the same color as Charmian's. It was called Clairol canary yellow. Even the flawless white gardenia which adorned his left ear didn't console me—I'd always imagined Constantine with a long, lustrous braid of Indian hair. I also regretted his shirt, a loose but clinging jade-green silk affair buttoned at the neck. On the other hand, Helga might prefer such ornamentation.

He kissed me on the cheek, and Helga too. "Is wonderful you coming," he said, guiding us into his apartment.

We were in a room that looked like a beach-town bar, the likes of which I had seen in the movie *Laguna Liz.* His little kitchen had a high counter and tall stools. Woven mats on the floors, a rattan couch and chairs, and a bamboo table were the apartment's mainstays. I noticed Helga's face stiffen and redden so I followed her gaze and saw the photographs that covered Constantine's entire west wall.

"This is disgusting," Helga whispered to me. "Try not to look. He's a dirty old man."

Ravishing women, or women who meant to be ravishing, most of whom wore skimpy tops or no tops, or no tops and no bottoms, and all of whom evidently knew Constantine quite well, smiled down at me. Pale-skinned women with tiny nipples and olive-complexioned girls with dark, pronounced nipples, blondes with long hair that covered their nipples, all of these women had two things in common—"gazonkas," as one of my nannies had once described Jayne Mansfield's overwrought breasts.

Some of the women wore lots of makeup, and some none. They posed with fans, bubbles, stuffed animals, and fur rugs; with combs, flowers, bows, and jewels in their hair, around their necks, and in their navels.

Almost all the photos were black and white, but the inks of the autographs ranged from flowery fuchsia to snappy orange. "To Constantine, you're my bosom buddy, Marnie" was written down one side of her burgeoning breasts. "For Constant Constantine, with love, anytime, Regina" was written across another's midriff as if not to cloak more important sections of her anatomy. "For Con, a toast to the most, Your Fiona." "To Connie, you're always welcome to make me moan, Lovey." "To Constantine, the Moldavian devil, from your Number One Disciple, Cici" (the dots of the "i"s circled her nipples). *True Confessions* magazine never featured anything like this.

Constantine looked at me looking at the photos and seemed to be on the verge of laughing. I wanted to laugh too. "Favorite kind of blossoms, right here," he announced.

"And you're a bumblebee, I suppose," Helga said. She looked immensely unhappy and she refused to sit down.

I felt as though I was back on our balcony at home, fascinated by something I wasn't supposed to see or hear. Should I pretend I didn't notice the photographs or comment on how they enhanced the room? What could I do to convince Helga that our gardener was a remarkable find? Assuming that my absence would improve the situation, I politely asked, "Please, where is the powder room?"

I had to walk through the bedroom, where I almost fell over the bed. It had a plush, red velvet coverlet and looked like an enormous valentine. It told me—if I didn't already know—that Constantine liked to enjoy himself. The heart-shaped bed and a huge set of dumbbells hogged the room. Again photographs lined an entire wall—a hundred more women with two hundred or so bare gazonkas. I set about reading the new batch of inscriptions.

"Dinner," Constantine's voice boomed with anticipated pleasure.

"Please start without me," I called to him.

"Are you all right?" Helga came to the bedroom to ask.

"I need a little rest," I weakly claimed as I climbed atop the valentine bed.

"These photos are too much for you, aren't they?"

I shook my head.

"Well, they're too much for me. I'll take you home."

"I don't want to go home," I pleaded, determined to give Constantine and Helga time alone. "I'll rest a little, and then I'll come in."

"All right," Helga said, "but rest quick. Please."

As I lay there wondering when I could safely examine the remainder of the photos, I glanced upward and met with a shock. On the ceiling directly above the bed hung a heart-shaped mirror with a fussy, red velvet frame. The girl reflected there wore a cloyingly childish dress, and her hair was cut in an undignified Dutch boy bob as dictated by her mother. She appeared to be encircled, no, *imprisoned,* by the froufrou of the frame.

Occasionally, on *The Charmian Leigh Radio Mystery Half-Hour,* mirrors had magical properties. Charmian would look in one, ask a question, and *voilà,* a truth was told in the announcer's most sterling tones. It was a device, of course, meant to be comical and to further the plot, but I took it seriously when *this* mirror talked to *me. The girl reflected is not the girl who is. Knock down the bars that confine you,* Constantine's mirror said.

I was five years old when he'd made his first foray into our house. I remembered the fragrant trail of sun, loam, and the Midas-cups he'd been trimming. The scent hung in his wake through the living room, up the staircase, and across the balcony, temporarily displacing the omnipresent odor of martinis and ashtrays.

It was strange to see Constantine climb the stairs, the same ones Charmian used when she led party guests through the house. My mother twirled her skirts à la Loretta Young while orating with the wide-eyed enthusiasm of Audrey Hepburn. Constantine's pace had been steadfast.

Even at that early age I was embarrassed when our gardener entered my room. I would have had him believe I lived in wigwam simplicity. Instead, Charmian compelled me to coexist with a red velvet settee, an eighteenth-century Chinese carpet, an antique sleigh bed, a carved mahogany dresser (in which I'd discovered the spacious secret drawer), and a "superb collection" of plein-air paintings. My mother's Edict on Décor forbade the use of thumbtacks or the taping of posters or photographs to my walls. And I wasn't allowed to move the furniture even by an inch.

My nanny at that time had been Miss Nora. She'd summoned Constantine to remove the crib from my room. "Fleur can hardly straighten her legs anymore. The crib has become a cage. So, if you'll just jettison the thing . . ."

"Is good bed right here," Constantine said pointing at the antique sleigh bed my mother had purchased before I was born.

"That's right," Miss Nora responded with a contemptuous sneer. "Mrs. Leigh says it's a 'museum piece too precious to be slept in,' but really she wants Fleur to remain a baby. Babies don't compete, you know, or, at least, their variety of competition can be easily controlled."

"Getting angry, the Missus, if we take away crib?" Constantine asked Miss Nora.

"Mrs. Leigh won't notice it's missing for months," the nanny assured him.

Constantine studied the meandering vine design embroidered on the one-hundred-year-old appliquéd quilt which lay stiff with starch across the elegant mahogany bed.

For a minute I was afraid he would agree I had no business sleeping in it, but Constantine looked back at the crib and said, "Is terrible thing keeping little girl behind bars all night."

My gratitude swelled as I watched him dismantle the frame from the pink-stenciled head- and footboards. The rows of bars appeared brittle and ineffectual under his husky arms.

I found it significant that Constantine paused on the balcony, where I so often skulked, and peered down into the living room below. I noticed the thick soles of his leather boots flatten the tapestry runner and saw his fingers stroke the banister. A radio technician on Charmian's show had told me that sound waves, even in a form as complex as the Gettysburg Address, remained in the atmosphere for eternity and would one day be recaptured. Could Constantine have picked up the conversations I'd heard, or the spectacles I'd seen, from that elevated station? And if he had received the signals, would he have responded with instructions to me: "You must never surrender your being to another living soul?"

Studying my face in Constantine's mirror, I saw someone who didn't please me at all. The children at school would call her a sissy, or worse. Then and there, I vowed that I would lead my life following our gardener's example.

Arising from the bed, I again pondered the smiling "blossoms." After a few minutes I realized that the photos were gifts of friendship from women who truly liked Constantine—if only I could make Helga understand. I headed for the living room, but since Helga and Constantine were at last engaged in conversation, I hung back near the bedroom door.

Constantine had placed wide, white plates full of food on the glass coffee table. I saw yellow wine, ivory yogurt, gray-green cooked greens, brown beans, and black bread. I saw Helga shift her position from the rattan couch to the floor and then back again to the couch.

"Speak of country you coming from, please. Parents? Sisters? Brothers? Ice skate in Norway? Ski? From city or countryside? Fish through ice?" Constantine questioned her while heartily chomping the roughage he'd cooked.

"The Norwegian people are the best in the world. Love for our fellow man—friendship—comes first with us. We aren't materialists. And the country's beauty is awe-inspiring. The mountain air is so pure that we have no word in our vocabulary for smog. Really, I come from the most wonderful place on the planet," she wound up her discourse on Norway. "So tell me," Helga said, turning her attention to Constantine's peculiar environment, "how did you happen to settle here for good?"

"Is land of free und home of brave. America. Like Constantine. Brave first, then free. Brave leaving homeland. Free in United States."

"But why did you choose Hollywood?" she accused him.

"Is Santa Monica here," he corrected her.

"But it's all really Hollywood," she said, making a hundred-and-eighty-degree gesture with her arm, "and it's just what my friends back home said it would be. Vulgar. Sinful." She took a wrathful bite of the black bread, and spitefully confided: "I'm going home soon, I'm very happy to say. I've already purchased my ticket."

The information tore at my calm resolve—my chest tightened with anger. Why weren't nannies forced to sign contracts with their employers like actors did with studios? Who'd emancipated them? And here I'd allowed myself to believe that Helga actually loved me, that for my sake she would give Constantine a chance.

I bounded into the living room. "You can't go yet, Helga." I was already hysterical. "You're supposed to give two months' notice so the agency can find a suitable replacement. They'll sue you for all you've got," I threatened. Unfortunately, tears defied the imperious posture I hoped to effect.

Constantine moved toward me and put his arms around my shoulders; it seemed to me my despair had garnered a reward. Then he turned to face Helga. "Is not fair you go like this. Why you are not telling Fleur?"

Helga stood up and, after a long pause, said, "You're right. I didn't mention it, Fleur, because I know I am deserting you." She was backing away from Constantine and me toward the wall of photos, but when her body brushed against them, she jumped forward again. "No one should grow up in this depraved town, Fleur. If I could take you home with me to Norway, I would."

"I've been told that before," I said caustically. Even if Helga had begged me to accompany her to Norway, I wouldn't have considered it. She'd lost all credibility as far as I was concerned.

Chilly sea air entered the car and stayed with us on the long ride home. It seemed to follow us into the house. I could feel its dank pressure even a few weeks later after Helga departed for Norway.

On the day we awaited the arrival of the new nanny, Charmian was in the butler's pantry arranging an exquisite bouquet of home-grown roses that were as white and delicate as whipped cream. She noticed me slipping out the breakfast room door and asked, "Where are you going?"

It was rare that she took an interest in my wanderings, so I answered honestly, "Out to talk to Constantine."

"Oh no you aren't, not after what Helga told me about him. *Écoutez,* Fleur. Wise up. A girl in your position . . . a girl your age . . . should not fraternize with the servants."

"Who else is there?" I asked contentiously.

Then Charmian turned coy. "*Ma petite chou-Fleur,* don't you think it's time you made some real friends?"

I thought of Daisy, of course, and bristled. A letter I'd written months before had been returned recently with the words "Address Unknown" scribbled on the envelope. And Charmian still hadn't lifted a finger to learn Daisy's whereabouts. But I didn't want to dwell on my loss, so I attempted to luxuriate in the beauty and fragrance of the roses. It was then I remembered the sacks of homemade fertilizer Constantine had carried up the hill just to give them a "boost."

"Constantine *is* a real friend," I said decisively.

"Right, if you are Lady Chatterley." Charmian could see I didn't understand her reference, so she explained, "He is a coarse, tasteless pervert who is preying on a child."

"I'm not a child."

"If I must, I'll remove him from the premises. He's a good gardener, but I must protect my child. For all I know, you've already been . . . ravished. I'm warning you, if you spend another second in his company, he's fired."

Here was something I hadn't bargained for: Charmian's change of attitude. My mother claimed to be a *modern thinker, a liberal* when it came to sex. She seemed to like discussing the subject day or night. How many times had she lambasted American museums for covering "statuary genitalia with those ludicrous fig leaves?" And what about her explaining to me when I was only eight years old that a famous movie star was divorcing his wife because she wouldn't have oral sex with him? I gathered, from her condemnation of the wife, that it was something Charmian did all the time.

I hadn't minded having these intimate conversations with Charmian until the night I saw her go all the way with Jeff. Never mind that my nanny was in love with the policeman, my mother had indulged herself. If Charmian deemed such antics appropriate for herself, why did she object to Constantine's gallery of girls?

And why shouldn't Constantine display likenesses of his friends? He had no wife and he might be very lonely. If I'd possessed any photos of Daisy, I would have tacked them up in my room or, most certainly, in my closet.

My heart pounding with fury, I had to wait until the new nanny arrived and settled into her room, and then for Charmian to leave for the radio station. As soon as this was accomplished, I ran outdoors. "Constantine!" I called to him plaintively. "Constantine!"

I hurried to the street and there, sure enough, was his yellow jalopy, but no Constantine. I rushed to the side garden and found the hose stretched to its fullest length. Water trickled out of a nozzle onto seedlings growing outside the sprinklers' arc, but Constantine wasn't directing it. Finally, up on the top of the hillside I spotted the sunny sheen of Constantine's stocking cap and the glow of his bare, Indian-red back.

As I climbed the steep trail, I remembered one of my parents' parties. From the balcony I'd overheard a screenwriter passionately telling Maurice about California's last wild Indian. "He called himself Ishi, his word for man," the writer had said. "His creed forbade him to speak his own name and he never gave it away. As a child, Ishi endured two massacres—saw family members shot and killed—and eventually outlived his entire tribe. The wretched, bedraggled man lived for years alone in the wilderness, surrounded by foes and isolated from all human contact.

"Can you imagine what it was like for him to decide to abandon his natural habitat, his home?" the writer groaned with pity. "Starvation and, I imagine, profound loneliness finally sent him stumbling into a white man's town to surrender himself. The sheriff jailed Ishi for 'his own protection' when word of the 'wild man' got around, but in a matter of weeks something astonishing occurred. An anthropologist named Kroeber—maybe you've heard of him—came to meet Ishi. In due course, Kroeber deservedly earned the Indian's trust. He prevailed on Ishi to teach him his language so that the anthropologist could record all aspects of the Indian's indigenous life. Best of all, Kroeber remained Ishi's friend and protector for the rest of his life."

"You're thinking action-adventure or exactly what?" Maurice had asked noncommittally.

"My script is about an innocent who becomes an outlaw in his own land," the writer said in an outburst of feeling. "Ishi's life would have been an unbearable tragedy if he hadn't been found by the one person in the world who knew how to help."

Maurice didn't let the writer down easily. "Even if you could convince Victor Mature or, say, Jeff Chandler, with just the right toupee, to play him, one desolate Indian is never going to sustain a feature film. Would you pay to see Tonto without the Lone Ranger? See what I mean? I'm afraid the only Indians who command attention nowadays are the ones in front of cigar stores."

Constantine was facing away from me, on his hands and

knees, close to the Barrymore wall. From the way his hands curled around a small, straggly plant, I knew it was something precious. Watching him, I promised myself to prevent his getting fired. I would defend the great man in any way I could. I would preserve his way of life; I would be his Kroeber. Protecting Constantine was the one way I could protect myself.

He heard my footfall and turned. "Look here," he urged me. "Look at jim-dandy volunteer."

I bent forward, hands resting on my knees, and gazed down at the plant that amazed Constantine. With its flat, gray-green leaves and small unremarkable buds, I found it uninteresting. "What's so great about it?" I asked sarcastically. I had more important subjects to discuss with him.

"Is weed. Get rid of. Use poison like Japanese," Constantine attempted—badly—to mimic my mother. Then he grew serious. "Has right living here little plant. Comes here before time of Indians."

"Constantine," I said, my small voice almost lost in the great out-of-doors, "my mother says that we can't be friends anymore. Otherwise she's going to fire you."

"Fire from job?" He laughed and said something in his own language that sounded like *"pshaw."*

"My mother is very strong-willed," I told him. "So we'll have to be very careful."

"No person telling Constantine what friends to have. And, is promise, Constantine never leaving Fleur Leigh."

Even though I knew all about restraining orders, which

were used liberally on *The Charmian Leigh Radio Mystery Half-Hour,* I didn't bring them up. "Will you promise? Will you swear? We'll only be able to talk to each other when she isn't here. Do you promise not to get her mad at you? So you can stay here always?"

"Fleur not trusting Constantine? Why?"

"Even though you're the strongest man I know and I'm positive you mean what you say, there are many forces outside your control. . . ." More than anything I wanted to trust him. But being the daughter of a detective, albeit not a real one, I seemed to require an affidavit or sworn testimony if I was to have any faith.

"Sometime," Constantine said, striving for clarity of pronunciation, "biggest force is inside you. Telling you don't believe. Or telling you . . . do."

V

Mr. Terwilliger

9/24/58

Even in twilight, if his brakes were on, the lighted tail fins of Maurice's Cadillac could make a whole city block glow red. Those fins reminded me of a lecture he liked to give. "There is no difference between marine life and what happens on good old terra firma," my father said. "Big fish the world over eat the little ones."

I thought he meant his *car* was a big fish, but that was only one of the reasons I didn't like to drive with him. Worry gushed through me like seawater in sand when I saw his Cadillac at the curb in front of me. The car hummed steadily, smugly squandering gas.

"Stop dawdling. Get in," Maurice hollered, further disrupting the twilight.

I was eleven years old now, too old to be treated that way, I silently pouted. Under one arm I carried new schoolbooks and an already dirty notebook stuffed with loose papers which threatened to fly away. I'm sure I was hungry; I was always hungry—my daydreams being studded with Oreos and Almond Joys. I had just left a medical building. Whenever Maurice was between pictures, he'd find something wrong with me, and off I'd be whisked to a doctor. He was picking me up now, but we weren't going home.

"Please don't make me go with you," I pleaded in my crankiest tone.

"No time to drive you home. Get in."

"Can't I call Tammy?" She was my nanny at the time. Tammy had replaced Melinda who came after Jeanne who had taken over after Helga departed.

"I can't leave you here," he protested. "Haven't I told you, the children of movie stars are top-of-the-line targets for kidnappers."

He knew whereof he spoke, I was convinced, because he'd consulted with experts in this field while producing the movie *Hollywood's Smallest Hostage* with Peggy Ann Garner. I *was* duly afraid, never mind the fact that neither of my parents qualified as movie stars. Maurice wasn't even in the picture business anymore; because of the demise of the studio system, he'd been, as my mother put it, *reduced* to producing television.

"There's plenty of moola in game shows," Maurice had justified his new business. "One set, one host, one announcer, and the contestants are free. All it costs is what they win, and *I* control that."

"Couldn't I go back into the medical building and wait behind the glass doors till I see Tammy's car?" I begged.

"I'm giving you a rare privilege. What other child gets to see television production from the inside out? And will you for Christsake comb your hair?"

I reluctantly climbed in, slamming the big, padded door as hard as I could. "Oops, sorry," I said.

We headed toward the KCOP studios where my father's show was broadcast; I remained silent while he gambled with the signals. The winner of this reckless game did not allow himself to be stopped by red lights. One moment Maurice flattened the gas pedal against the floor and we burst forward with the slick speed of a dolphin, racing the yellow glow of a traffic light. The next moment Maurice slowed way down, treading water, so to speak, until the light at the *next* intersection turned green.

Maurice's driving made me carsick, or maybe it was his lectures. "An ordinary driver will look at that first signal up ahead," he began. "He'll see it's red and, most of the time, he'll zip up to it anyway. Now, a driver with acumen—like me—sets his sights on the furthest visible signal, calculating and adjusting his speed accordingly. Then, too, I make sure to drive a straight line even if the road is curved—it saves both gas and time."

Need I say, his orations were accompanied by the constant, angry trumpeting of horns? Sometimes I noticed a siren and a pulsating light trailing us. At such moments Maurice, with a determined air, accelerated for a few seconds before lifting his foot from the gas pedal and coasting the Cadillac to a stop at the side of the road. He actually enjoyed confrontations with the law—I saw this repeatedly, how he lay in wait, motionless behind the wheel like some kind of preying amphibian, watching the cop wriggle around the car.

Maurice took his time before pushing the button that rolled down his window. Then, with a twinkle in his voice, he asked, "May I help you, officer?"

When the policeman asked for his driver's license, Maurice smiled, as if at a foolish child, and leaned across me to unlock the glove compartment. With a grunt of amusement he retrieved an elegantly stitched calfskin wallet. Holding it downward, then gracefully rotating his hand, he *presented* the wallet on his open palm. It was up to the cop to part the two resplendent flaps of leather and expose one of my father's most cherished possessions. No fairy-tale sword, cloak, shield, or shoes ever possessed such magical properties as Maurice's authentic Los Angeles Police Department badge. How my father had obtained it he would never tell, but the moment a policeman caught a glimpse of its gloss, he would quickly apologize, wish Maurice well, and send us on our way.

Sometimes I wished the cop would be unimpressed and arrest Maurice for placing a child in jeopardy. I pictured my father being manacled and carted off in a paddy wagon. Then

I would cautiously steer the Cadillac home by myself, straining only a little to see over the wheel. If I told Charmian my fantasy, I knew she would laugh heartily; I suspected she'd entertained the same thoughts herself.

Only when another car interfered with his game did Maurice become irate. He gunned his engine and muttered unintelligible epithets. When forced to make a sudden stop, his leviathan automobile fishtailed and, because cars were not equipped with seat belts at the time, Maurice held his arm ramrod-straight across my chest, absolutely certain he could break my momentum.

Sometimes when I fearfully cried out, "Maurice, please!" he'd laugh and chant, "There's a Ford born every minute with a sucker riding in it."

I knew *I* was the biggest chump of all because I'd allowed him to bully me into his car.

When the Cadillac passed the line of tourists waiting to get into his game show, Maurice whistled appreciatively. "The lemmings are out tonight," he said, floating his car into the executive parking lot.

We entered the KCOP studios through the rear door.

"The Wave Machine is giving us grief," the director greeted my father. Maurice responded by rolling his eyes; he thought the director was a nincompoop. "And Number Three"—the director referred to a contestant—"has the jitters. No, I'm putting it mildly. He's got the dry heaves."

Maurice's reaction was one of disgust. "Where is the coward?" he asked, and the director pointed.

I followed my father as he imperiously negotiated the production hubbub and made his way to the greenroom. I pitied whoever happened into his line of sight. Maurice had stern, sea-blue eyes that never wavered from you if he had a bone to pick. What little hair he had left looked like a feathery nest, the domicile of just one large, golden egg. Recently I had detected a slight slackness beneath the surface of his well-tanned skin, but Maurice's body was solid; he exercised. "Clothes hang on him so *très bien,*" Charmian often said, and I noticed how the contours of his strong, athletic frame momentarily smoothed and then pulled away from the precisely aligned creases in his fine new gabardine suit.

The greenroom at KCOP was a vast lounging space for the performers, full of open lockers and shabby, mismatched furniture. It featured an area for the makeup man to ply his art, and a few small dressing rooms were off to one side.

I thought I saw the makeup man cringe when Maurice came near. Why they made-up the contestants wasn't clear to me, but two chatty women, with smocks covering their clothes, were being pancaked and rouged. The third contestant, a short, wiry, horn-rimmed man, had balled his smock in his lap. He slumped in his chair, beads of perspiration ornamenting his garishly painted face.

Maurice glanced at a list of names the director had handed him and then asked in a courteous voice he rarely used at home, "Let me guess. You're James Terwilliger?"

"Uhuhuh-huh." Was it his fear that made the man stammer?

"I'm Maurice Leigh," my father said affably. "I produce this show. It is strictly for fun, you know, and, we hope for *you,* profitable." Mr. Terwilliger reached for Maurice's hand, but Maurice pulled it away. He didn't touch anyone unless he had to.

"Sir," Mr. Terwilliger said, his Adam's apple lunging, "see, the . . . thing is . . . I have . . . what . . . they call . . . stage fright."

"Why, it's perfectly normal," Maurice said as if they were talking about sneezing. "Now, Peggy Lee—she's a close friend of mine—says it's when you *don't* have stage fright you better worry." With that my father turned and winked at me so I'd know that what he said next was a product of his imagination. "Did they tell you that you've tested out as the smartest contestant we've ever had on the show?"

"I don't think so," Mr. Terwilliger said, looking miserable.

"And, as you know, if you've been watching the show, we like to have the smartest contestants go last—that's why we have you down as Number Three—but seeing your, eh, discomfort, I'm going to let you get this over with right away."

My father seemed to have a diaphoretic effect on the man. It was impossible to tell if it was sweat or tears that ran down Mr. Terwilliger's face and made polka dots on his lapels, but I didn't want to see him get wetter.

I was heading toward a dressing room to hide myself when the director grabbed me by the shoulders. "Fleur, sweetie, you'd be doing us a big favor if you'd go sit in the audience. Can't have empty seats now, can we, when Stewart pans the fans?"

"I have a lot of homework to do," I said, wishing I could tell him that I found the show painful to watch. Daisy would have said "Nothing doing" and gone her merry way.

"It's only half an hour out of your life, young lady. Come on. Do it for your dad. You know he'd do it for you." He steered me behind the stage, out a door, into the audience, and into a front-row seat.

Standing in the stage area in front of a closed curtain, a warm-up man, who I still believe had the hardest job, was "loosening up the audience," as my father called it, with a cavalcade of jokes. He also instructed them when to applaud and when to shout out the captions they would be seeing up on the screen. (Maurice encouraged as much audience participation as possible.) The fans tittered and guffawed beside and behind me—they were easy to please. I tried to read my assignment: an essay called "A History of Unknown Soldiers Far and Wide." At least that's what I remember as the title. I was a conscientious and curious student when my mind was not set awhirl in the eddies of my home life.

As the *Sink or Get Rich* theme music began to play, the theater darkened momentarily and I had to close my book lest the camera notice it. I dutifully looked up when the lights came up again and the host of the show, Larry Jeffries, walked out in front of the curtain and welcomed us to the next fun-filled half-hour.

Larry's makeup seemed to absorb the light so that he glowed like a small planet on a dark night. His resonant, relentlessly cheerful voice orbited the theater, hypnotizing the audience into accepting and embracing his lighthearted gibes at the contestants and themselves. As Larry himself often said, he let his smile be his umbrella. (To me, his oft-seen, perfectly parallel, refrigerator-white teeth did seem broad enough to keep the whole audience dry.)

As if one Larry Jeffries wasn't enough, there were multiple Larry Jeffries suspended on monitors above my head. This was because the business of shooting live often blocked the audience's view, although it sometimes seemed to me they'd come here just to see themselves on television as the credits rolled. Cameras, their operators, a dozen or so technicians, sometimes my father too, stood between the audience and the stage. Ordinarily, the producer and director remained in the control booth, watching the show on their own monitors and tersely signaling the show's host via a hidden microphone. Not Maurice—he called himself a "hands-on producer." (The phrase puzzled me since my father was so fastidious about not touching anyone.)

The technicians worked diligently, silently rolling cameras about in their efforts to capture a contestant's most subtle flashes of thought. They recorded and broadcast without creating any extraneous noise, never tripping over the snake pit of electrical cables that cluttered the floor, never dropping a sound boom or bumping into a light. To my mind, they performed a choreographed pantomime much more absorbing than the show itself.

A swell of canned music—four bars from "Victory at Sea"—signaled the stage hands to roll away the curtain, revealing Mr. Terwilliger center stage. Like all contestants, he had been placed on a small wooden platform—they called it a raft—in the middle of a circular, ten-foot-tall, ten-foot-wide transparent tank. The raft was attached to a vertical, telescoping post, like a mechanic's hoist, operated at Maurice's command, so that the contestant could be lowered or raised accordingly.

The tank itself, with a wide, blue-green screen behind it, was meant to look like an ocean on the TV sets at home. Someone had placed a heap of rubber seaweed and a faux octopus—leftover props from Maurice's picture *Murder Down Deep*—in the bottom of the tank, but this was mostly for the enjoyment of the studio audience.

"Our first contestant, James Owen Terwilliger, has an unusual hobby"—Larry paused and raised one eyebrow—"for a man. Yes, in his spare time, when he is not working at the Westchester Post Office, James Owen Terwilliger stays home and . . . cooks."

There were hoots of laughter from the audience woven into the applause. I didn't understand it at the time, but in the fifties men who cooked might as well have been interior decorators, hairdressers, or dancers.

"So, James, it seems only natural to give you some cooking questions," Larry declared.

"I'm only a hobbyist, sir," Mr. Terwilliger sputtered out. He was perspiring so profoundly his sweat seemed to emanate from a place deeper than ordinary pores.

"So, my first question to you is this: you've got an English muffin, a slice of ham, and a poached egg smothered in Hollandaise sauce. Put them together and what have you got?" He sang the line of an old tune so that the audience could fill in the concluding BIBETTY BOBETTY BOO.

I thought I saw a tremor run through Mr. Terwilliger's body before he cleared his throat and answered almost inaudibly, "Do you mean eggs Benedict?"

"Right you are!" Larry shouted over the now energized, speeded-up theme music. He gestured to the audience to applaud just as a yellow plastic bag with a dollar sign prominently printed on it splashed into the water. Trying to avoid the spray, Mr. Terwilliger lost his balance and almost toppled into the water. The audience howled.

I had once suggested that Maurice hire a pretty girl to present the prizes so that the contestants wouldn't be humiliated when they actually *won* something.

"Making fall guys of our winners is what makes us different," he explained impatiently. "Every other game show uses a pretty girl."

"Well, what if someone funny like . . . Suzie Duvic gave out the prizes? She could be dressed as a mermaid and maybe be swimming in the tank."

"Perish the thought," Maurice slapped his forehead with the heal of his hand.

Larry was beaming at the contestant. "Very good, James, now try this," he said, but I could see that Mr. Terwilliger's concentration had broken down. "You no doubt have a lot of zest in life, James, otherwise you wouldn't come on this show—would he, folks?"

"NO, NO, NO!" they shouted.

"But sometimes recipes call for zest. How would you describe the kind of zest used in cooking?"

Mr. Terwilliger looked stricken. "Gosh," he said, "that's not the kind of cooking I do. It sounds Moroccan or . . . from India?" Even his ears were perspiring.

"Go on, give it the old college try," Larry urged while showing off his exquisite teeth.

"I'm just a high school graduate," Mr. Terwilliger muttered with abject sadness.

"The show must go on," Larry said cheerfully and, as if to prove it, a wavelet rolled across the tank. Mr. Terwilliger had to jump in order to keep his shoes dry.

"I just don't know," Mr. Terwilliger lamented.

"I'm so sorry," Larry told him, not sounding sorry at all. And, as he explained to the audience that zest was the gratings from oranges, lemons, or tangerines, used to flavor and color fine sauces, the raft abruptly lowered, and water lapped at Mr. Terwilliger's cuffs. He reached down and tried to roll up his pants.

To the far side of the stage I could see my father, calm and composed, the creases in his trousers as straight as the roads he liked to drive. He circled his hands, one around the other. This meant: Let's roll the show along. I knew his signals well. He made them at the dinner table if someone talked too much. He made them at poolside when I ignored his shouts.

Nodding at Maurice and then tossing the contestant a smile as round and empty as a life ring, the *Sink or Get Rich* host posed another question. "Now James, we know you grew up in California. So it is likely there is a leafy, and I do mean leafy," he laughed knowingly, "green vegetable your mother probably cooked for you. She may have called it a 'cactus flower.' Its correct name is . . . ?"

"My mother never cooked a leafy, green vegetable in her life," Mr. Terwilliger demurred.

I tried very hard to think of the answer because, if I could come up with it, I would call it out to him.

"I must know it," Mr. Terwilliger whined as if in pain. "Heavens, I cook every single day."

The audience roared.

"Is it . . . asparagus? No, no, I take that back. Asparagus isn't leafy. *What* looks like cactus?"

"Are you asking *me*?" Larry Jeffries said jovially, nodding to the audience. "I thought *I* asked the questions around here. Well, I want you to know we're generous at *Sink or Get Rich,* so we'll give you a hint."

"Oh, thank you," Mr. Terwilliger said appreciatively.

Enunciating to the hilt, Larry said, "You have to be industrious to get to the *heart* of this vegetable."

The hint meant nothing to me.

Mr. Terwilliger mopped his brow, which was hard to do because he was still holding up his pant legs. But he looked relieved. "Artichokes," he said with a sigh.

"Right you are!" Larry Jeffries cried out. Another bag of money fell from the sky and the audience applauded. "But folks, what does he have to do now?"

"PAY FOR THE HINT," the audience cried out.

Before the words were out of their mouths, the raft lowered further and water surrounded Mr. Terwilliger's thighs. His shoulders slumped and he let go of his pant legs.

Despite the enmity of all those around him and the discomfort of the cold water, Mr. Terwilliger found the mental fortitude to answer "sarasota chips" to the question "What were potato chips called when they were first introduced in the United States?"

Larry Jeffries shot him a glance of disbelief and then pulled a piece of paper out of his pocket. He studied it with great care. "Oh, um, let me see, oh my, oh, so sorry, so very sorry," Larry said, his voice as liquid and eager to flow as Wesson oil on a hot griddle. "The correct answer is *saratoga* chips."

"But that's what I said. I mean that's what I meant to say," the contestant cried out, but he'd already begun to descend, so slowly the water seemed gelatinized. Though Mr. Terwilliger pulled up his suit coat and tried to tuck it under his arms, it quickly darkened in the ersatz ocean. His floating tie looked like a hooked fish.

It was the producer who decided whether a contestant would win or lose, and when. Maurice could make the "partipants" look like geniuses, but if he got sick of a competitor or if he felt the audience was tiring of one (sometimes they were held over for weeks and weeks going for bigger and bigger prize money), he'd decide to wipe them out. He'd pitched the opera buff three baseball questions. He'd punched out a boxing aficionado with a query on bullfighting. He'd ended the ten-week reign of a physics professor who collected art related to eruptions of Mount Vesuvius with questions on golf. I knew my father felt contempt for Mr. Terwilliger because the man's fear had usurped the prearranged sequence of events. I also knew what was coming.

Mr. Terwilliger was trying to say something, but no sound passed between his lips. His eyes were downcast as he stood in the tank water up to his armpits. I heard people in the audience titter and cackle. I wanted to know what was so funny about a man suffering? Seconds later, Maurice, like a Roman emperor in a movie epic calling for lions, gave Larry the high sign.

They didn't even bother to give Mr. Terwilliger a question that was outside his area of expertise. "What's the name of the sauce a Frenchman might eat along with the bread he has dipped into his bouillabaisse?" Larry asked, turning his face, just slightly, to grin at my father. "You have twelve seconds left," Larry interrupted Mr. Terwilliger's thinking process with a patronizing tone.

"Gee. Oh gosh."

Spooky organ music beat out the twelve seconds. *Boop boop boop boop booooooo boop boop boop boop boop.*

Up on the monitors, out of Mr. Terwilliger's sight, the correct answer flashed. *"Rouille,"* it said first. Then it was spelled out phonetically.

There was one scream of "I knew it," and the audience roared and applauded. Then "ROOW-EEE, ROOW-EEE, ROOW-EEE," the audience shouted gleefully in unison. A look of regret, then horror, flashed on the contestant's face before Larry, shaping his hands around his mouth like a megaphone, gave the audience the final signal.

"TSUNAMI, TSUNAMI, TSUNAMI," or rather "SUE-NAM-EE, SUE-NAM-EE, SUE-NAM-EE," the audience shouted. And sure enough, up on the big, blue-green screen behind him, the image of a fast-moving tidal wave appeared. Kettledrums rumbled with the musical equivalent of a deluge as Mr. Terwilliger sank languidly into the roiling waters.

As the curtain rolled in front of the tank and a commercial appeared on the monitors, I leapt from my seat and ran backstage, where someone was counting out the time, "Fifty-seven, fifty-six, fifty-five." They had to clear the tank and get the new contestant in place before the commercial's tag line.

I could see Mr. Terwilliger, enveloped in seaweed and rubber tentacles, near the bottom of the tank. Soon technicians, standing on a scaffolding, lifted him out as calmly as the gardeners at Will Rogers' Memorial Park removed dead goldfish from the ponds. They threw *those* fish in with the manure before they spread it on the lawns. Fortunately, Mr. Terwilliger showed signs of life. As soon as I heard him hiccup, I left the stage and escaped to the greenroom.

A few minutes later they brought him down. An old, shapeless, mud-brown robe had replaced his suit, though a rubber octopus tentacle was still wrapped around his throat. That, and his sloping shoulders, and his sad, unfocused eyes, made me think of a picture of the Ancient Mariner I'd seen in a textbook at school.

The director insisted that Mr. Terwilliger lie down on the threadbare, spring-loaded couch. "Keep an eye on him, will you?" the director directed me. "He'll be all right."

"*Will* you be all right?" I asked when we were alone.

"I guess now I know what they mean by water torture," he said sadly, and I felt so sorry I began to cry.

A moment later a hand rubbed my shoulder. "Hey there, honey, it wasn't *that* bad." Mr. Terwilliger put his arms around me until I calmed down.

"I kept thinking you were going to drown," I told him.

"You have quite an imagination," he sighed, "but I appreciate your concern. Now let me do something for you." He walked to an open locker, where he had stowed a large, red team bag which he set by the table in front of the couch. I heard a hiss when the teeth of its zipper parted.

"You know, I kind of thought there'd be a celebration, so I brought this," Mr. Terwilliger said ironically.

With the flourish and pomp of a magician, he shook a large red-and-white-checkered cloth into the air. We both watched as it floated down in a perfect square over the shabby greenroom table, dressing it up on contact. Next, Mr. Terwilliger produced two red-striped paper plates, jelly glasses festooned with remnants of colorful labels, red-striped paper napkins—he used one to wipe my tears—and bamboo silverware. He set the table for two and then pulled more tricks out of his bag. There was a gallon bottle of milk and a bulky package wrapped in wax paper and tied with colored string.

"Sit down," Mr. Terwilliger beckoned. In the few seconds it took me to follow his directions, he grew broader, taller, and confident. "First, I'll fill your glass with milk. Now I want you to close your eyes."

As it happened, milk was forbidden on the No Whites Inside Diet, along with bread, noodles, potatoes, the whites of eggs though not the yolks, matzo balls, macaroni, coconut, spaghetti, rice, and banana cream pie. Maurice prescribed T-bone steak, spinach, and vitamin pills as my regular regimen.

I heard the crinkling of wax paper and then the verbal go-ahead to open my eyes.

"Well, what do you think?" Mr. Terwilliger asked excitedly as I stared at a chocolate cake that must have been ten or twelve layers high. My mouth still waters at the thought of that Mount Everest of chocolate.

"It looks fabulous, but, really, I'm not supposed to eat this kind of stuff," I admitted.

"Do it for me," he urged. "This cake is my most outstanding accomplishment, and your eating it will be my *one* pleasant memory of this wretched evening."

I took a small, polite bite of the slice he'd placed on my plate. After the first taste, I had no control—the chocolate was threaded with sugared coconut and nuts just like an Almond Joy. "This is truly great," I kept telling him between mouthfuls of chocolate ambrosia and swallows of milk. "We usually have professional cooks at home, and this is better than anything they have ever made."

"You really think so? I started out in the most ordinary way. You know, using the regular recipe on the Baker's Chocolate wrapper, but somehow I got creative. I threw in some coconut—anyone can do that. Well, I hated to add plain old water to the recipe, so I came up with something else. Can you guess what my secret ingredient is?"

Mr. Terwilliger knew it would be impossible for me to guess. "One and a half cans of Campbell's tomato soup. Undiluted," he announced grandly.

"You should never tell your secret ingredients," I warned

him. "None of our cooks do." I wondered if it would be possible to get Mr. Terwilliger and Glendora together. They would make a perfect match, since he loved to cook and she loved to eat.

"Don't worry about me," he said before we parted. "It doesn't matter that I lost; nobody I know watches this show. And I'll always have my cooking; that's my passion. It's important in life to do what you love and stay away from what you don't. Like game shows," he added with a laugh.

If only I could have stayed away from Maurice's car, I might remember the evening more agreeably. But on the way home my father took a chance on a waning yellow traffic light at Sunset and Vine, just as an automotive behemoth, a Lincoln Continental, roared into the intersection from our right. The resultant noise sounded worse than a tsunami as the majestic black car rammed into the passenger's side—my side—of the Cadillac. The door crinkled like the loose papers in my notebook. The fender buckled and pierced the front tire. The windshield flew away from its frame and fell into the street in countless fragments. I went with it.

While I was out, a devious region of my mind gained control and, perhaps because it was familiar, spirited me to the Beverly Hills Hotel for swimming practice. There, I swam countless laps while Maurice mingled with the show business regulars who reclined in gaily striped canvas lounge chairs on a broad strip of sand trucked in from Malibu. The sand was strained, sanitized, and raked hourly.

In my benumbed state I mixed up my father with my swimming coach, Mr. Hughes, who rebuked me daily for turning my head to the left when I took a breath. "Lefties are the bane of my existence," Mr. Hughes asserted, but I obstinately clung to my habit, considering each leftward breath a declaration of my individuality.

Though each quarter rotation of my head was meant only to make an exchange of oxygen, I used my breaths to peek at the hotel sun-worshipers. I could smell sun-baked Bain de Soleil mingling with the aroma of Monte Cristo sandwiches from the Polo Lounge. And always, I quickly beheld the exclusive, tentlike cabanas. Though their circus of stripes suggested elephants and lions and men in tights, I had witnessed only minor spectacles there: Sophia Loren *et entourage,* Marilyn Monroe and her doctor, and Capucine as alone as her solitary name, parading in and out of them.

Skimming the surface of the pool, attempting to propel myself without displacing water, did have its pleasures. "You have good muscle memory," Mr. Hughes had once said. I liked the rhythmic flexing of my spine, the curling of my toes as I kicked, the drips that fell from my fingertips, the pleasant tugging of muscles away from bones. I enjoyed deciding when to restrict my energy and when to give my all to overcome a fluid's natural resistance. In fact, I was a speedy swimmer, but my sluggish flip-turns gave Mr. Hughes conniptions. "You will never be an Olympian, not flipping like that," he said.

Awakening, I felt as though I'd executed a hundred flip-turns in a row. My head was throbbing. My teeth ached. I could barely hear a man saying, "Can you open your eyes? Can you hear me? Can you comprehend my speech?"

My father answered for me: "Of course she can."

The stranger took my pulse.

When I opened my eyes, I saw Maurice walking around the Lincoln Continental, smiling as though he was pleased by the extent of the damage.

The stranger tucked a coat under me, then sat down on the sidewalk and cradled me in his arms. "I think we should call an ambulance," he told my father.

"Don't give her another thought. Get up," Maurice commanded. Then he quickly lifted me to my feet, saying, "I'll take care of her. She'll be fine."

Grasping that the stranger didn't accept this prognosis, Maurice reached into his pocket and whipped out his money clip. Only hundred-dollar bills were tucked into the gold clamp, and their bulk was a half-inch wide. (The obligatory fives, tens, and twenty-dollar bills my father carried were kept at the ready in his wallet as decoys in case he was robbed.) Maurice nimbly slid out a bill. "Just to thank you for your help," he dismissed the Samaritan.

But the man waved the money away.

"For your coat," Maurice explained.

"You trying to buy me off?" the stranger asked. "It's no go. I'm not leaving till I see this little girl is okay."

"Tell him you're okay," Maurice commanded.

Embarrassment overpowered my wobbliness and I blurted out, "Okay."

"You're sure?"

"I'm okay. Really. I'm okay," I said impolitely, trying to hide the humiliation I felt.

Then I had to stand around while my father argued with the owner of the Lincoln Continental. He called Maurice a "cretin," a "pip-squeak," a "retard," and a "first-class jerk."

"You addlepated, tumescent, oleaginous, fustigating, tendentious, onerous, objurgating excrescence of your mother's womb," Maurice strung out the adjectives with satisfaction.

The man responded as best he could with a "schmuck," a "schnook," a "schmo," and a "schlemiel."

"I see you've read at least one page of the dictionary," Maurice mocked him, turning to give me a wink.

I was supposed to laugh, but since I knew what it was like to be the recipient of my father's withering invectives, I felt only pity for the man.

While the two of them exchanged further slurs, I concentrated on my headache. When the Automobile Club finally arrived—hours later, it seemed—Maurice watched as his Cadillac's front tires were lifted off the ground. "I thank my lucky stars," I heard him say to the tow-truck man, "that my tail fins were saved. It would have cost an arm and a leg to replace them."

We took a cab to a car rental agency, and when we were finally on our way home, I twisted the rearview mirror so I could inspect any damage I had sustained. As soon as I saw myself, I shrieked.

"What's that all about?" Maurice asked, cueing me to keep quiet.

"Look at my face," I insisted.

He leaned over, and though he saw the violet, pulsing protuberance on my forehead, he continued to steer nonchalantly along Sunset Boulevard. "It's just an egg," he pooh-poohed.

It *was* the exact size of a grade-A medium chicken egg, but it pulsed and ached. It seemed very likely it would burst. "Aren't you going to take me to a doctor?" I asked, astonished. (Sending me to physicians was something Maurice did the moment he heard me sniffle.)

"For that little boo-boo?"

"If it were on your tail fin, you would," I lashed out.

"We're not going to tell anyone about our little accident, okay?" Maurice cautioned me as he made the right turn into our canyon. "If anyone asks, you can just say my car broke down and now it's in the shop. Is that understood?"

As we rode in the smaller, less responsive rental, Maurice's rapid acceleration and braking bounced me from one side of the car to the other. As long as he was in the driver's seat, I was at his mercy. I thought of Daisy's dream of driving an MG, and the freedom we had once anticipated. It was lost to me now, I felt certain. "What about my egg?" I asked pugnaciously. "What about my egg?"

"It'll go away."

"But people will ask where I got it."

"Say you fell on the playground."

"I didn't."

"Just say you did."

We passed the Beverly Hills Hotel and turned toward our house. Palm trees, evenly spaced and imposing like a colonnade marking the way to a palace, lined the sides of Benedict Canyon Drive. Maurice always counted them. If the sum of them didn't match his usual tally, he would drive back to Sunset and start over again. Though I knew nothing of obsessions, if that's what it was, I knew my father's rituals as surely as I knew he was going to make fun of my egg. He would joke with Charmian about *my* clumsiness, and at the Sand and Pool Club he would take bets on the size of the egg and the length of time before it would dissipate.

A painful throbbing filled my head, drumming out all commonplace thoughts. I remembered the day Mr. Hughes had forced me to practice flip-turns for hours on end. When my hand slapped the slick tiles and I tucked my knees close to my chest and ducked my head for the turn, I'd felt the water close over me like an airtight seal. And now, no matter how I tried not to picture it, I kept seeing my father bent under the Cadillac's hood, squeezing down hard on the radiator cap. A pulsing in my ears, a murkiness in my vision, and a sick dizziness overcame me. (Mr. Terwilliger on the bottom of the *Sink or Get Rich* tank must have felt just like this. I was angry, but anger was dangerous. Still, if I didn't do something, I would probably drown.)

"Maurice," I said, "I'm not your fish anymore."

"Of course," he responded absentmindedly. I was interrupting his count.

"No more swimming practice."

"Well, all right." He slowed way down so he could keep counting. "You don't want to be seen with that bump on your face, so I'll let you miss a day or two."

"I mean, I'm giving it up. I don't want to be an Olympian." Thinking of Constantine's disdain for them, I added, "I don't want to be anything that's in a pool." My voice had enough resolve in it to make Maurice stop counting.

"Of course you're going to keep swimming," he said.

"NO," I replied, wishing I was backed by the audience on *Sink or Get Rich.* Even if it meant I'd be sent off to boarding school, I was going to hold my ground.

"I've been waiting to see you in races, to see you win. Remember, I've put a lot into this. A lot is riding on you."

"No."

"All right then. All right. I can see you're in a slump. What you lack is an incentive. So . . . I'll pay you to go." He reached into his pocket and pulled out his money clip. "Did you hear *that*? How much do you want?"

The idea of possessing my own hundred-dollar bill excited me. And I knew exactly what I would spend it on: a month's supply of Monte Cristo sandwiches, Cokes, Oreos, and Almond Joys. Maybe I would invite Mr. Terwilliger to join me for lunch. But if I were to indulge in these delicacies, it would mean I'd have committed myself to being dunked under water for the rest of my life. "Thank you," I said, "but I don't need the money."

"You better accept my offer because with or without it you're going to swim."

I thought carefully before I replied. "You're forgetting something. I'm not a contestant on your show. I choose neither to sink nor to get rich. What I choose is not to play your game at all." To add insult to injury I threw in some *Mystery Half-Hour* jargon, "Really, it's an open-and-shut case."

Maurice never let anyone have the last word in a dispute, but, blame it on the egg, I immediately forgot what he said.

VI

CLOVER

11/29/58—12/29/58

On the Saturday after Thanksgiving, Charmian drove well beyond the borders of Beverly Hills into a ramshackle neighborhood, the kind, I'd been told, where dope fiends lurked and thrived. And looming over the district, like the *Viva Manhattan* backdrop at Twentieth Century Fox, were skyscrapers oblivious to the earthquake menace.

When Charmian parked the Oldsmobile in front of the Virginia G. and Knox P. Straithmore Foundling Home for Girls, she took the time to reapply lipstick and powder her nose. I climbed out into smoggy downtown air and went straight to the trunk to retrieve one of the many cardboard cartons we'd brought with us. "Aren't you going to carry one?" I asked when Charmian started up the walkway empty-handed.

"I can't make an entrance, not even at an orphanage, looking like . . . a peddler," she replied.

While we waited for someone to answer the door, which was sorely in need of paint, Charmian told me, "This was once considered an elegant mansion, can you imagine?" She shook her head with displeasure at its slippage into decrepitude.

My mother asked to see the director as soon as we were inside, but I was transfixed by the vision of numerous girls running or skipping through the wood-paneled rooms of the graceful old house. The thumping of their feet on the hardwood floors, the constant hum of voices, an occasional joyous shriek, and their giggling made me feel welcome.

"Why hello, Mrs. Leigh," the director greeted Charmian almost immediately. "How wonderful to see you again. Of course, I *listen* to you every Sunday night. I'm Elaine Ardemore, you may recall."

Since Charmian rarely remembered names, I was grateful to Mrs. Ardemore for making a gift of hers.

"And who is this, carrying such a heavy load?" the director asked sympathetically.

"This is Fleur de," Charmian announced.

"Just Fleur," I said firmly.

"You *are* a little flower," Mrs. Ardemore said, smiling her approval.

"Thank you," Charmian responded, and then added,

"We've come to make an end-of-the-year donation—clothes and such things for the children. They're in the car. The things, not the children, I mean. The trunk is open, so if you would have someone carry them in. . . . And I'll need a receipt; tax deduction, you know. Then off we must fly."

"You haven't been here in . . . heaven only knows how long. I'd like to show you what we've accomplished," Mrs. Ardemore said hopefully.

"Ellen," my mother incorrectly addressed the director, "of course I want to see everything, but I simply can't today. Really, I've got an hour-long show to prepare—it requires my full concentration. And to make matters worse, Fleur's nanny has just quit." She said it wearily, as if this fact alone would elicit commiseration. "Now," Charmian sighed, "I have to attend to all *her* responsibilities as well as my own."

It *was* true: Charmian's writers were working on her Christmas special round-the-clock. Later, Charmian would have to meet with them to "grout the holes in their plot, jimmy their platitudes, and stud their dialogue with wit."

Rather than the bruised look I had anticipated on Mrs. Ardemore's face, her eyebrows raised in what seemed to be inspiration. "You will have your receipt in a twinkling, I promise," she said to Charmian. "But first, let me do something for *you*. Come into my office. Please."

Mrs. Ardemore had sent me along with three orphans who were about my age—Jesse, Marge, and Sally—to carry the large cartons in from our car. All three girls wore navy blue cotton uniforms with matching Orlon sweaters. Despite my mother's saying I had a Nazi mentality, I loved uniforms. Uniforms demonstrated that the people in them were part of a distinct and singular entity wherein everyone played by the same rules.

"Hey, what's in these?" Jesse asked excitedly as the pile of boxes we were stacking in the entry hall grew higher than our chests.

"Yeah, what?" Marge and Sally harmonized.

"It's so fun to see what people send us even if it's a little bit used. Last year we got this huge box with diamond-studded high heels, a bunch of evening gowns, and white gloves that come up to your armpits," Marge related with delight.

"What did you do with them?" I asked.

"We use them for dress-up or when we're putting on a play. We got a hula skirt in that package too, remember?" Sally said fondly.

"How could I forget? You wear it every chance you get," Jesse said, crossing her eyes.

"Not everybody sends us something nice," Marge told me in a confidential tone. "Sometimes they give us this hodgepodge of shoddy hand-me-downs, stuff so crummy we have to throw it in the trash."

"Yeah, around two months ago we got about five boxes of nothing but junk," Jesse said gruffly. "Imagine some girl sending us worn-out dresses and this weird three-colored nightie. You should of seen her dilapidated penny loafers and, then, birds' nests, all coming apart, and this really icky old envelope of baby teeth."

I was stunned. Why hadn't Charmian told me? Why did she let me believe that Maurice had pulled off the job? Had my mother meant to hurt me or had she just forgotten my existence when she gave these things away? If only Daisy were here, she'd make sense of all this.

"Do you remember anything else?" I asked the girls as casually as possible. "You didn't happen to find a really nice shell or some silver dollars?"

"Uh-uh, just junk."

The cartons Charmian and I were delivering now became an even sorer subject for me. I didn't want the orphans to find out, not while I was present, what our "gifts" comprised. So, as a diversionary measure, I asked, "Would it be all right for you to show me around?"

"Sure thing, hon-bun," Jesse said. "Whatcha wanna see?"

It may have been situated in the midst of a dying neighborhood, but the orphange itself resounded with vitality. Wherever I looked, girls of, as was said in social studies class, every color and creed were playing and talking or decorating their rooms. They were apparently allowed to hang their own paintings and collages as well as photos and cutouts from fan magazines wherever they wished. Every girl had dolls, and whole zoos of stuffed animals inhabited some beds. Furthermore, there were enough bottles of toilet water on the dressers to sweeten the entire neighborhood.

"Do you mind having roommates?" I asked them, looking for the disadvantage in their living arrangements.

"Not me, silly," Marge responded. "It's like living with a whole bunch of sisters."

"You're never lonely. If one person is mad at you, someone else is your friend," Sally corroborated.

Their answer took me by surprise. I'd expected a complaint; I'd hoped for one. "Well, I suppose you aren't allowed in the kitchen except to do the cleaning up," I said, anticipating their disgruntled response to this at least.

My guides led me to the big, tidy, silvery kitchen where Jesse magnanimously opened what she called the snack locker. "You can eat any old thing you want. Go ahead, toodles, choose something nice. They keep it filled with goodies."

I scanned the larder, my mouth watering, admiring packages of Oreos, marshmallows, animal and graham crackers—all *store-bought sweets.* But in a thin, slightly stained cardboard box, I spotted four or five doughnuts. A sugar-coated, jelly-filled doughnut promptly found its way into my hand as though it had never heard of the No Whites Inside Diet.

"That's from days ago; you know, it's stale," Sally warned me, wrinkling her nose. "Better pick something else."

But I stuck with my choice. The doughnut was stiff and gooey at the same time, sweeter by far than any homemade cake; its taste, which I relished, wasn't the least bit subtle. The girls, I noticed, were watching me intently as I ate.

"You sure are hungry, girl," Marge remarked.

"Aren't you?" I asked, seeing they hadn't taken anything.

"Nah." "Uh-uh." "It's Saturday." "Guess not." "I'm saving

my hunger for dinner tonight." "We get cheeseburgers and fries." "Banana cream pie for dessert."

My throat tightened and tears seeped into my eyes. "The people who work here must really *like* kids. And you've got *each other* too. I wish I were an orphan," I burst forth in a gush of envy of which I was immediately ashamed. "I'm sorry," I apologized. "That didn't come out the way I meant."

"No, you're right," the three girls nodded agreement. "It's tons better living here than living with people who didn't want you in the first place."

Back in the reception hall I was again confronted by the conspicuous pile of cartons.

"Please, pretty please with spice on top," Jesse said, sashaying around them. "Can't we open 'em?"

I would have thrown myself atop the heap to prevent the unearthing of Charmian's torn raincoat, the dress that had sustained a cigarette burn, several of Father's ties too thin to be à la mode, the umbrella with a broken rib, Charmian's pink wool suit the belt of which George the cleaner had lost and paid for. Charmian had also spirited out of our house chipped dishes, a vase that leaked, a lamp that needed rewiring, a set of drink coasters she loathed, a waffle iron that, to the consternation of our cook, burned the batter, and any number of frayed lampshades, sheets, and pillow-cases.

Conveniently, Charmian, Mrs. Ardemore, and a girl several years older than I emerged from the office just then. The girl was carrying two battered suitcases, and although the day was warm, she wore a coat far too long to be fashionable. It looked like something that Charmian, in a previous year, might have donated.

"Fleur, I want you to meet Clover. We're very proud of her. She's only nineteen years old, a bit young to be a nanny, but then you're too old to really need one. Anyway, I'm sure you're going to enjoy her company," Mrs. Ardemore declared.

"Pleased to meet you," I said as I'd been taught. I skipped the curtsy, however.

Clover bowed her head and timidly replied, "Oh, the pleasure is completely mine. I'm so grateful for this opportunity."

When Clover served dinner that night, I had an inkling from the way she braced the heavy serving platter against her stomach that domestic work would not be her forte.

Maurice, fortunately, was oblivious. I watched as he skimmed a silver serving fork and spoon over blossoms of broccoli and the pale, regular slices of flesh he favored. He carved his meat, all at once, into precise, equal-sized bites, as though he were a surgeon who was mathematically inclined.

Clover didn't pay attention when she served the mashed potatoes; she kept moving the au gratin dish so that my parents had to swiftly scoop up the starch. I feared that if my father allowed me to partake of the potatoes, the peppercorn gravy–filled craters would be entirely demolished before I took my turn. Then, when she served the vegetables, a spoon fell from the aspic tureen and clattered onto the hardwood floor, spraying my father's white shirt with spinach leaves and gelatin.

"Oh," Clover said, hanging her head. "Forgive me. I'm such a butterfingers. At the orphanage we ate cafeteria style, so I didn't learn . . . Do you want to take off your shirt and have me wash it right now? I'd be happy to, really. I'll do anything . . ."

"That won't be necessary," Maurice said, making a show of tolerance.

"You're really too kind."

Oddly, Charmian didn't notice that after we were served, Clover remained in the room. Hugging the tureen to her breast, Clover pressed the small of her spine against the wall opposite me. Her head jutted forward as though to catch our every word.

The fact that Charmian did most of the talking did not discourage Clover. Far from it: Later, in the nanny's room, Clover recapitulated Charmian's every word, practicing her inflections and pitch. Clover chewed imaginary food and sipped from a nonexistent glass with lips pursed in the middle and turned up at the ends, just the way Charmian did. Clover also tried, with passable success, to imitate the coquettish motion of Charmian's shoulders and head. I was astounded.

"I've been listening to your mom on the radio for about a

hundred years. So I ought to have her voice down pretty pat," Clover explained. Clover was suddenly self-assured and talking freely. "It's too bad she can't dance. Or sing. *I* sing, you know, and I'm good."

"Would you sing something right now?"

"If there was a record player here, I would. At the orphanage I had one. I learned by singing along."

"Can't you sing a cappella?" I asked.

"What's that?"

"When you sing without musical accompaniment. We sing a cappella at our school Christmas pageant. It's so beautiful. You'd like it too, except that this year it won't be so good. Someone is trying to . . . sabotage it," I explained, using a word my father often employed.

Clover didn't sing that evening, but in the days that followed, she climbed our hillside and ran through her repertoire. Standing in the shadow of the Barrymore villa, with only me and a few lizards in the audience, she impersonated my mother, my father, and Constantine. Then, sans backup, she belted out tunes à la Ethel Merman or vocalized in the style of Doris Day. "Promise you won't tell your mother what I can do, okay? She needs to be the best at everything."

Normally, my mother had very little to say to my nannies, but Clover displayed such interest in *her,* clucking over Charmian's film credits, inquiring about her roles, sympathizing with complaints about producers and the sponsors of her show, and complimenting her so frequently that Charmian, as she readily admitted, warmed to the girl. This resulted in my mother making another philanthropic gesture. "Think what it will mean to an orphan to go Xmas shopping at Saks Fifth Avenue," Charmian enthused.

"Why do you always have to call it *Xmas* instead of Christmas?" I questioned my mother.

"I just do," she said.

Because I was accompanying Charmian where she'd surely be recognized, she selected *my* outfit too, dolling me up in an off-white wool coat-dress trimmed with an ermine collar and cuffs. I couldn't get out from under the white rabbit cap she slapped on my head "*Voilà*. You look just like Shirley Temple," Charmian exclaimed.

I was eleven years old and she'd made me look four. "I hate Shirley Temple. Who'd ever have heard of her now if there weren't a drink named after her?" I sassed my mother. How I hoped that none of my friends would see me, and when Charmian handed me an ermine muff to hide my callused hands and ragged cuticles, I staunchly refused to cooperate.

Only after we climbed into the Oldsmobile—Clover in the back seat, Charmian and I in front—did I consider the shabbiness of my nanny's appearance. By fifties' standards Clover was slim, but since her uniform bagged, I could tell little else about her figure. Her hair, however, had a mousy hue; she didn't wash it much. Her eyes, grayish and narrow, were expressive only when she was imitating someone. She had pasty skin that reddened around her undistinguished nose. Her face was unremarkable, but she'd told me, "All you need is a reasonable surface to work on. Then you can paint on any face you please."

"I wish Clover didn't have to wear her uniform to Saks. It must be embarrassing for her," I whispered to Charmian. "I'm sure that's why she's wearing a coat."

"Oh, I don't mind at all." Clover had overheard me and spoke right up. "The worst part of being an orphan is people knowing that you're taking charity. *Now* people see my uniform and know I have a job. I tell everyone I'm working for Charmian Leigh. They eat it up."

"Did you hear that?" Charmian said to me. "I wish *you'd* express some appreciation once in a while."

Just then the Oldsmobile neared the corner of Roxbury Drive and Santa Monica Boulevard. I glanced at the Church of the Good Shepherd and beheld a life-size crèche set up on the neatly nipped lawn. Under the swayback roof of a cutaway stable, the three kings, donkeys, dogs, cows, and even Jesus, Joseph, and Mary looked forlorn, as if they foresaw the inevitability of their child dying a young and violent death.

"Look," Clover whispered in my ear, "isn't everything about Jesus beautiful?"

"*Vraiment,*" Charmian remarked, "you'd think that church would have a set designer or an art director in its flock, someone who could make that . . . tasteless tableau more suited to Beverly Hills decorum."

I hoped Clover hadn't heard her and wondered if Charmian had scorned the crèche because it was so completely Christian. Surely my mother wouldn't mention her oft-repeated conviction that the Jews had invented Christmas. By that I assumed she meant the "Christmas" celebrated on radio, television, and in stores and towns throughout America.

But we moved on and the Oldsmobile bounced over the railroad tracks which had been laid, I often thought, to insulate the prosperous side of Beverly Hills from the poor one. Once a month a single locomotive chugged along the rails at a funereal pace.

Fortunately, the rich and impoverished could intermingle in another enticing buffer zone—the Beverly Hills commercial district—which was currently flaunting its own images of Christmas. Grinning Santas in Coca-Cola–red sleighs led by mayonnaise-colored reindeers had been strung over the boulevards. Angels had been affixed to signal lights, like figureheads on ships, and the lampposts had been transformed into Brobdingnagian snowflakes. Even the city palm trees had been wrapped in candy cane stripes all the way up to their topknots.

The novelty and the flair of Christmas in my hometown had always thrilled me, but suddenly, this year, I'd been compelled to see it from a different perspective. Rebecca Steiner, the smartest girl in my sixth-grade class and the very best singer in the school, had recently denounced our Christmas pageant. "I find it odd that we put on this big, gaudy tribute to Jesus Christ when the predominant religion in Beverly Hills is Jewish," she had told our choral director. "I opt not to participate."

For years Rebecca had been the only soprano capable of singing the Gloria Solo, my favorite portion of the evening, and I couldn't understand why she would forgo the pleasure of being the star of such a magnificent pageant. But gazing out the car windows at the Christmas flurry, Rebecca's criticism resounded in my ears and soiled it. Why *had* a community of mostly Jewish artists made Christmas into America's most important holiday?

We entered the Saks Fifth Avenue *parfumerie,* where simple pine boughs sprayed with gold gave a weaker nod to Christmas. As always, Charmian moved rapidly through this department. "You can't see perfume or hear it, so what's the point?" she declared as she waved away beckoning salesladies.

Charmian's disdain gave the *parfumerie* a forbidden and therefore enticing air. My sinuses might be assaulted in the skirmish of scents, but I ogled the amber-colored liquids in the thousands of vials, decanters, vessels, and beakers set out on every available surface. I could see them doubly and triply and quadruply reflected in the mirrored walls and ceiling. From the corners of my eyes, I spied rows of fancy atomizers with their mysterious tubing and lewd white netting around egg-shaped bulbs.

Displays of makeup embellished the counters too. Clover stopped to watch while a master of maquillage demonstrated blusher, shadow, and liner. The cosmeticians wore lavender smocks tailored to look like doctors' uniforms except for the darts at the bust.

We passed Stockings on our way to Gloves. "Gloves for the typists," Charmian proclaimed. "To hide their bedraggled fingernails."

I had to tell Charmian that we'd lost Clover, and by the time we retraced our steps to the *parfumerie,* Clover had received a new pair of lips and one enlarged and beautiful eye. "Don't blame me," Clover explained. "This woman wished me 'Merry Christmas,' then started drawing on me like I was a coloring book. And guess what? When I told her I worked for Charmian Leigh, she said, 'You mean the radio star?' and gave me this." Clover triumphantly held up a small, ribbed vial with the name Plaisir embossed on its side.

"I'm surprised they're giving free samples of Plaisir," Charmian frowned. "It's *trop cher.*"

"Maybe she could tell I'm an orphan," Clover murmured ruefully and lowered her mismatched eyelids. Then she dropped the delicate flask into one of the pockets of her coat.

As in past years, a lushly bearded Santa Claus held court in the lobby on an ornately gilded throne. Well-dressed children and their mothers stood patiently in line between cords of red velvet strung through stanchions of gold. The tongues of most of the children were quietly polishing all-day suckers purchased from an elf stationed nearby.

I'd been told by my parents almost as soon as I could talk that Santa Claus did not exist. "He was fabricated," my parents had said, and I assumed they meant by screenwriters. I admit to feeling superior to all the young believers waiting to sit on his lap.

"Oh look, there's Santa," Clover announced with genuine fervor.

I eyed the lollipops.

"You want one?" Clover asked me solicitously.

"At Saks they're going to be double the price," Charmian said, squelching Clover's impulse.

A photographer approached us and I saw Charmian rearrange the muscles in her face. "Hello, I'm Edward. Edward of Beverly Hills," he said, adjusting the elaborate camera that armored his chest. "I'd love to get a shot of your daughter with Santa. She's a beaut. Bears a keen resemblance to Shirley Temple."

"You're very kind," Charmian said without much interest.

"Wait a minute," Edward gasped. "I know that voice. You must be Charmian Leigh, the actress-detective."

I felt proud whenever Charmian was recognized. It meant she brought pleasure into other people's lives. But it also raised a disagreeable question: why didn't she bring more pleasure into mine?

Charmian's smile returned to her lips. "Well . . ." It was hard for her to strike the right attitude on occasions like this. On the one hand, she was the grande dame of radio, but, on the other, she wanted to be known for her cute-as-a-bug-in-a-rug style.

"I should have recognized you." The photographer socked his forehead with the heel of his hand. "I saw you in a couple of pictures a few years back. What was it, *Divorcée Something*? Is that right?"

"She was in *Growth Spurt, Chipewyan Chanteuse, Bigger Than Life, A Note for the Teller, Over Easy, Ivan the Marriageable, Divorcée Olé* . . . ," Clover said with wide-eyed veneration, listing Charmian's credits chronologically.

"Clover, we don't want to wear the poor man out," Charmian interrupted, cutting her off before Clover revealed the names of the movies *Variety* had said were fiascoes.

"Hey, Charmian, can I get some shots of you?"

"It's my day off," Charmian joshed, but she turned so that she faced the camera in a three-quarter pose, one guaranteed to remove pounds. Then she lowered her head slightly so she wouldn't be all chin, and smiled warmly with her eyes open wide.

While the flashbulbs sizzled, everyone, including Santa, stared. "Who is she? Who?" I heard children asking.

"Don't you listen to *The Charmian Leigh Radio Mystery Half-Hour* on Sunday night?" Clover said in a stage whisper that could be heard throughout the room. "You're looking at the great detective herself."

Edward persuaded Santa to leave his throne, just for a minute, and pose for a picture. "Why don't I get one with

Santa and your daughter. Then she won't have to wait in line."

"I'd rather not," I protested. "Other kids have been waiting in line. It's not really fair. They believe in him, and I don't."

Santa bent down so that his eyes were level with mine, and confided, "I believe in *you,* young lady, and that's what counts."

Edward pushed us together and worked fast. More flashbulbs popped, attracting other people to crowd around us. A woman pulling along her child approached Charmian. "Are you really Charmian Leigh?" she asked.

"Afraid so," Charmian replied, offering her rendition of modesty.

"May I have your autograph? I've got my book."

Charmian reluctantly consented, but she was spared further intercourse with fans because at that moment the instantly recognizable Linda Christian happened into the room. When Miss Christian saw the crowd eyeing her and ready to pounce, she quickly backed out. Regardless, she had been seen. Fans dashed after her in hot pursuit. The autograph hound next to Charmian grabbed back her book and hurriedly left the Santa room too.

On the fourth floor, in Lingerie, amid clouds of pastel chiffon and satin, Charmian said, "Guess I'll get the Suzie Duvic gift over with first."

"She's the actress who plays Miss Golly, right?" Clover asked. "Is she anything like she sounds?"

"She is exactly as she sounds," Charmian replied.

Clover began hunting around. She worked her way along the display tables, stroking material, lifting filmy undergarments to her cheek and, I noticed, checking price tags, all the while talking to Charmian. "Some people are just born with oddball personalities, don't you think? Suzie isn't like you, Mrs. Leigh. I'm sure *you* can play any role."

"I would adore to stretch my talents, test my abilities but . . . my audience requires me to be exactly the same from week to week."

Just then I saw Clover press a nightgown to her breast. I thought she meant to model it, but the front flaps of her coat slid closed over it as if they'd been pulled by a string.

Charmian happened to glance in her direction just then, and Clover threw open the coat and, as if she'd just unwrapped a package, exclaimed, "Isn't this just perfect? For Suzie, I mean. And it's only thirty-nine ninety-five."

Charmian studied the apricot satin gown edged with ostrich feathers. "They're faux," she said dismissively, but in a moment she changed her mind. "On the other hand, the price isn't bad, and Suzie won't know the difference."

Though Clover disappeared briefly a few times during the afternoon, she took far more interest in Charmian's selection of gifts than I ever had. She seemed to know every one of the *Mystery Half-Hour* cast members intimately and, as we moved from department to department, Clover picked out gift possibilities that flattered my mother's taste while respecting her hesitancy to spend money on others. All the while, Clover kept asking ingratiating questions about acting.

"Radio is the most difficult medium there is," Charmian confided. "You've nothing but sound waves to convey your emotions. You can breathe noisily. You can speed your speech or slow it down, stretch out your syllables, hum a tune, cough, sneeze, snort. Villains can belch occasionally. Now *this* is a little-known fact: with radio, silence can be your best friend. None of this is in the script, you understand."

When Charmian was giving the last saleslady her charge number, Clover handed me one of the all-day suckers we'd seen downstairs. She gave one to Charmian too.

"Why Clover, *c'est très gentil à vous,*" my mother commended her as she peeled off the cellophane.

"You know I'd do anything for you, Mrs. Leigh," Clover said, her one augmented eye beaming appreciation.

"Where did you get it?" I asked brusquely.

"Gosh, I was just walking by, on my way to the powder room, and one of Santa's helpers handed them to me. I guess she could tell I'm an orphan," Clover said with a little catch in her voice.

How old do you have to be before you're no longer an orphan, I wanted to know. Before I yielded to an angry snit, I remembered something important: there *was* no ladies' room on Saks's first floor.

* * *

Clover picked me up from school in the Buick, but drove it home as it if were a Porsche.

"Clover, do you have a driver's license?" I inquired nervously.

"Don't worry, I'm getting one," she said. "There's a booklet, or something, I have to read first. Or do you think I need a lesson?"

I understood Clover's haste once we arrived home. The living room was awash in a sea of gift-wrap paper, puffs of colored tissue paper, boxes of every shape, size, and design, clumps and balls and rolls of ribbon in kaleidoscopic hues, some of them pearlized so that they shimmered, pens with colored ink, reels of Scotch tape, Le Page's glue and Elmer's.

The contents of the Present Closet were spilled out onto the living room floor. Commingled with the gifts purchased at Saks were an accumulation of vaguely familiar objects, some of which my parents had received for Christmas the year before, as well as several bargain basement selections Charmian had picked up at an Ohrbach's sale.

Clover quickly knelt to the floor and resumed her job as assistant gift-wrapper, handing Charmian the tools of her trade while she assembled ingenious packages. Sinking into an uncluttered plat of carpeting, mesmerized by the sound of dueling scissor blades, paper resisting a fold, and strips of Scotch tape being wrenched from the roll, I watched

Charmian edge and fold and fringe paper so that one box lid sported a black tie on a frilly dress-shirt between the lapels of a tuxedo. (She placed a gift card in the pocket in lieu of a handkerchief.) I watched with awe when, after she wrapped one box conventionally, Charmian sliced a neat slot in the box lid. When she glued an actual gingerbread man halfway into it, she made him appear to be running away from pursuers.

"Oh, Mrs. Leigh, you can do anything!" Clover cried.

"Do you really think so?" Charmian replied.

Then, as if to offer yet another example of ingenuity, Charmian fashioned an entire package into a chimney with a waving Santa doll halfway inside. But while Charmian worked toward her artistic apotheosis, sprinkling on glitter to represent snow, my eyes were drawn to the slow movement of Clover's foot. She was using it to slide one of the packages away from the others. In a moment it disappeared behind the skirt of the couch.

Under ordinary circumstances I would have told my mother, but I couldn't shake the feeling that it served her right.

To my dismay, my parents attended, for the first time ever, the El Rodeo School Christmas pageant. They were generous enough to bring Clover along, but nothing pleased me that night. They had come because Charmian's hairdresser had informed her that the daughter of Hampton Friely, the new president of NBC, was an eighth-grader at my school. He guaranteed that the executive and his wife never missed any of their daughter's performances.

With its tall campanile, its azure mosaic cupola, and rippled roofs of earthen-red tile, El Rodeo Elementary School appeared to be part castle from Spain, part Moorish citadel, and part California mission. It was the perfect setting for a pageant like ours, but I didn't appreciate it. I quickly left my parents to their hunt for the television executive and trudged to the second floor.

We singers sat in the balcony so that the parents could sit downstairs close to the stage and the tableaux vivant. I joined the other sixth-grade altos under the vaulted ceiling of the auditorium. Everyone around me was breathing deeply and noisily because the choral director, Mr. Parks, had promised that this simple activity calmed nerves. I didn't bother breathing; I was too downhearted to be nervous.

Eons seemed to pass before the lights flickered and slowly dimmed to black and the hubbub of the audience ceased. I had loved our pageant not only because of the beautiful music but because, while we sang, the stage came to life with a stunning and new tableau vivant.

Each tableau, one per class, manifested the style of a particular artist. Breughel's skaters, for example, became life-size, taking the form of children I knew or recognized when the second-graders sang "Winter Wonderland," and a comical Norman Rockwell painting came to life during the fourth-grade rendition of "Sleigh Ride."

Still, I was gripped by melancholy. Even the high, energetic voices of the fifth-graders trilling out "Ring Christmas Bells," even the intricate harmony of the *din-dang-din-dangs*, held for several perfectly pitched counts, couldn't perk me up. Finally, I heard the applause from downstairs and saw Mr. Parks lift his pitch pipe to give us our C. The curtain rose on a tableau vivant so pretty I momentarily forgot to breathe. Angels, first- and second-graders who were intrinsically angelic, were perched like plump birds in nests of pink clouds that suggested Tiepolo. But what did I care? What was Christmas caroling without the full regalia of my favorite song? What was "Angels we have heard on high" without the Gloria Solo?

Rebecca, I wished to confront my classmate. *Why can't we be Jewish and at the same time perform the greatest music ever written? Why can't we have the best of both worlds?*

On the ride home, Clover enthused. "Hey, the singing was great, I loved the living pictures, and meeting the parents of Beverly Hills was a great treat."

Charmian called the pageant a "triumph," and I guiltily braced myself to hear more praise; I hadn't sung a note. But Charmian pulled a punch: *she* was rejoicing because she'd made a "solid" connection with the new president of NBC television.

Charmian had chosen the theme "Christmas in Ancient Egypt" for her party that year. Instead of the usual tent covering the front patio, a two-story, walk-in pyramid had been erected as a kind of entry hall. Guests, if they wished, could ride a real camel led by an appropriately costumed trainer or follow a silken cord through an exotic labyrinth of upended mummy cases, remnants from a picture called *The Mummy Steps Out.* At the end of the maze, guests would encounter our living room, which, to the consternation of those who'd been to our house before, had been stripped of all its furniture. In its place were Moroccan ottomans and low-slung tables nestled into—and this was my father's triumph—miniature sand dunes.

Workmen had spent an entire day covering our carpeting with a tarp and, thanks to the special effects department at MGM, a sandy substance had been spread throughout. "They developed it for *Darling of the Dunes,*" Maurice had informed us.

"How do you get rid of it?" Charmian had inquired skeptically.

"A special vacuum scoops it up," Maurice had explained, "and back it all goes to the studio."

Bartenders and waiters, hired directly from Central Casting and dressed by Western Costume in lots of white cotton gauze, circulated under a sky-blue canopy speckled with flashy gold stars that had been attached to the beams of our ceiling. They carried silver trays laden with olives, squares of cheese, and hard-boiled eggs sculpted into pyramids. "Use your imagination," Charmian had instructed the caterers. "*Je vous donne carte blanche.* Who's to know what Egyptians really ate?"

The guests included the cast members of *The Charmian Leigh Radio Mystery Half-Hour* and the *Sink or Get Rich* production staff, as well as anyone to whom my parents owed favors or wished to be indebted.

Those guests who could borrow from Wardrobe at various studios wore extravagant and seemingly authentic ancient Egyptian garb, while others were forced to be more innovative. Dido and Lottislaus Beck, more famous for their harrowing escape from a Nazi camp train than for the screenplays they wrote, had on the faded, shapeless togs they'd worn through much of the War. Though they looked nothing like the nomads I'd studied in school, Dido kept exclaiming in Zsa Zsa Gabor English, "We're Bedouins, Bedouins of Hollywood." They weren't even chagrined when the writer Irving Justman arrived in an authentic Egyptian djellaba, bought when he was bumming around the world. Because Irving had been blacklisted, Charmian felt she was making a political statement just by inviting him. Lester McAdam, who played the ever-cool Police Chief on *The Radio Mystery Half-Hour,* appeared to have borrowed a dressing gown from his wife. I didn't understand what it had to do with Egypt, and he didn't explain. The actress Deborah Talcome—her first name rhymed with Gomorrah—who had for years vied for the same movie roles as Charmian, came dressed as a Nile galley slave, one evidently so downtrodden she possessed scant clothing.

(I despised my own costume. I'd coveted a gauzy belly-dance ensemble and had begged Charmian to rent one or allow Clover and me to buy the materials and make one. Instead Charmian had sent Clover down to Newberry's Five, Ten, and Twenty-Five to purchase a factory-made costume, a leftover from Halloween. Mummy wrappings were crudely printed on the material, which was skimpy and cheap and scratched my skin.)

Despite the motif of their attire, women wore their furs. And, since we had no cloakroom, it was my job to take the wraps upstairs. Mink coats, fox stoles, and ocelot capes, as soft as they were, were also astoundingly heavy. I lugged them across the balcony into my parents' bedroom and arranged them tidily on the oversize bed.

Once the majority of the guests had arrived and the bed was a solid mound of fur, I stared at it until, instead of the dressy coats, I beheld living creatures who beckoned me to play. Locking the door, I quickly pulled off my costume, which was making me itch terribly. With nothing on but underpants, I, a casualty of the costume's cheap dye, discovered blotches of putrid colors all over my skin.

So, looking a bit bestial myself, I climbed onto the backs of the furs. Half swimming, half crawling, I slithered over them, sniffing their thousand and one scents. Deep down between the hairs, contrasting with the fragrance of perfumes dabbed on the linings and, in a few cases, the odor of mothballs, each fur had its own distinctive animal smell. Wherever my cheeks happened to brush, it seemed as though all the mammals had wedded into one, an all-embracing, warm-blooded creature that was petting *me.*

And yet where my hips and shoulders pressed more urgently against the pelts, I could discern an underlying toughness of unyielding, durable hide. I lay on the coats for some time until I realized that without its exquisitely concealed skin, the fur couldn't exist. Hair by hair, it would drift senselessly in the atmosphere like so much dandelion fuzz.

Rolling over onto my back, I remembered another bed I had lain in and felt immensely sad. Under Constantine's magical, heart-shaped mirror I had vowed to follow the great man's example and never surrender my being to anyone. Since then I'd wavered considerably. Why couldn't I have a hide as tough as those underneath me? Clover did. She'd recently said that if she were me she wouldn't give Daisy another thought. "Daisy made a cameo appearance in your life, and that's it," Clover had said. Feeling sad and alone, I stepped back into the ill-conceived and now badly wrinkled mummy costume and returned to the party.

Charmian had positioned herself center stage. It was hard to say which was more conspicuous, Charmian or the Christmas tree. The tree may have shimmered, but Charmian glistened, glimmered, and glowed in Claudette Colbert's renovated *Cleopatra* costume. A wardrobe mistress at Paramount had recently unearthed it and happened to mention to Charmian that she and Claudette were exactly the same size. It was this coincidence that had settled the theme of our party, though locating a Ramses II outfit for Maurice had presented quite a challenge.

Newly arrived guests found their way directly to Charmian. "You look radiant," the nice ones said. "If there's ever a remake of *Cleopatra,* you should have the part. And the house, it's . . . unbelievable." Everyone shook her hand, kissed it, or kissed her on both cheeks. Then they slid their Christmas offerings under the tree. The swelling pile reminded me of the orphans—how I wished they'd been invited.

"Darliiiing, you devil, when did you have time to arrange all this?" the unmistakable voice of Suzie Duvic squealed from across the room. "No wonder you won't come to my simple evenings around the pool." Suzie was dressed in a shoddy costume shop version of Charmian's ensemble. Her colors were more garish, more pronounced than Charmian's by far. Suzie also wore the traditional Egyptian blue-black blunt cut, though her wig seemed to be made of nylon, not real hair from Indonesia, as Charmian's was. It was a gesture, an imaginative addition to her costume, that enabled her to outdo Charmian: behind Suzie trailed a handsome, half-naked slave, an out-of-work actor, no doubt, who all through the night fanned Suzie with a spray of salmon-colored plumes.

I considered the kitchen to be the nerve center of the party, and I ran back and forth many times from the cool, star-capped desert of the living room to the kitchen, which was hotter than Cairo at noon. Clover had been reduced to a scullery maid because the caterers hadn't a minute to wash soiled glasses or scour their own baking sheets. Sweat trickled down Clover's cheeks, and her hair was stringier than ever even though she kept sneaking away "to take a gander" at the festivities.

All during the party, I noticed that no matter who engaged her in conversation, Charmian's eyes kept steering toward the pyramid. She wasn't looking for guests in need of greeting; she was searching for someone in particular.

The dinner itself was served buffet style, with the guests seated on a huge Persian carpet that had been laid over the sand dunes. I enjoyed eating with my fingers and balancing my Shirley Temple on the lumpy carpeting, but it didn't appear the adults delighted in sitting on the floor. And though Charmian had given the entrées Egyptian names like Lamb Alexandria, Fruit of the Nile, Tut's Treasure, and Nefertiti's Transgression, they tasted suspiciously like barbecued spareribs, fried won tons, and Waldorf salad.

I happened to look up just as an attractive couple trekked into the living room. They were not in costume and had the distressed look of neighbors we'd never met before coming to complain about cars blocking their driveway. (Of course, if they'd really been neighbors, they would have sent their maid.) The moment Charmian noticed them, she scrambled to her feet. "Oh, there you are. I'm so glad you could come," she greeted them in her warmest pitch. This surprised me because it was her custom to give latecomers the coldest of shoulders.

"Dear Anne and dear, dear Hamp Friely. I was beginning to fear you'd gotten tied up at NBC. Oh, did I forget to tell you this was a costume party? Forgive me. And please, take off those shoes. Then I'll introduce you to everyone."

"No, really, don't. We were in the neighborhood and decided to drop by for just a minute or two. We're really homebodies, you know. We like to spend time with our daughter before she goes to bed," Mr. Friely said.

"Well, you have to have a drink and a quick bite of our Egyptian fare," Charmian said as she shepherded them to an empty spot on the carpet next to me. "I'll be right back."

"Hello," they both very sweetly addressed me. Some people, I had discovered, liked me right off the bat for the sole reason that I was a child.

"We're the Frielys," Mrs. Friely said as she and her husband squirmed on the rug over the sand. "I understand you go to El Rodeo School. Do you know our daughter Ginger Anne? She knows you. Ginger Anne wants to be an architect when she grows up. What about you?"

"I want to be a housewife," I said candidly.

I was just about to ask the Frielys if by chance they knew of Daisy's parents and their whereabouts when Charmian returned. She handed them drinks jingling with pyramid-shaped ice cubes, but Anne went right on talking about her daughter. It was only when Mr. Friely unfolded his wallet and revealed a snapshot of their scion that Charmian looked miffed—she considered the discussion of one's children a waste of time.

As Mrs. Friely expounded upon Ginger Anne's tap-dancing prowess, I listened to her with one ear and saved the other for Charmian's launching of a subject just as dear to *her.*

"So you're running NBC. It's you who gives the green light to the series on your network, isn't that right?" my mother asked, coyly placing her hand on Mr. Friely's arm.

"I have some say in it, yes."

"Have you ever . . ." Charmian wavered, thinking how best to introduce her thought, "listened to *The Charmian Leigh Radio Mystery Half-Hour*? We've been on the radio for eleven years. Quite successfully, I might add. But now it's time to move on to a more suitable venue. With a few, minor adjustments, my series would be perfect for television."

"Uh-huh, I can understand your thinking," Mr. Friely said, his tone keeping her at a distance.

"Well then, when can we discuss it in detail?"

"I'm rather tied up these days, but you're welcome to call me at the office some time in the future." He handed her a card, and then glanced at his watch.

"Shall I send you a script right away? We've written a pilot and it's very good."

"Right now, I'm too preoccupied. We're developing a real humdinger, I'll tell you." Mr. Friely's enthusiasm for the project got the best of him and he went on: "It'll be called *The Singing Aviatrix.* The young and beautiful and talented star will fly a light plane solo around the world, and wherever she sets down, she'll resolve a conflict: a rift between a bucolic farmer and his wife one week, a native uprising the next. And she'll do it all with song—we have the Oscar and Hammerstein of television under contract."

"That sounds lovely," Charmian said apathetically.

"But the casting . . . ugh. It's hopeless. We've had hundred of singers come to the studio. I won't tell you about the ones who accost me, bursting into song when I'm having my shoes shined or getting gas. Our milkman's daughter arrived with the milk and wouldn't leave until I gave my ear to seven long songs. Still, we've found no one who . . ."

I was dying to see how Charmian would weave the topic of *The Radio Mystery Half-Hour* into Mr. Friely's thought pattern again, when I noticed a figure prominently posed on the balcony. She had heart-shaped lips, a turned-up nose, and large, lustrous blue eyes and lids. Foamy waves of yellow hair flowed down her shoulders, and her body was swathed in a whipped-cream fur, a full-length white mink similar to one I'd played with on my parents' bed.

"Who is that?" "Do you recognize her?" "What's she doing there?" The room erupted with questions. "She's the vision of an angel," someone said. And then there was quiet. Only the camel's muffled pacing in the pyramid could be heard.

The angel took several deep, unhurried breaths of the second-story air. As her lungs filled, her heart seemed to overflow with confidence. She sang "Angels we have heard on high," and her pure, sprightly a cappella soprano filled the living room. And then, unexpectedly, I received the missing element of my Christmas: *Glo–o-o-o-o o–o-o-o-o o–o-o-o-o o–ri-a, in excelsis de-e-o.* It was the Gloria Solo.

My heart sang its own tune of pleasure, but not so loud that I missed a single syllable. Somehow, I imagined, Charmian must have realized what I'd been mourning all month and arranged to have it sung for me.

The audience seemed to deplore the carol's end and remained absolutely still before breaking into rapturous applause. Shouts of "Bravo, bravo, bravissimo" soon followed. And, in another minute, everyone was clamoring, "Encore, encore."

When the angel finished her spirited rendition of "Que Sera, Sera," I noticed Mr. Friely brush past Charmian and bound up the stairs. He took the angel's hand and bowed deeply as if he were in the presence of the real Cleopatra. "I'm with NBC Television," he announced. "We're working on a very big project. Whoever you are, would you be able to come to the studio tomorrow? I think you're the answer to our prayers."

"Oh," a familiar voice said demurely, though loud enough for all to hear, "I'd be ever so honored."

Underneath the wig (filched from a Saks mannequin?) and the makeup (purloined from the *parfumerie*?) and the fur (pilfered from my parents' bedroom?) was someone I recognized.

My gaze turned toward Charmian, who was seething mad. She hated for anyone, other actresses especially, to get the best of her. And, until this moment, I'd never believed that anyone could.

"Well then," I heard Maurice tell Charmian after the last guests had departed. "You better call the employment agency right away. It'll be hard to find another nanny at this time of year."

"There's one good thing about this," Charmian told my father. "Hampton Friely is never going to forget this party and that he discovered Clover here. He might even be led to believe that I arranged Clover's . . . audition myself. And if he thinks that's so, then surely he'll know that he owes me one big whopping favor."

VII

Miss Hoate

1/5/59—1/6/59

Heels, high ones at that, clacked on the hardwood floors as Charmian paced the breakfast room. I watched cigarette smoke stripe the air until we heard the familiar scrape and thunk particular to Celebrity Taxi Service. I ran to the window just as a rattletrap cab turned into our driveway. Moments later a lean, scowling woman struggled with the door, worked it open, and closed it with a kick. After she paid the driver, she yanked her own suitcases out of the trunk.

"She has big bones, but they're good bones," my mother remarked.

Charmian had used this line, I remembered, only a week ago on her show. But how could she be expected to invent fresh dialogue when she was disconsolate because she couldn't advance her series from radio to television? Then too, just when her insurance company had agreed on a generous settlement to cover Glendora's heist, the police recovered everything. "Do you think the insurers will actually talk to the police?" I'd heard Charmian ask Maurice. "I mean, is there any chance they'd find out I kept the money *and* my objets d'art?"

Once our latest cook, Stephie, let the new nanny in, however, my mother shed her veneer of vexation and assumed the role of grande dame. "A pleasure to meet you, Miss Hoate," Charmian said.

"The *H* in my name is silent," Miss Hoate alerted her.

"How nice," Charmian muttered. "And now because I must leave momentarily, I'd like to introduce you to your charge. This is Fleur de."

"The 'de' is silent," I mimicked the nanny.

"Hello, you cute, adorable, precious little pet." Miss Hoate moved closer to me, too close, I thought, and she spoke as though I were a very small child. "Where did you get your wide blue eyes? And that honey-blond hair? Where did you get that button nose?"

"She inherited them from me," Charmian replied curtly.

"Oh, of course. I've read many treatises on genetics," Miss Hoate said, smiling a little too wide, so that her gums showed and her teeth glistened as though they were about to bite into a tender hide.

"Fleur de may be only eleven years old, but she is practically grown-up. We like to treat her as such. No baby talk, no coddling, no childish games." Once again, here was Charmian's spiel usually given to new help during the interview, but *this* time there'd been no interview. Since Clover had been discovered, Charmian had waited out the holidays, then thrown herself on the mercy of Her Ladyship's Domestic Employment Agency. And *voilà,* as my mother liked to say, they'd conjured up Miss Hoate. Having forgone the usual checking of references, they'd insisted that Charmian be at home when Miss Hoate arrived so she could give final approval.

"Since I'm running so late," my mother explained to Miss Hoate, "I've asked *ma petite chou-Fleur* to show you around. She will inform you of your duties."

"The agency told me what my duties are," Miss Hoate said stiffly before she remembered to smile again.

"I have a rehearsal and then a story conference that's going to last into the night," Charmian went on. "You can't imagine the script troubles I have. Well then, *au revoir.*"

I followed my mother out to her car. She grimaced when she climbed into the Oldsmobile—it truly wasn't swanky enough for her. "Please don't go yet," I begged.

"I'm hours late as it is."

"Charmian, when you said 'She has big bones but they're good bones' about a character on your show, didn't she turn out to be an assassin? Miss Hoate has got me kind of scared."

"Have I filled your head with *my* wild ideas?" Charmian

asked, looking helplessly toward the heavens. "When they're in *my* head, you see, they pay off. When *you* have them, they're a nuisance. *Tu comprends?*"

As I lumbered back into the house, I resolved to make a good impression. Demonstrating my good manners, I picked up the smaller of Miss Hoate's valises to carry it up the stairs. It was so heavy I had to use both my hands.

"Whatever you do, don't touch any of my things," Miss Hoate warned.

I let go of the leather handle fast, and the suitcase dropped to the floor.

"You better learn to start out on the right foot when you meet someone new, Fleur de."

"I always start on my left foot," I said automatically, and then decided I better explain. "Because I'm left-footed, see."

"I've never heard of such a thing."

"If you're left-handed, you're probably left-footed," I explained. "My left side is my best side."

"We'll see about *that,*" she said.

Empty-handed, I followed her across the living room. She didn't pay attention to my mother's recently returned bibelots or the authentic antique furniture. New nannies always commented on at least one item in this room. Her Ladyship's Domestic Employment Agency instructed them to do so, Charmian maintained.

I continued behind Miss Hoate as she climbed the stairs, studying the way her unfashionable, nubby wool dress softened her oblong rump. Everything about her was angular, including her thick, dark hair, which formed a three-sided box around her rectangular face. Four of her bones—big white knobs at her ankles and wrists—were highly visible and, I thought, quite gruesome.

"You turn at the first hallway," I said when she reached the top of the stairs and paused to look down at the living room. "You go through my room to get to yours. It's just beyond the French doors."

"Do you like ordering people around, or are you just a little know-it-all?" she asked (rhetorically, I assumed). She strode through my room and, once inside her cubicle, she scowled and announced, "This won't do."

It was four-thirty in the afternoon and the sun, orange and plump, rolled along the ridge of our hillside. At this time of day its rays, trapped momentarily by a yucca or a tumbleweed, somersaulted down the hill and burst through the patterns in the curtains, projecting wondrous designs on the walls and floor of the nanny's room.

"Doesn't the linoleum remind you of confetti?" I asked, stretching feebly for light conversation.

"It looks like vomit, and the curtains look like rags to wipe it up." Miss Hoate threw a suitcase down on the bed, and it bounced. "The bed's too soft."

"My last nanny said it was like sleeping on a powder puff."

"I don't want to hear about your last nanny. I don't want to hear about any nannies but me," she said fiercely.

"All my other nannies wanted to hear about the nannies before them," I foolishly persisted, trying to justify my words. Then, hoping to entice her, I whispered, "They especially wanted to know why the others left."

"Not me. Subject closed," she said, brushing past me. Once in the bathroom, she left the door ajar; I saw her turn the water on so hard it whooshed out of the faucet. Only when steam shimmied out of the basin did she pick up the soap. Her skin turned ripe red, but she soaped each long finger individually and rubbed every nail. "I'll be a doctor soon," Miss Hoate apprised me. "I'm only working *here*"—she pronounced the word as though she really meant Hell—"to pay off tuition for medical school."

"What kind of doctor are you going to be?"

"Do you know what plastic surgeons do?"

"Pretty much."

"Well, don't think I'm going to do face-lifts or nose jobs on rich girls like you," she said, leering at me.

"I'm not rich. I don't have *any* money at all," I explained.

Miss Hoate pulled her hands, now blotched and pruney, away from the sink and held them in the air the way surgeons did in movies. She looked at me strangely. "Hey, look at your knee. That's a grisly laceration. Come here."

"It's nothing. I scraped my knee on the playground and the scab's come open a few times. The nurse at school says it's a little infected but to leave it alone and it will be gone in a matter of days," I explained, standing my ground.

Without taking her eyes off my defect, she turned off

the tap with her elbows and dried her hands scrupulously as though she were about to pull on surgical gloves. "A nurse at school," she scoffed, "would know just about zero. I better lance that thing right now. Hmmm, what did I do with my . . . ?"

I started to run, but she grabbed me; I had to think fast. "Miss Hoate," I warned her, "my father knows almost every important doctor in the United States. He conferred with many medical schools when he made a movie about"—I seized on the first famous doctor's name I could think of—"Dr. Faustus. So if you do something he doesn't like, my father can get you kicked out."

She settled on wrapping a mile-long ribbon of gauze and some plasterlike substance around my knee and part of my thigh. While she worked, she explained, "My life plan is to work on victims who've been burned in apartment house fires, on ones who've been scarred in wars or maimed by their parents. There are lots of babies who come out looking like gargoyles. That's who *I'm* going to help."

"I'm sure they'll be lucky to have you," I said diplomatically. Charmian would have said I was spreading it thick.

"You can get lost now, Fleur de. Am-scray," she ordered as soon as she'd tied off the last of the gauze.

My instinct declared *run for your life*, but some perverse quirk in my nature caused me to stay and inquire sweetly, "Would you like some help getting settled?"

"Go stick your head down a toilet. Do you catch my drift?" she asked. "No one's allowed to see what I unpack."

She yanked the doors shut behind me, and I saw the sunlight disappear (the French doors were heavily draped). Then I heard her slip the bolt into the catch.

I had spent many an evening in the nanny's room. And in that room, sitting on the solitary twin bed, I listened to one nanny after another tell a unique version of the same story—how she'd come from faraway, defying her parents, to see Hollywood. I doubted I would hear this from Miss Hoate though; no previous nanny had ever locked me out of her room.

"I'm not like your other nannies." Miss Hoate's shout penetrated the drapes and glass as though she could read my thoughts. The harshness of her voice was not at all softened by the thick material between us. "And now it's time for you to take off your clothes."

"Why?" I cried, amazed.

"Because I told you to."

I went running downstairs. My shoes scuffed against the hardwood, clinked against the Spanish tiles, brushed the carpet, and thumped on the linoleum in the butler's pantry. Stephie wasn't in the kitchen, so I ran through the service porch and up the back steps to her room.

Stephie had one great interest in life. Her room was littered with racing forms and periodicals describing each horse scheduled to run at Santa Anita. She only liked cooking because she could do it while she listened to the goings-on at the track on the radio.

"What's that you've got on your leg?" Stephie asked as

soon as she opened her door. "Is your leg in a cast? Did you break something?"

"I think Miss Hoate wants to play doctor, and this bandage was the first move. Now she wants me to take off my clothes, and I'm scared."

Stephie's immediate answer was to make tea. "I'll bring it up to you in a minute," she said.

"I'm not going back up there alone."

"All right, go sit in the breakfast room."

Stephie had what they called in Westerns a "yellow streak"—she wouldn't break my parents' rule of keeping me out of the kitchen until she could be sure Miss Hoate wasn't a tattletale.

I was on my second heavily sugared and creamed cup of tea before Miss Hoate joined us in the breakfast room. She had changed her clothes. A white nylon uniform hung forlornly from her shoulders. Her calves were covered by sterile white stockings. Her hands were whiter still.

"There you are, Fleur," she said in a voice sweeter than my tea. "Hello again, Stephie. Did Fleur tell you we had a misunderstanding? It's made me terribly sad. All I want is for us to be friends, starting out on the *right* foot, Fleur."

"Fleur is an obedient child," Stephie said, reminding me of the reluctant witness for the defense on a November *Radio Mystery Half-Hour.* "Have some tea, Miss Hoate? Sugar? Cream?"

"Thank you ever so much," Miss Hoate responded. Then she took hold of my hand and said, "The agency told me I'm to do the laundry, so I am respectfully requesting that when you come home from school, you put on some old clothes or, better, your robe. Then I won't have so much washing to do."

"I can understand that," Stephie stuck up for her. "We used to have a laundress here twice a week, but Mrs. Leigh bought the new machines and fired her. Now laundry is the nanny's job."

As I dragged myself upstairs, forming the complaint I would make to Charmian, I realized she would say I was being *très, très* trivial. Then she would remind me what it was like to get a radio show ready for broadcasting each week. So I pulled on some jeans and an old blouse I didn't like. Then I returned to the breakfast room.

"Jeans need washing too," Miss Hoate told me in her syrupy voice. "And ironing. From now on when you get home from school, you take a bath, put on a robe. Only *then* can you have a snack. Stephie agrees with me. Isn't that right, Stephie? Go on up now, my pretty little pigeon, and put on your robe. Then Stephie says she will give you a nice piece of cake."

"I'm not allowed to have cake," I said defiantly. "And if I put on a robe, I won't be able to go outside and play." I didn't add that I could hardly spend time with Constantine in the garden wearing bedroom attire.

"You've been playing all day in school."

"If I put on a robe, I'll feel like I'm sick."

"I'll cure you. I know medicine, remember?"

"If I put on a robe, I won't be able to concentrate on my homework."

"You'll concentrate because I'll tell you to."

I ran upstairs and headed directly to the nanny's room. Miss Hoate couldn't lock it if she wasn't inside, and I was determined to find some evidence that would convince Charmian to fire her. I half-expected to find a hunting knife in a leather sheath or a pearl-handled pistol in her pocketbook. Had she been a character on Charmian's radio show, it would be a foregone conclusion.

The nanny's room, formerly a screened porch, abutted against the hillside. The wide expanses of screen had been glassed in, and if you didn't mind sitting in the dark, you could sometimes see animal families wander in and out of view. Sometimes wild deer would scamper down the slope and hop onto our tile roof. We'd hear what sounded like dishes breaking over our heads, and my father would call the police. Within minutes two or three squad cars would arrive and policemen with flashlights, shrill whistles, and voices like cowboys at roundup, would coerce mammals, rodents, and reptiles back into the hills.

Oh, how I wished I could have heard those voices just then because I found what I least expected. Miss Hoate had tacked blankets over all the windows, blacking them out as though there was a war.

My mother complained I wore my heart on my sleeve, but at that moment I could feel it throbbing against my blouse. Maybe, as Charmian contended, I'd been privy to too many of her story conferences where duplicity, roguery, and even heinous crimes were constantly being plotted, but here was a mystery that had yet to be explored on her show. I decided I'd better play the role of compliant child, at least until my mother came home. On went the briar-green flannel robe; on went the padded moccasins. I stayed well out of Miss Hoate's way for the rest of the afternoon.

I ate dinner alone in the breakfast room while Stephie and Miss Hoate shared their repast in the kitchen. Miss Hoate burst through the swinging door only occasionally to serve me. As I slurped—a pleasure I indulged in when eating alone—lentil soup, I felt myself seesaw between fear and curiosity. Somehow I couldn't help wanting to annoy Miss Hoate just a little so I redeemed a humdrum but fairly effective line Charmian had once written for a witless homicide investigator who was trying to nab a trigger man. "Have you got a moment?" I asked. "You're such an interesting specimen. Would you mind if I interviewed you?"

"You mean . . . for the job? You're too late."

"I mean about your life in general."

"What are you talking about?" she asked impatiently.

"Actually, I was wondering about those blankets over your windows," I said, trying to sound casual.

She groused, "You went in my room when I wasn't there?"

"Yes, I confess." Then using various bits and pieces of

dialogue from *The Radio Mystery Half-Hour,* I quickly added, "And by all the powers vested in me I swear not to go into your room again."

"Did you go through my things?" she asked.

"Of course not. All I did was marvel"—this was one of Charmian's pet American words—"at the blankets. They're such a unique addition to the décor, I was wondering where you got the idea."

"You really want to know?" she asked somberly. Then she dropped her voice so low I had to bend toward her to hear. "I told you I will soon be a doctor, right? Well, I've advanced by leaps and bounds in the medical field. Naturally, there are people who covet my research. Some will stop at nothing to get it. Communist agents are following me everywhere." Suddenly, she was treating me as her ally. "They followed me here. I could see them from the taxi. By the time I got to my room, they'd climbed up the hillside and were bivouacked on that high wall. They have telescopes."

"Telescopes?" I echoed dubiously. The wall she spoke of surrounded John Barrymore's vine-encased villa, which Charmian claimed had forty-seven rooms, each with dust and cobwebs thicker than the plaster. It was abandoned now and unsalable, having been designed by a set director instead of an architect. Padlocks hung from the gates, and the crumbling walls, mined with barbed wire, were too dangerous to scale. "Miss Hoate, no one would risk climbing that wall."

"The Commies need my notes. What I've done is only a

stopgap measure. They'll soon have telescopes that penetrate blanket fibers."

On Miss Hoate's next trip to the breakfast room, she served me a T-bone steak and scalloped potatoes. (Stephie, who hadn't been with us long, had not been informed about my No Whites Inside Diet, or perhaps, now that I no longer swam, Maurice had given it up.) I remembered my manners and said that the meal looked delicious. Then I attempted to calm Miss Hoate's fears. "The wall you're talking about is a part of the old Barrymore estate. He was a famous actor once, but, as is often said on my mother's radio show, he long ago joined the departed. Now there are guards patrolling all the time. And guard dogs."

"Nothing can stop the Commies. You've heard of the domino theory, haven't you?" she persisted. "And for all I know, you could be one of the fallen."

After dinner Miss Hoate behaved like a kidnapper keeping constant tabs on her hostage. She insisted I accompany her upstairs into the bathroom, where she again scrubbed her hands meticulously. When she'd finally dried them to her satisfaction, she beckoned me, "Come over here, I better get that dressing changed."

She unwound all the gauze around my leg and then wound it back again. This time it was a lot tighter, but I didn't complain. "Now then," she said cheerfully, as though exhilarated by her handiwork, "time to get ready for bed. Lights out at eight."

"I don't have a bedtime, Miss Hoate," I argued, my indignation giving me courage. "Remember, my mother told you I was to be treated as an adult? I don't get in bed until I'm tired, and then I'm allowed to read for as long as I like."

Miss Hoate peered into my face as though she were making a diagnosis. "That would explain why you look like walking gonorrhea," she said. "Children your age need at least twelve hours of sleep."

"No they don't, and our school nurse says reading is almost as restful as sleep."

"An elementary school nurse, ha," Miss Hoate spat out contemptuously. "*I* am an advanced practitioner in the medical field." Miss Hoate then began to pull my bedspread off my bed, almost tearing it away from behind the footboard.

"Watch out," I cautioned her. "That's my mother's favorite quilt. You see how it has an arbor of wisteria appliquéd all over it? Then there's all this embroidery, millions of stitches, some so tiny you can't see them. Every shade of purple and green imaginable." In an effort to distract Miss Hoate, I repeated a portion of the docent talk Charmian gave to guests touring our house. "Some of the stitches have special names. There's the French knot, the twisted chain, the satin stitch, the staggered stem—"

"I know all those stitches," Miss Hoate interrupted. "I'm practically a surgeon, remember? We have to know them."

"My mother says I should feel honored to have this spread on my bed. I have promised never to sit on it."

"She likes the quilt more than she likes you," Miss Hoate stated smugly, folding the material roughly as though it were a flag from a country whose government she despised. She threw the quilt across the room. It grazed a sconce and landed in a clump on the floor.

Believing I had no choice in the matter, I climbed into bed. Not until I heard her bolt the doors between our rooms did I creep out of the sheets toward my closet to retrieve my powerful flashlight. "In case of emergency," the nanny who'd placed it there had said, and until now I'd been anticipating one with pleasure.

Although I enjoyed reading under the covers in the bold beam of the flashlight, I remained alert for any sound from Miss Hoate's room, so my concentration suffered. And sure enough, she invaded my room twice before she turned out her lights. I pretended to be asleep when she splashed her hands in the bathroom sink and I counted the six minutes it took to dry them. Miss Hoate returned to her room. I heard a radio interlude of Hugo Winterhalter and his orchestra. Then nothing.

Fully awake and feeling safer, I occupied myself by studying my collections. I missed my silver dollars immensely—they were one currency that couldn't be counterfeited. I missed my birds' nests and my baby teeth. Trying to comfort myself, I played with my buttons, stirring them with my fingers and gently rubbing them against my lips. I touched the nicest ones with my tongue. Then I returned them to my secret drawer. Exposing anything I loved to Miss Hoate's evil eyes presented a risk I wouldn't take.

Then, by chance, I happened to glance at my bookshelves. The one valuable collection in my possession was a set of seven books in the *Wizard of Oz* series. Each Christmas Lester McAdam, the actor who played the Police Chief, presented me with a new volume. Except the books weren't new, he'd explained: "These books were published around nineteen ten through eighteen. They're 'first editions' that will get more and more precious. Think of them as savings bonds, except you can read them while you wait for them to mature."

I gazed at the books and then quickly counted them. How was it possible that one was missing? Charmian surely hadn't given it to the orphans.

When my mother finally came home, Miss Hoate was snoring, making a long, troubled but evenly spaced wheezing sound which couldn't have been duplicated even by the sound man who simulated the noises on *The Radio Mystery Half-Hour.* I tiptoed out of my room and found Charmian sitting in the *salle d'étudier* with a glass of milk, a cigarette, and a pill. The pills' reddish color told me they were the ones for sleeping.

I wanted to run to her, lay my head on her chest, and cry deeply and long, but I knew all too well that she found displays of emotion offensive.

"Damn, I missed Jack Paar again," she greeted me.

"There's something I have to tell you," I said, sounding as urgent as I dared.

Charmian looked at me with complete bewilderment. "What's that? Is your leg in a cast?"

"She bandaged me for no reason—that's what I want to tell you about," I explained, unwinding the gauze. "Charmian, this is important. I have to tell you about Miss Hoate."

"Who?"

"The new nanny. I think she has criminal tendencies," I stated, trying to speak the language my mother understood.

"I've got three days until airtime, and I don't have a script, let alone a story line. Leave me alone, will you? I have to think."

"When Stephie is around Miss Hoate is nice," I continued solemnly, "but when we're alone, she goes haywire. She purposely says things to scare me, and she's mean."

"Don't be melodramatic. She's . . . eccentric, granted, but eccentricity dost not a criminal make. You really must learn to get along with all sorts of people."

Clover had taught me that Charmian could be manipulated, and that's what I set out to do. "Honestly, you sweet, adorable actress-writer-producer with those big blue eyes, I'd be a perfect suspect for your show," I mimicked Miss Hoate. Then I climbed up on a chair and teetered comically as I pretended to hammer nails into the wall. "Please don't mind the holes in the walls—this is a necessity. I'm covering my windows with blankets, you see, to the chagrin of my enemies." Then, jumping down, I pantomimed the nanny's labored ablutions over the sink, saying with dismay, "I washed my hands about thirty times today, but they just didn't get clean."

Charmian laughed, "You're quite the mime."

"I tried to get your daughter to play doctor with me, but she wouldn't remove her clothes. So I swiped one of her *Wizard of Oz* books to teach her a lesson."

"Good characterization," my mother chuckled.

"Charmian," I said her name gravely. Then I paused to gather my courage. "I'm trying to tell you how scared I am. You're acting as if you don't care what happens to me."

"Don't be silly. Of course I care. How can you say such a thing?"

Despite myself, I lost my composure. "You're never here when I need you. You've hardly spent a minute with me since the day I was born," I announced bitterly.

"After all I went through just to *have* you—how can you say such a thing?" Rather than being angry at my outburst, Charmian seemed almost amused. She'd had drinks at a party and now, I guessed, her pills were doing their job. "Come here," she patted the seat next to her. "Let me tell you something. . . ." My mother was in a story-telling mood.

"If only I could have hired a stuntman or a stand-in to give birth to you. . . . That's how harrowing it was. I was in labor for days and days before they chloroformed me and gave you a cesarean delivery. They put me out cold. When I awoke and determined that I was in a private hospital room, there were absolutely no clues as to the sex, status, or whereabouts of my baby. In fact, I couldn't be certain I'd given birth! 'Is there a doctor in the house? I need assistance right now,' I called out while I sat on the nurse's buzzer for an hour or longer.

"Well, the passage of time gave me the chance to regain control of my many faculties. I *am* an actress *and* a writer, am I not? So I made a grand gesture on your behalf—I picked up the phone next to the bed and dialed the hospital's number.

"Cedars of Lebanon, Hollywood," Charmian parroted the receptionist's response.

"Allo, allo," Charmian now mimicked *herself* using a French telephone operator's accent. "Paris ees calling long distance. *Comprenez-vous?* On the line I have, er, Contessa Katrina Marina Farina Vanderhilt. She ees the mother of the world-renowned actress Charmian Leigh. Madame, you may *parlez maintenant*."

Quickly, Charmian changed roles. Both at the hospital and now here at home, she assumed her most erudite Continental diction. "Hello, is this California? I am given to understand that my daughter has just produced a baby. Now, I can't let you disturb her—I know how poorly she sleeps—so can you tell me, did she have a boy or a girl?"

The hospital receptionist checked with the nursery, Charmian explained, then came back on the line. "I'm not supposed to give out information regarding celebrities, but seeing as you're the granny and calling from overseas . . . Oh well, what the hell. A little girl has joined Miss Leigh's cast of players."

"Did she really put it like that?" I asked.

"Well, it's a *Hollywood* hospital. Anyway, I asked her this: 'Are mummy and infant faring well?' And can you guess what she said?"

"What?" I asked, playing the straight man, thrilled to have a story that was just for me.

"They both came through in fine fettle. The baby is healthy, and Miss Leigh is as beautiful as ever," Charmian, playing the receptionist, exclaimed. Then the two of us burst into laughter.

As had happened in the past, just when I could no longer pretend I didn't despise my mother, she beguiled me. I could have sat in her *salle d'étudier* for the rest of my life, listening to her tell stories and laugh at herself.

"So you see what I went through for *you*? Becoming a mother is no laughing matter. Which reminds me . . . there's something you ought to see."

I followed her into the bedroom and into the largest closet. Feeling for something on the shelf above her furs, she finally pulled out a medium-size manila envelope. "Take a gander at this," she urged me. "This is your birth announcement. You can keep it if you want."

Charmian and Maurice Leigh

present

for the first time anywhere

their daughter

Fleur de Leigh

now showing at

The Cedars of Lebanon Hospital

for a limited time only

(All Seats Reserved)

thereafter by appointment only at

The Beverly Hills Hotel

Beverly Hills, California

Fleur de Leigh

Produced by CHARMIAN LEIGH
Directed by MAURICE LEIGH
Original Play by MAURICE LEIGH
Based on an Idea by CHARMIAN LEIGH

Vital Statistics

Weight in pounds: 7
Months in Production: 10

Any resemblance to characters other than Charmian or Maurice Leigh is purely coincidental.

"You'll simply love her!" —*Louella Parsons*

"Howl of the season." —Hollywood Reporter

"A bellyful of laughs." —*Hedda Hopper*

(Advertisement)

Be sure to listen to

The Charmian Leigh
Radio Mystery Half-Hour

Sunday nights at seven

After I read it, Charmian yawned. "What a day," she said, "and now this. You are going to have to work things out with Miss Hoate yourself—I don't have time. And now, my sleep pills are starting to hit me. Mr. Seconal is kicking in. I better get in bed before I conk out."

I saw that she was speaking the truth because when she stood up, she wobbled. "Stop worrying about the nanny," my mother urged. "A hundred years from now you'll laugh at this."

When I came home from school the next day, I realized it was Stephie's day off. I considered calling Charmian at the studio, but the receptionists at CBS usually had difficulty locating her. Besides, Charmian's advice would probably have been useless.

Miss Hoate was writing in a notebook so vigorously with such concentrated movement that, although it was risky, I just had to glance at the pages.

"What are you looking at?" she bellowed, slamming her notebook. The smack made me flinch. Then Miss Hoate cradled her notebook against her chest. "You think just because you're rich you can get away with anything."

"Believe me, I'm not rich. If I had *any* money, I'd give it to you. So you could take a long trip."

"You're not rich?" she asked as though this might be a fact worth pondering. "You're not rich?" Her eyes narrowed to gashes. "Then you have good reason to try and steal my medical theories, the ones I have proven right here." She tapped her notebook vehemently with her pointer finger. "You'd just love to sell them to the Communists, wouldn't you? Because you know they'd pay millions."

What I had seen in her notebook—slashes, dashes, and tiny loops all cramped together—looked like gibberish, but since she called her scribbling "medical theories," I thought possibly she could be right: it *could* be a kind of formula. Whatever the case, I knew it would be best for me to get out of her sight. "Guess I'll go upstairs and do homework," I offered. If I could have whistled casually, I would have.

Earlier, Miss Hoate had draped an old bedspread from the cook's room over my bed. (She'd torn Charmian's good quilt and had set about repairing it herself.) The change pleased me because the new spread was plain white chenille, machine washable, like the ones sold at Woolworth's, my favorite store in Beverly Hills. I threw myself on it and rolled on my back. The sensation of the tufts gently tickling the back of my knees and my thighs made me giggle.

It seems impossible that I fell asleep, but then I'd never had a place to lie down during the day. The next thing I knew, I woke up to find Miss Hoate leaning over me. Her hands were on my shoulders, close to my neck; her face looked red and strained. Her lips pulled back from her teeth so that she looked like a snarling dog.

I screamed. Then I wrenched my body away from her and rolled off the bed. I was in a situation comparable to those Charmian got into on her show, but *I* didn't have any writers to pull me out. "What do you want?" I asked shakily.

"I came upstairs because I realized the dressing on your leg had come off. But when I saw you on the bedspread, I was really afraid for you," she said, sounding quite sincere.

"Afraid of what?"

"You fell asleep on the bedspread," she declared with horror.

"I thought you put it on the bed *so* I could lie on it."

"I never dreamed you'd lie on it," she said gravely. "No one lies on chenille spreads. The tufts are too dangerous."

"Why?" I asked warily.

"I know medicine, remember?" She scrutinized me for the longest time, but, as always, there was a cast to her eyes, as though she were seeing me in El Greco elongations or Dali droops, not at all accurately. "I have personally examined the cadaver of a man killed by his chenille coverlet. I have viewed a film, taken through a microscope, that showed how the flocci can work their way through the finest porcelain. With a human, they ease into the body through the pores. Then they glide through the veins like little sailing ships. Within minutes they're bunched around the heart."

Keeping the bed between us, I tried to reason with her. "But Miss Hoate, that's impossible. Look how big the tufts are and look at my tiny pores." Even while I was speaking with bravado, some wee, doubting-Thomas segment of my brain was asking, "Are you sure? How do you know she's not right?"

"Don't contradict," she shouted, lunging toward me. Her knuckles made two deep, nasty dents in my bed.

When characters behaved like this on *The Radio Mystery Half-Hour,* Charmian said they'd come *unhinged.* Only when they killed someone were they upgraded, or downgraded, I wasn't sure which, to *psychopaths.* To my mind, Miss Hoate was closer to the second category. She would need special handling, as Charmian often remarked.

Miss Hoate's eyes were flashing, and she began pulling the spread off the bed, twisting it so that a part of it became a cord.

"You say and do things no one else would think of." I tried to make my statement sound like a compliment.

Miss Hoate looked startled, almost pleased. "The only admiration I've received in years is from the Communists. And it's backhanded, naturally."

"Gee, Miss Hoate, you must have some friends. To admire you, I mean."

"One friend. I have one friend. Her name is Margaret, but I had to leave her behind." Miss Hoate used a corner of the bedspread to pat her eyes, and I found myself feeling sorry for the enemy, something Charmian Leigh maintained that a person in danger should avoid.

"Where *is* Margaret?" I asked softly.

"At the hospital."

"Which hospital did you work in?" I asked, wondering if it was where I'd been born.

"Camarillo State Hospital," she answered.

"Is Margaret a doctor or a nurse?"

"Oh, she's a patient."

It took me minutes, it seemed, to grasp this paramount clue, and then everything about Miss Hoate made sense. Camarillo was an insane asylum about a hundred miles away. I knew this because comedians often made jokes about it.

"They teamed me up with her, made me Margaret's roommate. So I could take care of her, see. Instead, I have to take care of you."

There was something so threatening in her tone that I made a beeline to the bathroom, where I slammed and locked the door. I crept softly across the mustard-colored tile and opened the door at the opposite side of the room. As I stealthily exited our house and ventured out onto the hill-side, I considered running over to Pickfair. I could climb the hill through the brush and enter through the rear. Someone in the kitchen would let me use the phone. But would phoning my father achieve anything? Since I'd stopped swimming, he'd refused to talk to me.

If only Daisy had been available, I would have hiked or hitchhiked to her house. Thinking of my loss brought tears to my eyes. Daisy had endured some fairly zany nannies herself. She would have commiserated and known what action to take.

To my joy and partial relief, I spied Constantine's gleaming yellow jalopy parked in our driveway. The only trouble was I couldn't see *him*. I didn't dare call his name aloud because I could hear Miss Hoate calling mine. "Fleur de, Fleur de, Fleur de. Don't you dare hide from me. It's time for your bath, and then I have a little surprise for you," she shouted menacingly.

Please, Constantine, please show yourself, I prayed to my powerful friend as I scanned our hillside, hoping to glimpse one little splotch of bare skin. Miss Hoate was about to round the corner of the house, and I had to find somewhere to hide. I looked again at Constantine's car. As usual, the top was down, so it provided no place to conceal myself; then I remembered that I'd always wanted to ride in the rumble seat.

It was terribly cramped in there. I might as well have climbed under the hood; I couldn't bend my knees or shift positions. Soon my neck was aching and cramps were fettering my legs. Then, what may have been hours later, the bubble of air that was my lifeline heated up like a pottery kiln. The motor had started and gas fumes swirled around so that my eyes began to burn.

Because I believed Miss Hoate quite capable of following Constantine in the Buick, I didn't dare move. But then my fear that the great man might not forgive me if I upchucked in his car forced my shoulder against the rumble seat door. My heart pounded as I strained against it, but it was tightly latched. More afraid than ever, I cried out, "Constantine, Constantine, stop the car."

The motor knocked so loudly it drowned out my voice. Finally, with one hand pressed tight against my mouth, I thumped my head against the back of Constantine's seat. Nothing could have gratified me more than feeling the jalopy coast to the side of the road.

When he pulled the rumble seat open and I popped up, Constantine jumped back in alarm. His face looked white, and his eyes were stunned. As honking cars whizzed passed us, I realized that he'd parked the jalopy on one of Sunset Boulevard's most dangerous curves. Though horribly embarrassed, I stood on the curb and vomited all the food and fear and fury I'd swallowed in the last two days.

"Is big shock finding small girl in car," Constantine explained himself when we were under way again. This time I was sitting next to him. He listened sympathetically to my tale of woe.

"So, nanny is crazy person?"

"I'm afraid so."

He thought for a moment before he gravely said, "Is best thing if Fleur comes home with Constantine."

"Really?" It sounded so cozy, so ideal, my staying at his apartment. I imagined mornings with him—the two of us swimming toward a rising sun, our bodies gliding through an ocean that shimmered with gold. Afternoons, while Constantine worked, I would leisurely browse through his gallery of "blossoms" and perhaps meet some of his free-spirited friends. In the evenings we would feast on the rustic viands he would provide and later we'd lift the dumbbells in his bedroom. The two of us would live a wholesome life, free from conflict.

Then I remembered. "But Constantine, we're not supposed to be friends. My mother doesn't want me hanging around with you. She'd split a gut if I went to your apartment again. And she'll never believe what I just told you about Miss Hoate. Oh gosh," I started crying again, "what can we do?"

"Don't cry, Fleur Leigh," he tried to console me, "Constantine taking care of everything."

I wanted to believe that he could save me from any catastrophe, just as I'd seen Howard Keel as Wild Bill Hickok suavely rescue Calamity Jane.

Constantine parked his jalopy directly in front of Beverly Hills police headquarters.

"I think we're supposed to park across the street," I urged him. "I don't want to break any laws."

"Is okay," he said and took hold of my hand. "Fleur Leigh having business here."

As we approached the desk of the officer on duty, it occurred to me that Constantine and I made an odd pair. Our gardener's bare chest might appear out of place in a government office. Worse, the accumulated aroma of his all-day, outdoor exertion pervaded the room. Constantine's splintered English and my age were going to count against us too.

"So what do your *parents* have to say about your nasty nanny?" the sergeant asked in a kindly, though slightly mocking manner after Constantine and I had described my predicament. He didn't seem to be taking us seriously.

"My mother is an actress. She's very busy with her show," I tried to explain.

"Which show?"

"It's called *The Charmian Leigh Radio Mystery Half-Hour.*"

"Oh, right, Charmian Leigh, the radio detective," the sergeant said sarcastically. "She makes a point of outsmarting the police in every episode. Can't say she's exactly popular in these here parts, but it seems to me that a loony nanny ought to be right up her ally. So why are you bothering with us?"

"Well, it's just that Miss Hoate says she lived at Camarillo. That's a *mental* hospital," I said. "Couldn't you check your records just to see if she's wanted for anything? Maybe there's an APB out on her or something."

"Sounds to me like that little girl listens to too much radio," another officer mouthed off. He was sitting at a desk with his back to me, but I could see that he was a very corpulent man.

"Is no way to talk to frightened child," Constantine reproached him.

The fat officer slowly arose from his chair and made his way toward us, saying, "There's no good reason for this department to help out Charmian Leigh or any of her immediate family."

The voice was familiar and I looked at him carefully.

No, it couldn't be. The officer waddling in our direction, the officer bursting his uniform, the officer who looked ten times fatter than Glendora ever had, was Jeff. "Charmian Leigh ruined my life," he hissed at us. "She left me on the cutting room floor. But don't think I didn't get even. I sent a copy of the stolen property file to her insurance company, and you can be sure I let them know it had all been recovered."

"Jeff," I said earnestly, "would you like Glendora's address? I bet if you wrote to her, she'd take you back."

"The best thing you can do is get out of here. Scram," he said.

"Shame on you, not helping little girl," Constantine reproached him as we turned away.

I didn't see Miss Hoate again until later that evening when she served dinner to my parents and me. While she was collecting our soiled salad plates, the doorbell rang.

"Damn, who would bother us at dinnertime? I guess you better see who it is," Maurice instructed Miss Hoate.

"Perhaps it's a telegram," Charmian said hopefully. She was always awaiting word that her show was going on TV.

"I really don't like answering the door when I don't know who's outside," Miss Hoate argued with my father. "You never can tell what kind of weirdo's out there."

"We won't know until you open it," Maurice said.

"But . . ."

My mother couldn't stand the suspense and brushed past Miss Hoate. I was standing behind Charmian when she opened the door.

On the threshold were two ordinary-looking men who affected a casual attitude as though they'd just happened by, tourists looking for an autograph, most likely. "We're looking for Miss Evelyn Hoate," one of them said. He spoke very softly to Charmian.

"I really don't approve of our help having visitors during working hours," my mother said harshly.

"This is not what you'd call a visit, ma'am. We're here on official business," the same man said. "I'm Officer Charles Gordon and this is Dr. Gregory Mandell. He's a psychiatrist." The policeman swiftly showed Charmian a badge while the doctor furtively held out a parka with arms long enough to fit an orangutan. I recognized it as a straitjacket because such contraptions were used liberally on *The Radio Mystery Half-Hour.*

"I'll tell you quite frankly, I loathe pranks," Charmian spoke harshly.

Miss Hoate must have seen the straitjacket too, because she dropped the plates she was holding. I thought she would start screaming and run for the back door or grab and crush me to her chest the way criminals on the lam seized hostages on Charmian's show. But that was not what Miss Hoate had in mind. She walked toward us and, with a kindly look and a sorrowful shake of her head, said, "Mrs. Leigh, I must apologize about Fleur de. I really cherish this child, but when she became, uh, physical and threatened to push me into your oubliette, I became frightened. I was alone in the house with her after all, and she was hysterical. I could think of nothing to do but call Camarillo State Hospital. It's probably all my fault. How I wish I hadn't chosen to be a plastic surgeon; psychiatry would have been a much more useful field."

"Oubliette? What on earth is going on here?" Charmian asked me, irritation bouncing her speech around. *"Mon Dieu."*

"I'm sure the psychiatric evaluation will show Fleur de is only the slightest bit insane, and I'm positive that with help, she'll be right as rain. And, if it means anything to you, I promise that when I complete my medical degree I will offer you and Fleur de my full assistance." Miss Hoate spoke so convincingly that for a moment even *I* believed her.

"Oh, I see, so it was *you* who called," Dr. Mandell said to Miss Hoate in a gentle, paternal tone. "I'm afraid I had it backwards. I am sorry. Will you accept my apology? Now, Evelyn, would you let me impose on you one more time?"

"Ask and ye shall receive," she responded.

"Some people, especially children," he said, looking at me, "become terrorized by straitjackets. So could I ask you to slip into this? For a second or two? Just to demonstrate to the young lady she has nothing to fear? We don't want to get Fleur all riled up. We don't want her to repeat her hysteria."

"I'd like to help you," Miss Hoate told him, "but, really, I can't. I'm embarrassed to admit this—and please don't tell any of my colleagues—but I suffer from claustrophobia. Putting on a straitjacket, even for a minute or two, could easily aggravate my condition."

My father, who was now standing close by, spoke almost in unison with Charmian. "Hysterical child, my eye." "No child of mine gets hysterical."

"Miss Hoate, if you malign my daughter any further, I shall take it up with Her Ladyship's Domestic Employment Agency," my mother added.

"I know a darn sight more about Fleur de than you do," Miss Hoate countered. "I've spent more time with her in two days than you have in a lifetime."

"How dare you!" Charmian's voice resounded through the living room. "You're fired! Get her out of here," my mother ordered the officer and the psychiatrist as though they were mere actors playing supporting roles on her show.

"They're here for Fleur de," Miss Hoate reminded her.

"Then you can just leave on your own two feet," Charmian lashed out at the nanny.

"Nothing would make me happier," Miss Hoate gloated. Seizing the moment, she spun past me like a hard-hit croquet ball. She squeezed between the officer and the doctor, then whirled over the threshold. She would have rolled out of their grasp forever had not a dark figure moved from out of the shadows of our entry porch. A voice rang out. "You. Nanny. Stopping right here, not run from police. Not now."

Miss Hoate wailed. "You see. What did I tell you?

There're Communist agents everywhere. They're after me. Hurry, hurrry, call the FBI."

Fortunately, I wasn't misled. I recognized the large, powerful hand of Constantine as it reached out and attached itself to my soon-to-be former nanny's bony arm.

VIII

Gilda

2/5/59–4/21/59

Because Trina, the nanny who replaced Miss Hoate, was the only applicant for the job, my mother bowed to her demand of a half-day Saturday and all of Sunday off. Consequently, during Trina's tenure, Charmian was forced to make provisions which would keep me occupied; she routinely left orders for Trina to pack a lunch and drive me to the Academy.

In the fifties, the Academy of Motion Picture Arts and Sciences Theatre was housed in an unobtrusive building on Melrose Avenue next to a Carl's Market. Neither the neighborhood nor the theater's facade gave any indication that inside, as Charmian phrased it, "*culture* awaited." Yes, an entire year of movies, four of them a day, all that could possibly be nominated for awards, were screened on the premises.

"Kids are supposed to play outside or they won't get their Vitamin D. That's what they tell us at school," I protested just to be troublesome.

"You get ample sunshine on weekdays," my mother replied. She also advised me to thank my lucky stars because only the most privileged children had access to the Academy.

A few other youths were deposited there as well. We developed a strained camaraderie, getting to know each other in the dark without disturbing the adults in the audience. Throughout the afternoon, as soon as a picture bogged down in excessive dialogue or smooching, the older, braver youths left to forage at the market. When they returned, I traded my lunch for four or five Almond Joys.

By no measure did I consider my biweekly internment in the auditorium an ordeal. Satiated with candy and mesmerized by the wide screen, I came to believe that at one of these movie marathons I'd be seeing a Todd-AO Technirama production about me. The film version would winnow the true drama from the bedlam of everyday existence, thus imbuing my life with a clarity I failed to find. How eagerly I awaited *The Fleur de Leigh Story*, with perhaps Sandra Dee in the lead, wherein all, *all*, would be happily resolved.

One Saturday morning, however, Trina turned the Buick in a westerly direction instead of heading east toward the Academy. "How come?" I asked her, thinking of the moron jokes that were popular at school just then.

"Oh, didn't your parents tell you?"

"Tell me what?"

"They've signed you up for some sort of, I don't know, acting class. No wait, maybe it's one of those psychological *groups.* Guess I wasn't paying attention. What I do know is that you kids from Hollywood have all the advantages. Anyway, I'm taking you early because I have an appointment of my own."

I had grown accustomed to my parents springing surprises on me, but habituation somehow never softened the blow and I watched sorrowfully as our broad-tailed Buick lurched away from the curb. Then, timidly, I rang the doorbell at a private home on a hill in Brentwood. It was doubtful that my parents wished me to study acting when, in response to my offering to play a small part on Charmian's show, she had theatrically expounded, "Acting is simply venomous for children, *chou-Fleur,* and there's one thing that's truly important to me—I want you to lead the life of a *complètement normale* child."

Trina's second supposition as to where we were going seemed more probable. Charmian was annoyed by my endless inquiries about Daisy; in turn, she believed my psyche had been seriously injured by Constantine. And no doubt, now that Miss Hoate had revealed *her* looniness, it was just like my parents to get *my* head examined.

The door was answered by a frail, shabbily dressed old

man. His eyes were hooded and pouched with age. His hair grew in wisps, and his gray, claylike skin was reminiscent of a pre-Columbian funereal figure, a scary one I'd seen on a field trip to the Southwest Museum. I fretted that Trina had delivered me to the wrong address.

"Vait here," he told me before I had time to say a word.

After a minute, a boy—a full-fledged teenager about four years older than I—arrived on the threshold and assumed the role of greeter with aplomb. He had a pleasant enough face and the kind of teenage savoir faire that appealed to adults rather than fellow students. "Hi, you must be Fleur. I'm Gilda's son, John," he welcomed me. "Come on in. You're early, but it's quite all right."

He led me into a sunny, sunken living room, a fashionable architectural contrivance at the time. I looked about with Charmian's critical eyes, the only way I knew to assess interior decoration, appreciating the wide, white bookshelves, the spotless windows, the profusion of frilly-leafed plants. Indian pottery and carvings and a few antiquities on stands shared space with books on the coffee table and the shelves. On the walls were primitive paintings, a solitary African mask, and what, I realize now, must have been an original Ben Shahn sketch.

John and I sat down on a comfortable semicircular couch. Nubby, sand-colored material covered it. I would have felt at ease in these surroundings had it not been for the man I'd met at the door inching toward me with a vacuum. A roaring canister at the end of a hose trailed him like an unruly pet.

"I guess my father didn't introduce himself," John shouted over the continuous blast. "Sometimes he talks a blue streak. Other days he says nothing at all."

"*He's* your father?"

"Yeah. He was a famous psychoanalyst in the old country. Have you heard of Freud or Jung?"

I nodded.

"You would have heard of my father too if Hitler hadn't come along. In the old country, they called my dad Herr Doktor Feder." John's pronunciation of it gave the name grandeur. "But here he's just Old Fritz."

Psychoanalysts occasionally haunted my parents' soirées. Charmian courted them, as did many other actors who waited in line to shake hands with sages. But instead of joining what Charmian termed *the badinage,* the psychoanalysts remained aloof. Perhaps they'd allow a sycophant to bring them another martini and some blini coated in caviar, or maybe a chicken liver wrapped in sugar-coated bacon and secured with a feathered toothpick. Sometimes Charmian hired Javanese hula girls to entertain her guests. At other parties a magician mingled with the crowd stealing watches, jewelry, money clips, or keys—of course, he later returned the objects to the astonished owners. Shunning the entertainment, the analysts stared at the party-goers with brooding, red-streaked eyes as though anyone well acquainted with angst could not possibly derive pleasure from a fête. "They don't have time to be civil," Charmian excused them, "they're busy . . . associating." Most of them were graying and frumpy. One of them had a hump.

"So, who *is* Gilda? Aside from being your mother, I mean," I asked John.

He looked amazed. "You don't know that she leads the psychodrama workshop?" John tried to explain the purpose of psychodrama as Old Fritz vacuumed, dusted, and plumped cushions with a fierceness that belied his frail frame. Then, just before the doorbell rang, the doctor carried away his cleaning implements and vanished.

The members of the workshop must have carpooled to Gilda's house because they arrived en masse. There were five of them, between ten and fifteen years of age, neatly dressed as if for school. The boys wore slacks and long-sleeved shirts and the girls sported straight skirts and cashmere sweater sets. Polished pennies gleamed in the slots of their well-shined loafers. Anyone as well groomed as they would realize that my hair wasn't professionally cut, just evened up by a scissors-happy maid. I saw the girls examining my fussy blouse with its Peter Pan collar and three-quarter sleeves, and wondered whether I should explain that I was wearing a dirndl skirt because after a few hours at the Academy and two or three Almond Joys, a straight skirt turned into a girdle.

Charmian had trained me to memorize names to relieve her of the burden, but even if she hadn't I shall always remember: Sharon, Ophelia, Robert, Malcolm, and Todd. They were a solemn lot, cool and snobbish, the kind of kids Daisy probably met at boarding school. They said hello perfunctorily and were indifferent when we traded the names of our schools. Despite the fact that they lived in Beverly Hills where, as Charmian said, the school system was *superlatif,* they attended private institutions. This indicated they were gentiles or from that echelon of Hollywood Jews who had reason to fear kidnappings.

"So . . . um . . . what does your father do?" Sharon asked me casually.

Charmian had advised me to always mention my connection to show business. "It gets you better tables at restaurants, nicer rooms in hotels, deluxe treatment from *tout le monde,*" she asserted. I rarely accepted my mother's counsel on this, but I wished to dazzle the group; I explained that Maurice was a producer and that Charmian was, well, who she was.

The boys and girls were not impressed. They *all* had movie parents even more renowned than my own. "Show biz families are Gilda's specialty," Sharon disclosed.

All the while we conversed, I couldn't help but notice the eyes of the workshop constituents continually glancing toward a large, uncarpeted area two steps above the living room. The space looked very much like a stage.

Eventually, a stunning woman appeared on this landing. She paused, as though giving us time to ogle her. The woman was wearing what Charmian would have described as Oriental lounging pajamas of loose but clinging silk that showed off her slim figure to advantage. Its burnt orange color clashed chicly with her hair, which framed a flawless face with a pinkish tinge suggestive of pistachio shell dye.

Full lips, a narrow nose, and artfully tweezed eyebrows complimented smart green irises showcased in red-fringed ovals.

Sharon and Ophelia ran to Gilda and threw their arms around her. Brushing the girls aside, Gilda swept in my direction and encapsulated me in a warm, magnetic hug. "You've all met Fleur, haven't you?" she asked. A second later she let me go. I watched her glide around the coffee table and seat herself on an ottoman. She fluffed out the ends of her overblouse like a pianist with tuxedo tails.

"Fleur, dear heart, I hope you understand that your entrance into our fold is highly unorthodox. Members usually work with me for months so I can inculcate them with the philosophy of psychodrama. However, your father, a brilliant man, guaranteed your voluminous mental capacity. He assured me you could pick up what we do practically by . . . osmosis."

"He did?"

"Now let's get started, shall we? So, who has material today?" Gilda looked around.

There was silence until Ophelia spoke up.

"Ophelia's mom just happens to be Zoellyn Darton," Sharon whispered, giving me the name of a stellar performer, comedienne, and enduring glamour-puss whom I'd seen in innumerable movies at the Academy.

Ophelia was a tall, pretty girl, almost an exact replica of her mother. The daughter could have been a model of the Breck hair girl breed were it not for the braces on her teeth, her sloppy posture, and the fact she lumbered when she walked.

"I really got into it with Zoellyn this time," Ophelia said. "Gilda already knows. So, Gil, do you want me to really go into it?"

"Of course you should," Gilda declared. "I think a reconstitution of the incident would be beneficial for you *and* the rest of us. Now, let me see . . ." Gilda scrutinized the group. "Malcolm, why don't you play Ophelia today?"

"Me? Play a girl?" Malcolm's voice cracked. His brow furrowed and his eyelids crimped as though to prevent him from crying. "I can't. Please don't make me."

"All boys need to get in touch with their feminine aspect," Gilda prodded. "But if you feel that strongly . . ."

"Malcolm's father is a mogul," Sharon informed me.

Gilda looked around again and sweetly beseeched, "Todd, *you* wouldn't mind the role. Will you do it?"

"Gladly," Todd said, "if Oph will lend me her boobs."

"Shut up," Ophelia said.

Todd stood up and immediately assumed Ophelia's slouch and lumbering walk.

"*His* father is Roland Ramos," Sharon whispered. "Have you heard of him? He won a best-supporting-actor Oscar."

"Now let me see," Gilda mused. "Fleur, why don't you play Zoellyn? The fastest way for you to learn psychodrama technique is to do it."

My first impulse was to rebuff her, but the truth was I'd always wanted to act. Having observed so many actors competently ply their trade had made good acting seem a simple feat. Besides, if Ophelia's mother was anything like mine, a portrayal wouldn't be difficult. I followed Gilda, Ophelia, and Todd into the dining room and listened to their sketchy instructions.

"All right, thespians, let the playlet begin," Gilda proclaimed before taking a seat with the "audience."

Stiffly, Ophelia set the scene. "Zoellyn is taking her weekly bath in a tub of warm milk, and I'm screaming at her," she announced. Then she stepped down to join Gilda.

Dryness overpowered my mouth and pasted my tongue to my teeth, but the show must go on, I could hear Charmian say. Reflexively, I sat down on the hardwood floor and pretended to splash. I even hummed what I hoped was a bathtubby tune. Using what Charmian called the Stanislavsky Method of Acting, I tried to imagine the feel of warm milk permeating my skin. While I patted my face and shoulders delicately with an imaginary sponge, I couldn't help but notice that Old Fritz had stationed himself in the hallway, close to me, but out of sight of the audience.

Todd, a remarkably comfortable actor even while playing a girl, stepped to the side of my "tub." Facing away from Old Fritz, Todd towered over me, and when he shook a magazine threateningly, I flinched appropriately. "You don't give two figs about me, you big fat cow," he began.

He was so at ease playing the role that he relaxed me. I felt grateful and wanted to please him with a snappy retort.

My tongue resisted, but I succeeded in ad-libbing the lines, "I'm hardly a cow, *chéri*. I'm a size three."

"Zoellyn's more like a twelve," Ophelia cried out.

"When you're at home, you want to get me out of the house. So you can completely forget I exist," Todd whined.

"My poor, dear . . . dope," I responded, trying to play Zoellyn Darton's hautiness, which I'd seen in many a movie, to the hilt. "I can't"—I pronounced it "cawnt"—"possibly forget you. You're so . . . boisterous."

"Yeah? When did you hear me in the last three days?" he asked, his voice weighted with vitriol.

"*Je ne sais pas*," I said, stretching and yawning as I assumed a beautiful actress would do if she were relaxing in a bath of milk. I noticed that Old Fritz seemed to be whirling his hands, one around the other, as a signal to speed things up, but I was enjoying my first acting stint and didn't want it to end. "To the best of my recollection, you were outside watching the workmen reshingle the roof, which was paid for, by the way, entirely by my talent."

"You see, you see, that's how much you think of me." Then Todd as Ophelia bent down and shouted sassily into my ear: "I ran away three days ago, you old battle-ax. I was roaming Coldwater Canyon three whole days and nights. You didn't notice. Neither did my creepy nurse. Only the cook missed me—because she had to toss out food. And now you don't notice my scratches and bruises. Do you even know the police brought me home?"

"Oh, Ophelia, your histrionics get me down," I sighed,

trying to mimic the sound of Charmian's ennui with me.

Then Todd made a surprise move and pulled a knife from out of the tube he'd made of his magazine. It had an ominous gleam. "Do you see what you're making me do?" he screamed. I saw the knife coming toward me and I screamed too. Surely Ophelia hadn't pulled a knife on her mother, or did Gilda allow kids of Miss Hoate's ilk into her group?

I covered my face and tried to roll away from Todd's reach, ignoring the bathtub walls I had so vividly imagined. No blow struck me, but there *was* a struggle, with much panting and grunting. "What the hay?" Todd managed to shout at Old Fritz, who had him in a stranglehold. Seconds later the weapon bounced by my feet.

Gilda was on the stage. "Get the hell out of here," she growled at her husband. "I've told you not to interfere."

"He saved my life," I explained, stepping out of character.

"He saved you? He saved you?" Gilda repeated in a huff as she swooped down and scooped up the object in question. In her hand the butter knife looked picayune. How had I failed to see it for what it was?

"Shouldn't everyone know that I was about to slash my *own* wrists? I mean, as Ophelia. That's what she did, right?" Todd asked, diverting attention from the doctor to himself.

Ophelia, in the audience, pushed her sleeves up and raised her arms high into the air, revealing two thoroughly bandaged wrists. I heard murmurs of approval.

Gilda smiled uncomfortably. "Ophelia, maybe it would be best if you just described the rest."

"Well . . . Zoellyn has this telephone right by the tub," Ophelia eagerly informed the group. "She reached for it. I was hoping she'd get electrocuted, but no such luck. Notice, I couldn't even kill *myself*! So Zoellyn called Gilda. Like she always does when I act up. They talked forever, and then the two of them went out to the Coconut Grove."

"Zoellyn is a very dear friend of mine," Gilda said proudly, "but that doesn't mean I can't be objective. Dr. Freud socialized with many of his patients, and look what he achieved."

"Anyway, the next day Zoellyn bought me a fur coat," Ophelia continued. "To shut me up. So I shut up. For a while anyhow."

At that, Gilda began applauding to indicate the close of the playlet. "What can we learn from this little scene?" she asked.

"Get in trouble, get a fur coat," Sharon said. "What kind of fur is it, Oph?"

"Rabbit, probably," Ophelia said mirthlessly.

If Gilda had asked me personally what I thought of the scene, I would have said, "Ophelia lives in a viper's nest. But what's the point of trying to understand her supposedly glamorous mother when Ophelia doesn't have the power to change a thing?" I didn't wonder, not just then, if my axiom applied to my own mother too.

Old Fritz had left the stage and now reappeared. On his

shoulder rested a heavy silver tray heaped with cookies. He was also carrying a large pitcher of milk. Maybe he *was* a great psychiatrist—he'd hit upon the one element that might possibly cheer us up.

"Not now," Gilda snapped at her husband, but Todd had already snatched a handful of sweets. "I told you not to bring in the pastry until I called. Old Fritz, I'm warning you."

The old doctor, I noticed, was wearing a smoking jacket. With frayed and faded lapels and cuffs, and elbows that had thinned to translucency, the jacket was a remnant from another time. Like the death-defying diver poised on a jagged cliff over a promontory, as featured in *Acapulco Confidential,* which was up for best special effects that year, he hesitated for only a moment, then rushed down the steps into the living room. His jaw quivered with determination as he set the cookies and milk on the coffee table.

There were macaroons, divinity fudge, pfeffernuesses, hermits, chocolate chips, almond squares, topsy-turtles, brownies and blondies, petticoat tails, cinnamon pinwheels, oatmeal gems, cocoa kisses, and ginger thins. I took a few, but what I really craved was an Almond Joy. I missed the chocolate-smothered coconut goo and the dependable nut embedded therein. Even now I miss nibbling candy in the darkness of the Academy Theatre, amid the constant flux of music, images, and people, where I could focus my thoughts on the languid unraveling of flavors on my tongue and await the rapprochement of my life in a movie about me.

Gilda hissed at her husband: "This is taking passive-aggression too far. Members of the workshop, do you see what he's done? Old Fritz, if you think I'll continue to put up with this, you're an imbecile."

I felt embarrassed and concerned. My parents had a rule, and I suddenly admired them for it—they never reproached, bickered, or battled in public.

Gilda stormed out of the living room, leaving the rest of the troupe with nothing to do but indulge ourselves. After a minute or two, I noticed Old Fritz's yellow teeth and realized he was grinning.

My parents insisted that I also see Gilda privately once a week. I had a feeling they simply wanted to brag to their friends that I was seeing an analyst, but Maurice said he thought a dose of self-discovery might improve my disposition, which had lately become "contumacious." He added, "I'm contemplating doing a television series with Gilda as the host. *Someone* has to try her out. Besides, Gilda has offered you psychotherapy at a cut-rate price."

I turned to Charmian. "I don't want to be a guinea pig."

"You'd better start oinking," she said.

"What in the world would we talk about?" I asked, ignoring her little joke.

"*My* analyst started *me* out with penis envy," Charmian happily mused. "You know what it is? Well, it turned out I'm free of that nasty disease. My analyst says I don't have a jealous bone in my body."

"If the kids at school find out I am seeing a psychologist, they're going to . . . ostracize me."

"*Tant pis,*" Charmian rejoined.

The following Tuesday found me scuffing my shoes as I journeyed from El Rodeo School along Wilshire Boulevard to Gilda's office in the heart of Beverly Hills. I was pondering my upcoming visit, hoping that, despite what I'd seen of Gilda in the psychodrama group, she could still be my champion, my Kroeber, when the two of us were alone. Maybe I wouldn't have to wait for a movie to explain my life; possibly Gilda, with her psychology background, could help me see the sense of it.

The glow of a fish tank lit the waiting room. I killed time admiring the gaudy colors and zany fins of exotic, aquatic bodies doing their laps. I kept imagining diving in, surprising myself with the realization that I missed the water. But when Gilda entered the room, my fantasy abruptly changed; I wanted to squirm into the sand and conceal myself behind the plastic shrubbery.

Instead, I let Gilda shepherd me through a dark, narrow hallway into a small office which had an entirely different appearance than her home. For one thing it wasn't immaculate. It smelled of cigarettes, and I saw overburdened ashtrays strewn around the room. Ragged envelopes, loose papers, and several crumpled Fig Newton wrappers were scattered about the floor. Gilda's open, oversized pocketbook lay in a heap. The wastebasket was filled to the brim with crumpled Kleenexes, some of which had spilled down the sides like a runaway soufflé.

When I glanced at her desk, I received even more of a jolt. Resting on a tiny pedestal was an apparently authentic shrunken head, the work, no doubt, of one of those barbarous South American tribes we'd studied at school. My parents would have delighted in this macabre psychiatrist's gag, but not me. Even more shocking than the head were the thick black spears of hair shooting out of its scalp. On that tiny pate they looked gargantuan.

Gilda led me to the couch. "Go on, lie down, little one," she said, tenderly impelling me as if she were about to tuck me in for the night. She turned down the lights and closed the blinds.

"I thought we were going to talk."

"You bet we're going to talk. Relax."

The couch was sticky and it smelled. I cautiously lowered my head onto the headrest, using my hair as a kind of shield from germs. But once I was prone, my eyes were assailed by shafts of light sneaking in through the lopsided Venetian blinds. The effect suggested all those tense interrogation scenes I'd witnessed at the Academy.

"Are you comfy?" Gilda asked in a honeyed tone as she seated herself behind me, hidden from view. "Now tell me anything that comes to mind, no matter how trivial." She waited, then gave me a verbal nudge. "Well, dear heart? What occurs to you?"

"Does this mean I'm in analysis?" I asked. "I hadn't expected a couch."

"Yes, that's right, sweetheart. It's easy with a young patient as precocious as you. Now then," Gilda cleared her throat, "shall we get down to brass tacks and talk about what's going on between your gardener and you?"

"What do you mean? What did my parents tell you?" I asked, affecting a casual tone meant to hide my curiosity.

"Oh, they just gave me a sketchy idea. They didn't tell me anything you need feel ashamed about. Besides, we all have . . . urges. Psychologists like me consider them healthy."

"What urges? I don't understand."

"Well, your parents mentioned the gardener having a great many girlie photographs. You found them fascinating, didn't you?"

Because she was paying such close attention to me, the part of myself that sought a parent in every adult I met stepped into action. I *was* terribly eager to please her. "Well . . . yes, I guess so."

"Would you consider posing for photos like that?" she asked, her tone suggesting it would be perfectly all right.

I was embarrassed, but the idea struck me funny too. "I don't . . . have anything to show. Besides, I don't think Constantine *takes* the pictures. He just *has* them. Girls give them to him, I think."

"So, tell me, has this gardener ever touched any of your body parts? Remember, sweetie, you can tell everything to me."

"Once or twice he combed my hair and washed my face."

"Now there's a new one," Gilda muttered appreciatively. "Do you have any idea why?"

"Because nobody else did it, I guess."

Suddenly, Gilda slid next to me on the couch. "My poor, dear babe-in-arms, I had an idea you were a neglected child. But not anymore." She gave me a little shove, saying, "Move over, sweetie-beetie. Make some room. Let me make up for the affection you've never received."

We lay uneasily together on a couch that was designed for one occupant only. It was a funny thing: I was so unused to physical contact that when actually experiencing it I felt exceedingly uncomfortable. "Let's imagine we're at a slumber party," Gilda pampered me with her voice as she stroked my neck and hair, "and we're lying together in the dark. Think of me as your best girlfriend. I'll ask you a silly question and you say whatever you want."

As soon as she said this, tears flooded my eyes. Memories of pleasant nights I'd spent talking to Daisy, and being heard, in her bedroom or mine, poured into my head. It was two years since we'd had a tête-à-tête but I still found Daisy's absence unendurable. Quite suddenly, a propitious idea formed in my mind—surely Gilda could contact the Belmonts and get the lowdown on my friend. Maybe Gilda could even coerce them to have Daisy write to me.

"All right? Now about those photos; which appealed to you, the big breasts or the small ones?" Gilda interrupted my musings.

Her question mortified me, and I despised our arrangement on the couch. But I didn't complain—I assumed that provoking the patient was part and parcel of the treatment.

"Do we have to talk about breasts?" I complained.

"We can talk about anything you want."

But Gilda had broken the spell. I didn't want to talk to her about Daisy now. I didn't want to talk to her about anything.

The following Tuesday, though Gilda had her arm under my neck and across my chest, I discovered she could smoke with one hand. As the room filled with Chesterfield smog, Gilda assailed Charmian's character.

I wasn't sure where my loyalties were supposed to belong, so I did my best to change the subject. "Is it true you're going to do a TV show with my father?" I asked.

Gilda sat up quickly—she was that excited—and almost swept me off the couch. "Your father and I are just ironing out the details of our partnership. Included is a special low price for my work with you. That's because I really want to know you, pumpkin. Although"—her voice became dreamy as her thoughts moved into the future—"once I'm enmeshed in the thick of the show, I may not have time to see patients. But don't worry, I do not intend to give up my psychodrama workshop. On the contrary, it's going on the air. The workshop you are in, Fleur, will be on television. With a live audience and a sponsor. And listen to this: Your dad thinks that soon after the show's inauguration, psychodrama workshops will be the rage throughout America. Each one will pay me a share of their proceeds just the way the Arthur Murray Dance Studios pay him."

I hesitated, but my curiosity won out. "What if some of the parents get mad? Maybe they wouldn't want just anyone to know their children don't, um, aren't . . . happy at home."

"The parents *will* run the risk of having whatever they say reenacted on the show, now won't they? But you know a lot of people believe that any publicity is better than no publicity at all."

As Gilda detailed other proposed highlights of her show, I let my eyes reconnoiter her office. So Constantine wasn't the only person who liked to display photographs: framed glossies on Gilda's desk and walls featured her in the company of movie stars. It was clear that Ophelia's mother and Audrey Totter and Linda Darnell, among others, were Gilda's customers.

"Speaking of your mother, did I mention I ran into her at a party the other night? Your father is the dearest, sweetest, most brilliant man, but, let's face it, Charmian is—how shall I say it?—egomaniacal. You see it too, don't you?"

The smoke from her cigarette was causing my eyes to tear and perhaps it clouded my mind, because the only way I could conceive of to defend Charmian was to let Gilda know that Maurice wasn't all sweetness and light. There was his habit of looking at me and making it known he didn't like what he saw. The year before, he'd handed me a paper sack from a pharmacy. "I'm seeing fuzzy shadows under your arms and it isn't ladylike," he'd said when I pulled a razor out of the bag. And should I disclose the fact that after Maurice had fallen into my talcum powder trap, I'd caught him several more times—if only snooping—in my room? When I'd walked in on him fishing in my drawers, I felt too ashamed to accuse him so I'd pestered him instead. "What are you looking for? What do you want to find?"

Only once did Maurice respond. "*Someone* has to keep an eye on you," he'd sighed. Perhaps he and Gilda were in cahoots to uncover what he alone couldn't find.

"With a mother like yours, any daughter would be looking for a mother in every woman she meets. Why don't you let that mother be me?" Gilda asked sweetly.

At any other time I would have been seduced by her empathy. But I was considering whether to let Gilda know that while Maurice showed no interest in my daily routine, he exhibited a morbid fascination in my health or, as he saw it, my lack of it. Just a little sneeze and my father was on the telephone making appointments with doctors. "I feel fine, really," I'd protested just the week before, but Maurice insisted on sending me to a specialist. After I'd undergone a thorough examination, the physician, rather than telling *me* what he'd found, called my father. Colloquies with doctors were Maurice's hobby, it seemed.

And although Maurice never revealed the diagnoses of my "cases," he disbursed pills with an eager hand. My only form of protest was to shove the pills to the side of my mouth between teeth and cheek until I could escape his gaze. The acrid, nauseating taste of melting medicine remains with me today.

"Anyway, we *must* explore your interior geography emanating from the maternal region," Gilda said provocatively, and I assumed she would ask for a dream.

Maurice often badgered me to tell him my dreams. He spoke as though they told him so much more than I could possibly know about myself, that any normal conversation between us was superfluous. Eventually, no matter how hard Maurice probed, my subconscious prevailed: I stopped dreaming for twenty years.

As much as I detested private therapy sessions with Gilda, I relished psychodrama. The sagas-in-the-making, the constant upsets in familial alliances, the emotional upheavals, as reported by the other thespians, were every bit as absorbing as films shown at the Academy. What reenacting these incidents had to do with gaining psychological insight, I had no notion. Chiefly, the acting thrilled me and I threw myself wholeheartedly into all my roles, whether I played a parent, a child, or a servant. I'd even played—quite brilliantly—an old, deaf dog being consigned to the pound because the new decorator at Todd's house had condemned his mangy coat.

Only once was I too baffled to do justice to a role; Gilda assigned me to play Sharon's mother in bed with her new boyfriend. "If I do it, I'll probably barf," I said. Other than that one, I gave each portrayal my complete concentration, using whatever physical and mental capacity I had. No one seemed to notice I never contributed a playlet of my own.

"Thespians, order please. Today we're going to concentrate on Malcolm's life," Gilda announced one Saturday.

Malcolm, the mogul's son, was a thin boy, small for his age of fourteen. He had dark curly hair that rarely honored the part he tried to comb into it, and his deep-set eyes were surrounded by dark circles and disorderly eyebrows.

"I wrote out a script for the person who gets to play me. It's easier than me trying to explain the scene," Malcolm murmured as he unhappily handed a sheet of paper to Gilda.

Gilda scanned it quickly. "This is a *very* juicy role. I hope you appreciate my giving it to . . ." Gilda looked at each of us, then handed the paper to me.

"The best parts *always* go to the girls," Todd remarked.

"Fleur celebrated her twelfth birthday last Wednesday, and this role is my birthday present to her," Gilda said, squelching Todd's protest.

After I read his sketchy script, I asked Malcolm, "Do you want me to recite it verbatim?"

"Oh no, jazz it up."

"Use the script as an outline. Let your imagination soar," Gilda coached. Then, breaking the workshop tradition, she proposed, "Shall we retire to the bedroom?"

Gilda's bedroom had been painted a monastic white.

Twin beds with coverlets, white on white, were neatly made, though one of them was piled high with satin and moiré and lace pillows. Just behind the door, I was surprised to encounter Old Fritz hunched in a straight-back chair as close to the reading lamp as was physically possible.

"All right, Old Fritz, you can go," Gilda snarled.

The look on the doctor's face said we were marauders, but he was unarmed. As he scrambled out of his chair, the heavy volume he'd been reading fell to the floor, but he ignored it; he squeezed hurriedly past the thespians and retreated down the hall.

Gilda removed the coverlet from the pillowless bed. "This will be the stage," she said, motioning for "the audience" to sit on the floor. While Gilda seated herself in her husband's chair, with Ophelia and Sharon leaning their heads on her lap, Malcolm flattened himself against the wall. Near the undraped "stage," I bent down and removed my shoes.

"Quiet in the theater. Ready, begin," Gilda directed as I climbed atop the bed. Once again, my tongue stuck to the sides of my mouth. Even my teeth were dry, and I had an urge to run. But as I allowed Malcolm's persona to overtake me, I became so engrossed I forgot my own rattled nerves.

Like a diver acquainting himself with a new board, I took several practice jumps and was rewarded by the squeaking of bedsprings. The sound unnerved me, as did Old Fritz, who had reestablished himself just outside the open door. His head was bobbing as if synchronized to the rhythm of my bouncing. Oddly, it was the doctor, not Malcolm or Gilda, who gestured for me to begin.

"Are you wondering why, at my age, I'm jumping on a bed?" I addressed the audience to the accompaniment of the rhythmic squeak. "Well, get this. My father says that everything in this house belongs to him. Yup, that's right. He earned the dough, working goddamn hard to pay for the bed I'm not sleeping in. He worked goddamn hard for the table we feed our faces at, the goddamn chairs we plop our bottoms into, the goddamn piano that none of us play, the goddamn clocks that keep the wrong time, the goddamn *everything,*" I recited, giving my impression of the moguls Charmian had described, while bouncing steadily. I liked what it did to the timbre of my voice.

"He paid for the big refrigerator in the kitchen and the small one in Mom's dressing room. He paid for all the food we eat. The plates and the silverware and the glasses and the towels and the sheets and the toilet paper, the pens and pencils, all my school supplies. You name it, it's his," I proclaimed, hoping I had made some writerly additions to Malcolm's script.

"But did you know my father doesn't like people touching his things? He especially doesn't like me to. That's why I jump and I jump and I jump as high as I can and stay in the air as long as I can. See?" I did some extra hard jumps to demonstrate. "I stay in the air. Sometimes all night. It's exhausting being Malcolm Senior's son."

That was all the script called for, and I could see that Malcolm looked fairly pleased, but Old Fritz was signaling at the door. Go on, tie it up, give us a finale, his hands seemed to say as he tied an imaginary knot and bow.

Having no inkling of what would happen next, but—and this was a feeling I've never forgotten—confident I could do something appropriate, I bounded off the bed. My thump was hardly heard because of the applause, but I ignored it as best I could and once again puffed myself up to play the mogul. Placing myself directly in front of Malcolm, I gazed heartlessly into his eyes. Without my planning or willing it, a cold and cruel yet familiar voice arose from my throat. It was supposed to be Malcolm's father sounding off, but I knew it really wasn't. "You tenebrous, lachrymose, profligate, solipsistic, onanistic, fetid excrescence of your mother's womb. Don't you realize that even the air in this house belongs to me?"

Malcolm flinched and pressed himself against the wall. His eyes, for once, widened. "Wow," he declared. "My father isn't *that* bad."

From the hallway I heard clapping, and then Old Doctor Fritz made his way into the room. "You, my friend, are the finest practitioner of psychodramatic technique I haf ever seen," he announced, and shook my hand.

"What did you do? Stay up all night reading *Twenty Minutes a Day to a More Powerful Whatchamacallit?*" Todd asked.

"Where *did* you learn all those words?" Ophelia asked, awestruck.

"I don't know," I answered. I really didn't. "And don't ask me what they mean."

Gilda, who had positioned herself between her husband and me, turned to the other thespians still sitting on the floor. "This is an important moment. No one say a word. Including you, Old Fritz," she said in a nasty tone. "Fleur, dearest, think. You've heard those words somewhere, spoken to you in just the same stony-hearted tone you used on Malcolm. Try to hear them again."

I listened carefully to the air around me. The words swarmed and, sure enough, I felt their sting again. But I didn't want to listen. Why should I? I wanted only to celebrate the triumph of my performance.

It was odd, I thought several Tuesdays later, that I had always wanted at least one affectionate parent, but now that Gilda—calling herself my "re-parent"—cuddled with me on the couch once a week, I wasn't so sure.

"Here you have an educated adult all to yourself. Isn't there something you'd like to ask her about?" Gilda suggested.

Again, I thought of Daisy. If she wasn't dead or terribly sick, why hadn't she written to me? Did she consider me too much of a baby to bother me with *her* problems? This was the one subject that affected me deeply, but I answered Gilda by saying, "Not that I can think of."

"Come come, there must be a thousand things. Ask me

any question. Think of a subject you wouldn't discuss with another living soul."

"Soul. Mole. Down a hole."

"What?"

"It's just a saying. It doesn't really mean anything." But, with my grandmother suddenly occupying my mind, I had an urge to throw caution to the wind. What did I have to lose? "I have this friend . . . ," I began.

"Yes? Boy or girl or *man*?"

"Girl. It's more like I *had* her—she's disappeared."

"Go on," Gilda urged.

I explained about Daisy and the letter and what the caretaker said, and then I made my request. "Could you track down her parents and call and ask what happened to her? If you said you were a psychologist, the Belmonts might confide in you. If Daisy was all right, I know she would have written. I'm afraid she's had a nervous breakdown. Or maybe she's dead."

"If her parents aren't talking about her, they're not going to talk to me. But I could ask around among my psychiatric colleagues. If your friend is having emotional problems, one of them is bound to know."

"I'd really appreciate it," I said.

"Though it isn't exactly kosher, I'll do this for you, if you'll tell me the truth about your gardener and yourself."

I certainly wanted to accommodate Gilda, but what could I say? As a newly turned twelve-year-old, I *was* attracted to Constantine. I loved the man. I loved his strength and kindness and the way he dressed. I loved the way he'd saved me from Miss Hoate. And also, I thought his gallery of girls was funny as could be. Most important of all, I thought our gardener was the one person in my life now who truly loved me. What if I told Gilda that, in my mind, Constantine was the last wild Indian in Beverly Hills, and that I'd sworn to protect him always?

Gilda infused an element of casualness into her next question, but that didn't make it easier to stomach. "Do you ever think about Constantine when you masturbate?"

I felt frightened. This was something *no one* talked about. I'd actually heard the word only once before: Charmian had come home from a bridge party and told about the hostess's little boy and how relentlessly he had disturbed their game. The hostess had plied her son with candy and a new toy, and turned on the TV, but nothing stopped him from bothering the players. Finally, Charmian could stand it no longer; she took the boy upstairs. About ten minutes later she returned alone. The house was quiet, and the cardplayers didn't see the child for the rest of the afternoon. "What did you do?" the hostess asked when she was saying good-bye to Charmian.

"Taught him to masturbate" was the punch line, and Charmian had laughed heartily as she repeated it.

I'd laughed too, as if I knew what it meant. Then, as soon as I could, I'd looked up the word in the dictionary.

"I hope I didn't embarrass you," Gilda said. "But everyone masturbates whether they admit it or not. There have been studies to prove that most girls start masturbating when they are three or four years old."

"How do they study *that*?" I sat up to challenge her.

"Now there's an interesting question. What do *you* think?" she asked. "Look, sweetheart. Let me reassure you. Everyone masturbates. If they don't . . . that's when there's something wrong. It's even possible that sometimes thoughts about *me* stimulate you. So tell me. About you."

I like to think now that I would have told her she was crossing boundaries for which she had no visa. In truth, I probably would have broken down and admitted engaging in what I thought was sinful behavior, though it never involved fantasies of Gilda or Constantine. Frankly, at that stage, the Sleekèd Boy epitomized sexiness to me. But I was saved because just then I heard odd, high-pitched sounds, something like little men jabbering on faraway planets. Gilda leapt from the couch. Then I heard an electronic groan and several metallic clicks. "Goddamn it to Hell," Gilda bellowed.

I turned and asked, "What *is* that?"

"It's a recording machine that inevitably tangles everything, for Christsake," she cursed as a mass of thin, tightly looped tape cascaded out of a drawer in a cabinet next to her. It looked like the scissors-curled ribbon on cheaply wrapped gifts.

On *The Charmian Leigh Radio Mystery Half-Hour,* whenever Charmian was stuck for a plot, a blackmailer would turn up with an incriminating recording of one of her clients. A man could lose his fortune. A government could topple. A wife could lose the husband she suddenly realized she loved. Each one came to Charmian who, at peril to her life, burglarized the ruinous tape recordings from a menacing felon, a foreign power, or a vault guarded by a python. If there was one thing I'd learned from the weekly broadcasts, it was never, never to allow any of the words—no matter how innocent—that fell out of my mouth to be captured by enemy hands.

I fled from Gilda's office. Standing on Bedford Drive, in the heart of Beverly Hills, I'd never felt so alone in my life.

The following Saturday when I climbed into the Buick, I buttered up Trina with a new moron joke. "Why did the moron wear red suspenders?" I prompted her, and she couldn't figure it out. After I gave her the answer, I sighed and said, "Well, Trina, it's back to the old Academy Theatre for me."

"What about your acting lessons? Or whatever they are? Aren't you going there today?" she asked.

"Oh, didn't my parents tell you?" I replied. "Psychodrama is a thing of the past."

"Amazing how you Hollywood youngsters can just try things on and cast them off as if they were dresses in a bargain basement," Trina said with a shake of her head.

Twenty minutes later I nestled into a comfortable Academy seat and looked up at the big, enticing screen. For months to come I spent two days a week sitting in the dark, dropping Almond Joy wrappers on the floor, saturating my mind with movie characters and plots.

Meanwhile, Gilda's bills kept coming, and Maurice, believing Gilda's word that I was making great progress, paid them. By the time he found out I had abandoned her therapy ship, it made no difference to him; the networks had put the kibosh on psychodrama TV. "No audience wants to see children maligning their parents—no matter how famous they are. And they certainly don't want to hear strangers reveal intimate secrets about themselves," one television executive after another told Maurice.

It took weeks, if not months, of hibernating in my Academy seat to realize that movies wouldn't provide the answers to my life's puzzles. How could they when they were concocted by scriptwriters just like my mother? And yet, even on Charmian's show, there were occasional lessons to be learned when she and Miss Golly wrapped up the loose ends. Then, on one particular Sunday, the picture scheduled for exhibit wasn't delivered on time, so the projectionist ran an older one that he had on hand. At first I found *The Man Who Knew Too Much* annoying because, contrary to the title, the man played by Jimmy Stewart knew so little about his predicament—he was practically an innocent bystander. Then it came as a surprise to me that he didn't seek any whys and wherefores; instead he depended on his own ingenuity, and a little help from Doris Day, to outsmart the enemy.

Maybe, I thought, Gilda was mistaken. Maybe understanding the mysteries of my life wasn't the point. Maybe, in order to triumph in life, I needed to learn resourcefulness.

IX

Thea Roy

6/26/59–11/12/59

Previously, when Thea Roy had come to our house for cocktails or a soirée, she'd waited in grand style under our tiled portico until the front door was opened by a butler or the maid. Then, striding majestically into the living room, like a pasha or a potentate, Thea commanded attention without uttering a word. "All these beautiful faces and they're all looking at *me,*" she might eventually declare with feigned amazement. Her delivery flaunted the decisive enunciation of an actress who'd made a determined transition from silents to talkies.

As a result, it distressed me to be leading Thea to the service end of our house, where a narrow set of linoleum-covered stairs dead-ended in the cook's tiny room. With its lack of embellishment, its economical Venetian blinds, and its cast-off cast-iron bed elbowed into a corner, the room seemed so unworthy of Thea that I apologized.

"It's a well-scrubbed hotel room at the end of an arduous trip," she said. And since she neither tested the bed nor peeked at the bathroom, I knew she was resigned.

Although it was broad daylight, Thea was wearing one of her evening capes—a figure-hiding stratagem, Charmian claimed. The cape hung from Thea's shoulders monarch style. She unfastened it and let it drop to the floor.

The two men who had accompanied her entered the room. They were in their autumnal years, as Thea might have said, and had suffered similar slippage of their brows and jowls. This didn't prevent them from being jaunty dressers in double-breasted suits, red ties, and matching handkerchiefs. They carried Thea's brass-hinged leather trunk on their shoulders in the manner of pallbearers. I watched them set it down gingerly in the only possible space, noisily uncouple the locks, and ease it open.

"Where're the rest of your things?" I asked Thea.

"Sweet William is taking care of everything. I didn't think I'd need much . . . here."

William had been the third of Thea's five husbands, and she had been the first of his six wives. "May you be the first of all your husbands' wives," she'd wished me many times. "Every man remembers his first wife; after that they blur." Thea and William had stayed married less than a year—

"Not a bad run, really," she'd said—and remained lifelong friends. William had even provided the two men who were helping Thea move.

"Where do they come from?" I whispered.

"They were actors before the War. William brought them over here to save them from the camps. But just listen to their English; they could never find work. They've become William's janissaries, so to speak."

"What are janissaries?"

"Fleur, dear, isn t there a dictionary in this house?"

As the janissaries unpacked Thea's scant belongings and put them away, I felt embarrassed by the rattle of wire hangers in the closet and the hollow clatter of the cheap, unpapered dresser drawers. Thea, however, lowered her thick, unyielding body into the only chair in the room, tilted her head against the chair top, and closed her eyes. The placid smile on her face resembled that of the great stone Buddha pictured in my geography book.

My mother had purposefully named the one spare bedroom in our house *la salle d'étudier* and filled it with books, a desk, and a television console. No comfortable chair or davenport, and certainly no bed, was in evidence, lest someone think we had room for a guest. ("I can't bear to get up in the morning and have to *recevoir,*" Charmian had explained the subterfuge to me many times.)

Thea knew my mother's disposition on the subject of

houseguests when she discovered she no longer had a place to live nor any means to support herself. Therefore, Thea had to employ an elaborate stratagem that bypassed the spare bedroom altogether when she wangled her way under our roof and into the room meant for the cook. First, she'd persuaded Margaret, our current cook, to move on. (Charmian found out later she'd gone to work for William.) Then Thea had set about replacing Margaret with "the most coveted domestic chef in Hollywood."

"If this dame has cooked for all the stars you say she has, why would she want to cook for me?" Charmian had inquired suspiciously. "I have yet to reach my professional zenith, I'm afraid."

"Madame Tzu wants to try cooking for a, eh, normal, American family. Charmian, you must admit you don't entertain nearly so often as Debbie Reynolds or Robert Young."

"I'm not sure I like Chinese food," my mother had countered.

"Really dear, she's a professional. If you order Cream of Wheat, and I'm sure you will, it will be the best you've ever tasted. She's a magician in the kitchen."

Only after Madame Tzu was ensconced in our house, cooking up unappreciated slivered scallops in oyster sauce and bird's nest soup before accidentally hitting upon what became one of Charmian's addictions—sweet and sour pork over plain, white rice—did she confess to Charmian that she was married and wanted to live *out*. The following day Thea had paid Charmian a visit during which she said she understood the cook's room was vacant. The day after that Thea moved in.

William's janissaries tiptoed away, and Thea's eyes remained closed. I stayed with her, pleased to have the company even if she slept. School was out for the summer and, except for weekends at the Academy, the time before it opened again seemed eternal. After a while, without opening her eyes, Thea said, "Do something for me, please. Get me out of my earrings."

I had never seen Thea without earrings. Unless she was playing a role in a movie, she always wore the same pair. They looked like the age-tarnished censers hung in Gothic cathedrals during medieval times.

Unused to touching anyone older than my schoolmates, I struggled to unhook the earrings from Thea's withered lobes without causing harm. "What about the rest?" I asked referring to the great coils of jewelry that lay like ornate armor on her chest and must have been weighing her down. She nodded her consent to remove it.

As I placed the jumble of jewelry in the top dresser drawer, Thea mumbled, "What's the name of your nanny again? Will you ask her to come up?"

"Lorna isn't home. She took Madame Tzu to do the marketing."

"In that case, would *you* mind bringing me a little fruit and cheese? On a tray?"

"I'd be glad to," I answered eagerly.

"And remember, whatever fruit you bring, it must be peeled."

"Even grapes?"

"Especially grapes. And pitted."

Charmian warned me to keep away from Thea. So now it was Constantine *and* Thea I was supposed to avoid. "She'll make you into her servant, waiting on her hand and foot. That's not what I had you for."

"What *did* you have me for?"

"Just keep in mind, Thea is enormously spoiled. Fame made her an *enfant terrible*. But the *loss* of fame has convinced her she deserves pampering all the more."

"I think she might be sick," I defended her.

"Aren't you the observant child."

"What is it? What's wrong?"

"Oh, well, a lingering disease," Charmian said, placing the emphasis on the word *lingering*, as though she meant it was *Thea* who lingered, not the disease. "If I had known about it when she asked to stay here, I definitely would have said no. I thought it was just a matter of time—until she could clip a coupon or two—and she'd be on her way. Really, she railroaded me into this."

"Why couldn't Thea stay at William's house?" I asked.

"Let me tell you—Thea earned plenty in her heyday, but, as I have just ascertained, she never bothered to save a red cent. Instead she made poor William pay over and over again just for being married to her for seven months. I suppose he's had enough. If not, William's new wife has put her foot down. As well she should."

I should have known better than to raise the subject just then, but Thea's welfare was uppermost in my mind. "Thea says that being in a room so far from a telephone is the way she imagines life after death, so—I was wondering—could we have a phone installed in her room?"

There was a pause and then, "*Voilà,* you see how she pushes. I'm giving her free room and board, and she's angling for more. Keep away from her, I'm telling you."

Thea spent most of her time in bed. She had coughing spells and intervals of gasping for breath which terrified me. So when she wished for a glass of buttermilk over shaved ice, or a shot of Chivas Regal in hot tea, or a cigarette from the basket in the living room, I retrieved it for her. And when Thea didn't have enough physical fortitude to walk to the butler's pantry where the closest phone happened to be, I carried messages back and forth. I felt important, as though I were gainfully employed. In addition, the telephone decorum of Thea's mysterious callers, a Lady Evangeline Pryce-Jones and a Swami Siddheswarananda, impressed me more than any movie star's. William called two or three times every day, and Suzie Duvic called too.

"What do you know about this Suzie Duvic? Have *I* known her?" Thea asked as the messages piled up.

In between errands I studied the photographs in Thea's scrapbooks. Already a beauty by the age of seventeen, she had boasted eloquent eyes, enameled skin, and an elfin waist. Still, I wondered about her speech, "Thea, did you always talk the way you do?"

This struck her as funny. "Oh, oh my, oh God, no. But fortune favored me with a demanding coach. See if you can't find a photo of Dame Ottoline Evans there. In my line of work elocution is everything. Do you know? I *still* do my exercises every day."

It was true. I'd listened to her. Sometimes she did them in her sleep. "*Ba pa, ba pa, ba-pa, bapa bapa bapa, la row, la row, la-row, larow larow larow, fo ma, fo ma fo-ma, foma foma foma,*" she'd repeat, her tempo increasing to a breakneck pace. Even at high speed she never blurred her syllables—it was said Thea Roy could mimic any human sound. I attempted to execute her tongue twisters, but I could never combine accuracy with speed.

On her fifth day with us I asked if she really could cry at will. Thea responded by demonstrating one of her legendary acting feats. "How do you wish my tears to appear? A stream? A trickle? A single pearl-shaped drop?"

"Just one tear would be fine," I said. I didn't want to tax her.

Thea looked off into the distance for a few seconds. Then, quite sorrowfully, it seemed, she looked me straight in the eye. Dumbfounded, I watched one small droplet form in the corner of her left eye and dribble down her cheek.

"Or would you prefer something more substantial coming from my right eye?" she asked. A moment later a fuller, rounder tear etched a path down her right cheek. "Not good enough?" Several more followed while her left eye dried.

"That's amazing!" I exclaimed. "How do you do it?"

"Next time you're crying, watch yourself in the mirror and try to control the flow. Make use of your misery, that's my motto. Then, all you have to do is practice, practice, practice."

In her photographs, mostly studio stills, Thea wore gowns bedizened with jewels, or tatters designed by Givenchy or Chanel, while men in the background or by her side posed as kings, pilots, road workers, tribal chiefs, pirates, bakers, cowboys, or bishops. "There is nothing I haven't done in this life," Thea said.

One day when Thea was in a restless half-doze, I unearthed a photograph in her scrapbook that had been lodged behind another. Here was a radiant, young Thea holding a baby exquisitely dressed in a regal, white christening gown. "Thea," I said excitedly, "did you have a baby in a movie? Or was this your baby in real life?"

Thea sat up abruptly, leaned over the bed, and snatched the photo from my hand. "Where did you find this?" she angrily inquired. Then she tore it into more pieces than I could count.

I was mystified by her conduct and miserable that I'd caused her grief. "I'm sorry. I didn't know . . . It was just that you looked so beautiful and the . . ."

But Thea's head had sunk down onto her pillow again

and her eyes were closed tight enough to shut out my apology and bury the subject for a while.

My mother said that Thea had preceded her into this world by a good quarter century. I didn't think either woman was honest about her age, so the math might have been inadvertently accurate. Thea's body had thickened and slowed, her snaky coil of hair had grayed and thinned, and her skin no longer appeared to be enameled but had the appearance of crazed crockery.

"Face it, Thea's the Wreck of the Hesperus. If I look like that when I reach her age, I promise you, I'll shoot myself," Charmian threatened.

I'd asked Thea why she'd never had a face-lift, and she'd responded, "Me? But I'm proud of the lines in my face. Every one of them tells a story, and together they prove I've *lived.*"

I told Charmian, "To me, Thea is really beautiful. When I talk, her eyes never leave my face. She really listens."

But Charmian scoffed, "That's acting technique. I can do it too."

"Then why don't you? With me, I mean?"

"Because you're just my little girl. I'm not on the job."

It was futile to try to further this discussion—nothing would change Charmian's attitudes—so I changed the subject by asking, "Did Thea ever have a child?"

Charmian thought for a moment and then recollected, "She had one child, a girl, and that's it."

"A daughter? What's her name?"

"Can't recall."

"Well, do you know where she is? Maybe we should call her. She might not know that Thea's sick."

"Thea's daughter committed suicide about twenty years ago," Charmian said in a furious tone. "A really stinking trick for a child to play on a parent."

Charmian's anger on the subject caught me by surprise and made me wonder if she knew something she wasn't telling about Daisy Belmont. But I also wanted to know about Thea's daughter. "How old was the girl when she . . . ?"

"Full-grown. You can't call someone *that* foolish an adult, now can you?"

It took Thea a few weeks to grow weary of me, but finally she asked, "Don't you have any friends?"

"Not until school starts in September. And even then I'm not positive."

"How is that possible?"

"Well, I *had* a friend, my best friend. We used to say we were two flowers growing in the same field. Because her name is Daisy. But two years ago she got sent away." As I tried to explain my loss, I burst into tears.

"This sounds serious," Thea said sympathetically. Then, after giving me time to dry my tears, she asked. "Where did Daisy go?"

When I finished relating Daisy's history as I knew it,

Thea made the effort to crawl out of her bed. She bade me wrap a cape around her shoulders and help her trudge to the telephone. Although Thea seemed quite weak, once I'd dialed Daisy's old Beverly Hills phone number, her professional persona took over and she assumed the role of a bewitching tyrant. "This is Thea Roy," her voice boomeranged into the receiver and throughout the butlers' pantry. "I am calling for either one of the Belmonts and I've only one minute to allot to this call."

Thea held the receiver close to my ear so that I could hear the caretaker's adoring voice filter through the telephone: "Thea Roy? The actress? Oh, Miss Roy, I've been loving your pictures since I was a little girl."

"If you truly enjoyed my pictures, you'll help me by calling one of the Belmonts to the telephone immediately."

"I can give you their number in Switzerland. They've moved, you see. They're only going to use this house when they're in town making a movie."

"And the child?" Thea quickly came to the point.

"She's living there too. Very happy from what I hear. Shall I give you the number then?"

Thea slowly repeated the number and I wrote it down. After she'd returned the receiver to its cradle, she said, "I'm sure you'll call your friend when the time is right."

Though Thea exhibited great sensitivity about my star-crossed friendship, she didn't withhold her opinion on many other matters. "Your mother warned me you are a clingy child," Thea complained the next morning. "I really don't need a constant companion just now. Ah well, I suppose it's up to me to teach you how to make better use of your time."

"How?"

"Hmmmm, we'll have to see. Now think. Tell me one thing that really interests you."

My personal inclinations were so rarely taken into account that the only response I could offer was, "Well, you."

She smiled. "That's very sweet. I thank you. Now go get me a cigarette from the living room, will you? And on your way, try to think of something that captured your fancy before I arrived on the scene."

There were my collections, of course, and food, but I didn't think she'd be interested. I was curious about people, but who? "Tourists," I told Thea when I returned.

"Tourists?" She sounded perplexed. "Where? Who?"

Even now, I find it difficult to admit how many idle hours I spent sitting in front of our house watching for the few stargazers who found their way into our canyon. With a desert water bag tied to their bumpers in case their radiator blew up, they rode on slow-rolling tires that popped the brittle leaves and dried seed pods scattered about the canyon. All through the pre-air-conditioning summers, they drove with their wind-wings flapped forward like tongues lapping up the breeze, their eyes open as wide as their windows. Mopping away speckles of perspiration and crackling their movie star maps, tourists made pilgrimages to Hollywood. Our house might as well have been chock-full of plaster saints and the reliquaries of apostles. Whenever tourists spotted me, they slowed to a stop and asked, "Is this where Charmian Leigh lives?"

"And what do you tell them?" Thea probed.

"I say *no*."

"Why is that?"

"Because Charmian doesn't want anyone pestering her, and my father thinks I'll be kidnapped."

"You'll have no success in Hollywood with an attitude like that," Thea chastised me.

"I don't know if I want success in Hollywood."

"But you're here. You might as well . . . imbibe."

"What should I do?"

"Let me rest now, and I'll give you an answer tomorrow."

Three days later, when Thea was able to finally rouse herself, I helped her get dressed. She had already dispatched Lorna and Madame Tzu to the market, and soon they returned with a bushel of lemons.

I watched with fascination as Madame Tzu whacked lemons in half with a butcher knife. Her short, midnight-black hair reminded me of a lampshade, and when she spoke, her tight black eyes seemed to light up. "Joan Crawfor, I no like," she regaled us in her Chinese-American shorthanded English. "All she eat is stew and bread pudd. You no need chef for cook white goo, I tell her but she no listen."

Like Charmian, Madame Tzu seemed to require an audience, so despite my parents' rule, she welcomed me into the kitchen. While she talked, she allowed me to rub the lemon halves back and forth against the ribbed, porcelain juicing form. Together we strained the seeds from the juice and poured the clear, pastel-yellow liquid, along with sugar and ice, into one of my mother's most ornate crystal pitchers.

Still following Thea's directions, Lorna and I carried a Queen Anne tea table from the living room, a Louis Philippe chair, a hand-rolled linen tablecloth, a set of cut-crystal tumblers (purchased "as a favor" from impoverished émigrés), and a set of silver soda spoons out to the curb.

"My mother isn't going to like this," I told Thea. "What if something gets broken?"

Thea looked at me sternly and said, "If you want the best, you must give it." Then she dictated our new business motto, which I dutifully transcribed onto a shirt cardboard:

Stop
at This Spot
for a Draught . . .
of Lemonade.
Only a Dime,
It Tastes Divine.

I sat down alone at my elegant lemonade table and saw the house across the street soaking in a pool of gold as sunlight poured over the west hill into the tub of our canyon. After a while, a shimmering square of light began to travel along the rocky hillside opposite me. I heard the pleasant, rhythmic tapping of Constantine's jalopy.

"Is fresh. Having bang-up flavor," my first customer praised the lemonade. A few minutes later Constantine brought me a bouquet of nasturtiums to brighten my table.

There was nothing to do but wait patiently until a sedan pulled up and stopped by my table.

"Hi there, kiddo," the driver hailed me as he blotted the driblets of sweat that clung to his forehead. The movie star map his wife held had grown limp, and their children were red in the face. "Say, tell me: is this where Charmian Leigh lives?"

Thea had scripted my answer, and I stuck to it, saying, "As a matter of fact, it is."

I made four dollars that first day. But soon I discovered that if I told personal anecdotes about my mother, my father, our famous neighbors, and other movie stars who didn't live near us at all, the tourists would tip me—the more embellished and animated the story, the more generous the gratuity. I was able to take in twenty-seven dollars my first week.

"You take after your mother," Thea remarked when I laid out the cash, like Monopoly holdings, beside her on the bed. "I mean that you write *and* act. You just do it on your feet. We call that *improvisation* where I come from."

Soon Thea suggested I make some additions to the menu, so I began carrying a line of avocados I had picked from Charlie Chaplin's trees; Asian pears, removed after dark from Jerry Lewis's yard; and loquats from Danny Kaye's. Madame Tzu crushed the fruits, and we served them as a beverage. My new sign urged tourists to: "Stop Here and Drink THE FRUIT OF STARS."

I learned something about cooking that summer: if you add sugar, anything tastes scrumptious. I learned something about business too when Maurice charged me for Madame Tzu's labor, the sugar and lemons, the laundering of the tablecloth, and the use of my parents' furniture and utensils. But the longer I kept my customers entertained, the more drinks I sold. The following week I grossed thirty-five dollars and netted twenty-seven.

On the nights my parents came home for dinner, Thea always said she felt "too weak" to join them. Maurice liked to eat meals in shirtsleeves, and Charmian had a different mien altogether when she had guests, so they didn't entirely regret Thea's absence from our table.

One night, not long after school had begun and my seasonal business had come to a halt, Maurice and I were eating a repast of five willowy shreds on sea bass and la pa congee, while Charmian concentrated on her sweet and sour pork. Suddenly, the swinging door between the butler's pantry and dining room flapped open and smacked against the wall so hard I thought both the door and the wall had cracked. Madame Tzu burst in, crying something out in agitated Chinese.

My father raised his voice. "Slow down," he said to Madame Tzu. "You're spouting gibberish."

Madame Tzu, too unnerved to muster any English, started tugging at my mother's clothes, and Charmian, decoding her charade, said, "I think she wants us to follow her."

"A kitchen fire," Maurice speculated.

But Madame Tzu didn't pause in the butler's pantry or the kitchen. She pulled Charmian on through to the service porch and up the back steps to Thea's room. Maurice and I followed behind.

As we paused in the doorway, I saw Thea's body lying graceless and immobile on the floor, her eyes and mouth wide open. I ran in and flung myself down next to her. Then, because I didn't know what to do, I began whimpering.

"Stop that," my father ordered.

Madame Tzu leaned over my friend and put her ear to Thea's heart. Neither of my parents ventured over the threshold.

"I knew I shouldn't let her stay here," Charmian lamented. "Anyway, we can't let her die. Not here. I don't want my name associated with . . . death."

"She got pulse," our cook said with elation and clarity. "You call doctor righ now." Then she began the application of what I believed was Chinese artificial respiration.

"I'll call an ambulance. If she's dying, she'll be better off in a hospital," Charmian responded and started down the stairs.

"You call doctor righ now so she don die. Else I call *Hollywoo Reporter* and *Variety* and tell evelythin what you say," Madame Tzu threatened.

While my parents went off to the telephone, I helped Madame Tzu lift Thea onto the bed. Her body was heavy and unresponsive, as if Death was trying to pull her out of our hands. I felt immensely afraid, angry too.

To my consternation, my parents didn't phone that year's physician-to-the-stars, the doctor they would have called for themselves; they settled on an obscure doctor, a distant relative of Maurice's secretary. When he finally arrived hours later, Maurice wouldn't let me stay in the room during the medical examination.

While Charmian and Maurice made martinis and prepared to settle in the living room, I crept to their bedroom. When the telephone operator asked for it, I gave her the number with no trouble. Though I'd never used it, I knew it by heart. It was early morning in Switzerland, but a maid answered at the Belmont household and summoned Daisy to the phone.

"Oh, I've been meaning to write to you," Daisy said in the same deep and amused voice I'd always known. Only now she seemed to have an English accent. "I'm afraid I haven't been much of a friend. I've just been so busy . . . becoming . . . mature."

"The last time I heard from you, you wanted to commit suicide. That was two years ago," I scolded her. "Well, it sounds like you lived."

"Did I ever," she laughed. "But I *was* miserable in that boarding school and I got very sick. Heartsick, the doctor called it. So guess what? When my parents found out how bad off I was, they decided to move to Switzerland too. So now we live together and I'm going to a different school. It's an *international* school, and it's spectacular. We're being steeped in European culture as well as Italian *and* French. I'll be able to talk to your *mother* one of these days," she teased. "And, Fleur, I'm all developed. I'm beautiful. Mother and I went to a couturier in Paris and bought the most gorgeous clothes. I have a boyfriend too, Fleur. He's English and he's a duke. He's cousins with just about everyone in Europe who counts. Anyway, I have to go. It takes me an hour to get dressed for school. You should try to come to Switzerland. I'd love to see you. Well then, *au revoir.*"

So I'd found Daisy only to discover how lost to me she really was. This realization made Thea's state of health all the more important. Even if it meant a hundred injections, even if it meant the bitterest pills, the doctor would have to do everything in his power to make Thea well.

Dr. Saltzman kept us waiting almost an hour, an eternity for a child in anguish, before he joined my parents and me in the living room.

"Do you charge by the hour or by the case?" my father asked.

"If she dies, I don't want it to get around that it happened here, do you understand?" Charmian told the physician. The smoke from the twelve or so cigarettes she'd just smoked hovered over him.

"Is Thea going to be all right?" My anxiety made me bold.

"I don't think we have to worry about death just yet," Dr. Saltzman said. I realize now he was a young doctor who didn't know how to deliver bad news. "She's conscious and alert. We talked. Gosh, I wish I'd known her when she was a star. She must have been stunning. Well, anyway, I'm going to get some oxygen brought over here right away. Eight or nine hours of it every day will get her over this hurdle. And maybe the next."

"Oxygen? Isn't that highly flammable?" Charmian sounded alarmed, as though the doctor had proposed bringing dynamite into our house. "All that equipment? Who will administer it? *I* certainly can't be responsible. I don't have time. I have a weekly show on the radio."

I left the living room without being noticed and crept into Thea's room.

"She too weak talk," Madame Tzu warned me, so I sat down on the floor and leaned against the bed. Thea's breathing was disturbingly labored, but as long as it was audible, I relaxed.

I'd lost track of time, but eventually the doctor returned with several cylinders of oxygen and a small plastic tent. He showed Madame Tzu how to connect the valves and drape the tent over Thea.

I'd learned, on Charmian's show, that people gave off a sound like a rattle before they died. I sincerely believed that if I heard it I could leap up and shake Thea back to life. When the doctor left and Madame Tzu began to doze in the chair, I climbed into Thea's bed, pushed my arm in under the tent, and placed it gently across her chest. "Thea," I whispered, "I just want you to know that I called my friend Daisy in Switzerland. And she's fine. She's doing fine. So you see it really was worthwhile that you got her number for me. Thank you so much. Thank you. Can you hear me, Thea?" I watched over my friend that night with the vigilance I had in the past devoted to my collections of inanimate objects. I lay with my arm around Thea all night.

My parents gave me no choice. Even Thea weakly urged that I attend school the next day. But I didn't hear a word my teachers uttered; I didn't even try. I didn't talk to a single chum. I didn't taste my lunch or go near the playground. I kept my thoughts wrapped tight around Thea.

It seemed an eternity, forty days and nights in the desert, at least, or ten years at sea, before I was finally allowed to return home. Once inside, I ran toward Thea's room, only to find William's janissaries seated on the back stairs outside her door. Their handkerchiefs were soggy and balled, and tears had striped their ties. Behind them, through the open door, I saw that Thea's bed had been stripped.

"Where is she? Where is she?" I screamed as I ran through our house.

My mother, who was sitting at her dressing room table preparing to go out, calmly explained. "Thea died this morning before I woke up. There was nothing to do but call the mortuary. They came for her a little while ago."

Of course, I'd known the moment I'd walked into the house, but now that Charmian put it into words, I couldn't deny what had happened. "Thea died? She died? You let her die without coming to get me? How could you be so cruel? Why don't you ever, ever think of me?"

"You saw for yourself. She was hardly in *plus-parfait* condition. She was old. She was ready."

"Well, *I* wasn't. I wanted to say good-bye." I was screaming at Charmian, forgetting in my anger that screaming wasn't tolerated here, that it could get me thrown out of the house. In my heart of hearts I held my mother responsible.

"Look at your face," Charmian accused me, of what I couldn't be sure. "It's as red as a lobster and you're all puffed up like a blimp. Let's have no histrionics, please. Thea wouldn't have heard you even if you yelled as loud as you are yelling now. Once you're dead, you're dead. Curtain down. *Finis.* The end," she translated.

The image weakened my resolve and I could no longer hold back my tears. "I wanted to say good-bye whether she heard me or not," I sobbed.

Her lipstick fully extended from its cylinder and pressed between her fingers, Charmian sat facing her mirror. Even at a moment like this I could appreciate her beauty. Suddenly, the image of Madame Tzu's somber face appeared above Charmian's. As far as I knew, our cook had never before ventured upstairs.

"I give message ver importan," Madame Tzu said. "Miss Roy say to do. She say make sure Fleur get evelythin. All her thins. All what store in Mr. Wirliam's garage. Scrapbooks specially, but evelythin for her."

"Is that true?" I said.

"She talk bou you before she die. She worry."

"Thea worried about *me* at a time like that? When she was dying?" In some small way I felt consoled.

"It was very sweet of her," Charmian said. "But really, Fleur, where would we put her things? There's no room. You know how I hate clutter. Even *you* wouldn't like Thea's . . . detritus littering the house. Let's donate her memorabilia to a university . . . or, better, the Academy. Yes, let's, we can claim it as a deduction."

"That's what you do with *all* my things, the ones that keep disappearing. All this time you let me think that Maurice was stealing from me."

"I don't know what you're talking about."

"Just tell me what you did with my Madagascar shell."

"Which shell is that?" Charmian asked, sounding entirely uninterested.

"You know very well," I challenged her.

"Not that big one with the pink and brown swirls. You don't mean *that*? I thought I told you it should be in a museum. Surely you'd want as many people as possible to enjoy it. It's at the Natural History Museum now."

"So you could take it off your income tax?"

"It wasn't that valuable, *chérie*."

"So where are my silver dollars?" I asked sternly. In this case I still harbored a little suspicion of Maurice.

"My goodness, it seemed such a waste that you weren't earning interest on your capital. I put that money in the bank for you. I suspect you'll be thanking me in a few years."

Charmian sounded so reasonable, so positive, that I was compelled to ask, "But can I get them back?"

"If you want the money now, you can get it."

"I want the same silver dollars I had."

"That, I'm afraid, would be impossible."

"You took them away without even asking me!" I lashed out again, but I was thinking of Thea more than anything else. This is how Charmian was. "And you took one of my volumes of *The Wizard of Oz*."

"You'd already read it many times and I needed a gift in a hurry. I was going to a dinner party and they had a sick child."

"Did you give that poor, sick, dinner-party child my baby teeth too?"

"They were disgusting, Fleur. Little mounds of decaying bone."

"Those teeth came out of *my* mouth. So, no doubt, they were a nuisance to you." I moved to the doorway, a position in Charmian's bedroom just then comparable to center stage and, like an actress in total control of a scene, I blocked Charmian's exit. For once, I would make her listen to me. "Thea was a nuisance too, wasn't she? You're glad she's out of your hair. You don't care if I already miss her horribly. And no matter what you say or do, I'm keeping Thea's belongings. Possession is nine-tenths of the law—

that's what you say on your show. So if you try to take them away, if you try to send *me* away, I'll . . . go to the police. Jeff is still a Beverly Hills cop and he hates you."

I didn't wait for Charmian's reaction; I'd given myself a superb exit line.

In front of our house Constantine's jalopy looked like a giant piece of butterscotch candy; its reddish upholstery gleamed under the sun's warm rays. "Constantine, Constantine, Constantine," I called as I circled our property. I shouted his name again and again. I was on the warpath, silently daring Charmian to try and stop me from tracking him down.

I found Constantine working at the top of our hill. A vigorous vine had crept over the Barrymore villa walls, and it threatened to strangle the more staid foliage Charmian wanted to grow on the hill. Constantine was constantly cutting it back; he squatted down to show me how it had already sent out little shoots that now were sprouting out of the ground. "Is passion flower vine. Too *much* passion," he said, and then laughed as though he'd surprised himself by saying such a thing.

"Do you know what happened?" I asked him solemnly.

"You tell," he urged.

I meant to express myself in a calm, dispassionate manner, my usual defense for fending off a blow. But I blurted out my sad lament: "Thea died this morning."

Constantine startled me. Without a word, he put his

hands around my waist and lifted me up so that our two cheeks met. He held me tightly, and I leaned my head on his shoulder and felt his sun-warmed flesh all around me. I didn't know if the sweet, robust scent I smelled was his or that of the passion-flower vine.

"Is terrible thing when friend dies," he said softly.

If I could have, I would have had us frozen together just like that, my only regret being that Thea had to die before I could receive the reward of his embrace. "Every time I like someone, they go away," I said, knowing I sounded like a whiny child, but unable to stop myself as my tears fell on Constantine's chest. "They leave me all alone, surrounded by enemies, and they never come back. They don't even send me a card."

Constantine set me on my feet, and we sat down together on the warm soil. Again he wrapped his arms around me. "Is terrible thing being left lonesome. But I coming here. Three days a week. Coming much more if you want. Anytime."

"But that doesn't mean you will always be here," I complained.

"I say, yes"—he chose his words carefully—"I will be here always."

"But Constantine, you might get a better job, you could die, or, probably, my mother will fire you."

He sighed and looked at the ground, "Constantine giving you promise."

I was wishing I could trust him. I was wishing I could believe each of his sparse words when he took my cheeks in his hands and tried to direct my gaze. "Look here," he excitedly urged.

A splotch of sun had filled the little trough I'd just dug with my feet, and I noticed a flat, whitish stone imbedded in the newly turned dirt. In the moment it took me to discern what it could be and gingerly pull it away from the earth, I didn't breathe. Then I brushed the arrowhead against my lips and placed it in the nest of my palm.

Constantine had sworn that Indians once lived in Beverly Hills, and now I held proof. I'd always assumed I would have to be Constantine's Kroeber, but sitting on the warm earth with the great man, I realized that all along Constantine had been mine. I leaned my face against his chest and heard the muffled, steadfast beat of his heart. I hear it now.

Though Charmian was enraged that Suzie Duvic's name was mentioned as one of Thea's grieving friends in all of her coast-to-coast obituaries, she was heartened that the *Hollywood Reporter* and *Variety* confirmed that Thea Roy had died peacefully in Beverly Hills in the elegant home of her closest acting confrère, the actress Charmian Leigh.

Tourists read about it too. During the Thanksgiving vacation they arrived in droves.

Wishing to make use of the pumpkins I'd found growing wild on the hill below Fred Astaire's house, I employed all my persuasive powers to convince Rosemary, our new cook, to fry them up as fritters. Out at my table, I kept them hot in a silver chafing dish with a canister of Sterno placed strategically underneath. I'd wanted to serve the pumpkin fritters flambé, but due to the perpetual fire danger in the canyon, I was not allowed.

Rosemary cleverly utilized the plump rose hips I'd found flourishing at the Barrymore villa when I'd finally managed to scale the crumbling wall. With a flourish worthy of John Barrymore, I turned the spigot in the silver samovar and poured rose hips tea made from the roses growing over his wall. I served it in Charmian's best Haviland teacups.

"Is this where Charmian Leigh lives?" the tourists chanted. "Is this where Thea Roy died?"

"It most certainly is," I said repeatedly that weekend, resolute in my entrepreneurial role.

"Is it true Charmian Leigh's show is going on television?" the savvy visitors asked.

"That's right. On NBC," I answered cheerily. I didn't explain that at the very moment when Mr. Frieley read Thea's obituary and spied my mother's name he happened to be desparate to find a replacement for a viewerless sitcom that was spoiling his ratings average.

Another tourist approached me. He was dressed impeccably in a white suit and tie, and had the manners of a southern gentleman. "Is this where Thea Roy spent her final days?" he inquired, studying the display of her earrings and jewelry, which I'd arranged on a pink satin cushion.

"It is."

"Gosh, I think I saw every picture Thea Roy ever made,"

the modern-day pilgrim told me. He ordered tea and a fritter. "She was the greatest, but I heard she was down and out by the time she died. Charmian Leigh must be a very kind person taking her in like that."

Afraid I might spill out the entire story, I asked, "Would you like to see some photographs of Thea?"

"Yes, ma'am, I'd be delighted," he said.

Behind my table, I had installed Thea's upright open trunk. Its drawers were now filled with her scrapbooks, which I brought out one at a time and placed on the table.

For the most part, tourists were overwhelmed. Many brought along flowers, which they laid around the table and on top of Thea's trunk. Some of the well-wishers had been in her fan club and brought letters expressing their sorrow. Others told stories about Thea and described in detail movies she'd starred in that I'd never seen. Other sightseers wanted to visit her grave and asked for directions. A select few knew the names of Thea's husbands and identified them in the scrapbooks so that I could write them down. Everyone remembered aspects of Thea's life that I felt certain she herself had long ago forgotten.

During these exchanges, I felt a gentle happiness overtaking me, as though I were regaining Thea, gaining admittance to sides of her I could never have known.

"And by the way, who are you?" the southern gentleman asked, posing the one question for which I had no ready reply.

Who was I? Before Thea came to stay with us, I might have answered, "Oh, well, me? I'm nobody." But I didn't feel like nobody now. Thea had taught me to accept life as it came, then make use of what I could, improvise, and, above all, stand up for myself.

The kindly southerner realized that he had stumped me and said, "I just mean, how do you happen to be here?"

He was so nice, I wanted to give him the gift of a sensational response. I considered a moment and then said, "I'm Thea Roy's daughter. She adopted me very late in life, but not so late she didn t fill me up with her wisdom."

"You're a very lucky little lady," he said.

"I heartily agree," said I, and meant it.

"And will you remain here living with Charmian Leigh?"

"Until I reach majority, unless Charmian sends me to a boarding school," I said, realizing that I no longer saw this possibility as a threat.

"You know something?" the tourist said. "I was planning on going to Hollywood Boulevard to sink my shoes into the footprints of the stars at Grauman's Chinese, but coming here to this beautiful canyon and meeting you has been by far the better treat."

"Why, thank you."

"So, how much do I owe you?" he asked in his silky southern drawl, politely winding up our chat.

"Let's see, you had two cups of tea and a pumpkin fritter. That's eighty-five cents."

"And how much for looking at those fabulous photo albums?"

"For that there is no charge," I told him graciously.

SIMON & SCHUSTER PAPERBACKS READING GROUP GUIDE

FLEUR DE LEIGH'S LIFE OF CRIME

DISCUSSION POINTS

1. Many nannies and other authority figures pass through Fleur's life. Who is your least and most favorite and why? How do these transient authority figures shape Fleur's life? Do you think they cause her to become more self-reliant? Cynical? Insightful? Wary of attachments?
2. How does Fleur's understanding of her father change after she gets to know Grandma Glo? What does she learn about her parents' relationship from Glo's visit?
3. Charmian is a complex character and certainly a challenge to Fleur. What do you think motherhood means to Charmian? Is Fleur stronger than Charmian? If so, in what ways?
4. Why is Fleur so strongly drawn to Constantine? What does their relationship teach her?
5. How does living with her parents affect Fleur's outlook on life?
6. What effect does Daisy's disappearance and Fleur's rediscovery of her have on Fleur? Do you think it would have been better or worse if Fleur hadn't found her?
7. Fleur has been in many ways transformed by the end of the book. Is she still the same person inside? What major differences are there between the Fleur we first meet and the Fleur at the end of the book?
8. The word *crime* in the title is used as a metaphor. What crimes take place in Fleur's household? What is Fleur's crime?
9. Discuss the role that Hollywood plays in this novel.
10. Why did the author choose to use the comings and goings of Fleur's nannies as the structure of her novel?
11. After the story ends, what do you think happens to Fleur later in life?

WHY I WROTE *FLEUR DE LEIGH'S LIFE OF CRIME*

As a child I was frequently told to thank my lucky stars because I was so privileged. That I may have been ignored and unloved crossed no one's mind. Writing this novel enabled me to comprehend, appreciate, and have the fun of re-creating my past.

About the Author

Diane Leslie was born in Hollywood and by age nineteen was working as a television researcher and story analyst. Soon, however, she found herself sailing halfway around the world and marrying a sailboat rigger. Home in Los Angeles at last, she began writing fiction while raising two sons. For the last decade she has worked at Dutton's Brentwood Bookstore, where she sells books, hosts the frequent author readings, and leads numerous book groups.

Printed in the United States
By Bookmasters